NOW WE SURVIVE

THE KILLING SANDS · BOOK 3

DANIEL P. WILDE

Now We Survive (The Killing Sands, Book 3)
Daniel P. Wilde
Paperback ISBN 978-1-77342-062-2
Hardcover ISBN 978-1-77342-063-9

Produced by IndieBookLauncher.com
www.IndieBookLauncher.com
Cover Design: Saul Bottcher
Interior Design and Typesetting: Saul Bottcher

The body text of this book is set in Adobe Minion.

Also Available
EPUB edition, ISBN 978-1-77342-060-8
Kindle edition, ISBN 978-1-77342-061-5

CONTENTS

This book is dedicated to Chandi.
I would do anything for her.

PROLOGUE

"No price is too high," the man with the German accent said to his host. "I must find it at any cost."

"I will not send my men out on a fool's errand," the Egyptian replied solemnly, staring out toward the orange sand dunes along the edge of his village. The two men sat on portable, reclining chairs under a sturdy cloth canopy. The heat had tapered off as night approached, and a chilly wind wisped fine grains of sand in small torrents along the ground at their feet. Flying insects buzzed and looped around the low-level light fixture above the men's heads.

"I assure you, it is not a fool's errand. It exists, here in your desert. When you find it, you and your people will be greatly rewarded."

The Egyptian looked over at his visitor, as if trying to discern whether he could trust a man with such prestige and political clout. "I will ask for volunteers," the Egyptian finally said. "If any want to search for this thing, they will have my blessing. But I will not force my people to undertake this expedition. We are happy here, and we do not need your money."

"*Needing* my money is not the issue. But surely, some of your people would like more than they have."

"I'm sure that is true. I will give you my answer in two days—and my price. Until then, please leave my village. My people must not be influenced by you or your position with the IWO. It must be a decision each makes of his own free will."

"I understand. I will take my leave of your beautiful village. I will return upon your word, with plans and all information I have at my disposal. And your price will be met, whatever it is. I promise you that."

1

"Are we nearly there?" Ms. Allison Thompson asked. The tour director squinted at her guide as the sun beat down upon her uncovered head.

"We are," Mr. Riyad Shafik replied dourly. He was fed up with Ms. Thompson's constant nagging. He was guiding her small group through the Depression toward The Project, but they had stopped several times for people to take pictures or relieve themselves. It wasn't his fault they were taking so long.

Riyad understood the people—he was a tour guide after all; and he had led hundreds of these kinds of trips through the Qattara Depression over the last few years. Everyone wanted to see the now-defunct "Qattara Depression Project"—a huge hydroelectric project within the Depression. There was nothing else like it in the world. Along the way, every group made several stops to take pictures of the massive sand dunes and the fech fech, the fine powdery sand that lined the desert floor for miles around. Once they got closer to The Project, the people wanted to take pictures of the hypersaline saltpans that stretched across a vast, mostly flat basin. Occasionally, the saltpans would be partially covered by sand, but most of the time, the saltpans were impressive to behold. And everyone wanted photographic evidence to prove that they had been there.

So, on this occasion, nothing was different, except the constant pestering of Ms. Thompson. She was relentless.

"Why is it taking so long?" Ms. Thompson asked again, her high-pitched voice grating on Riyad's nerves.

"As I've already explained to you, Ms. Thompson, your colleagues would like to take pictures. They paid for this tour, and the opportunity to see something truly unique. We must let them see it. Please be patient."

Ms. Thompson slouched on the back of her camel, sulking. Riyad enjoyed that very much, but his face remained passive. He swatted at a fly that had landed on the sleeve of his shirt. The only thing that ever bothered him about these trips was the bugs. The heat or cold—depending on the season—was always bearable, if one wore appropriate clothing. But the bugs—they were relentless, and truly unforgivable at times. On this trip, thankfully, the bugs were a minor inconvenience. It was the incessant buzzing of Ms. Thompson that Riyad loathed. He just wanted to get this over with and return to his home in El-Alamein.

Several minutes passed and the people began to return to their camels. They had fourteen camels in this procession, each ridden by one person. Most of the camels had laid down while their riders wandered away. When the riders returned, it was easy to climb back on before Riyad helped each camel to stand. For those people whose camels had remained standing, Riyad helped them up into the stirrups. It was a process Riyad had carried out many times. He walked between the hardy camels, making sure everyone was seated properly, and then climbed back onto his own mount.

"Come along ladies and gentlemen," Riyad called back over his shoulder from the front of the caravan. "We are very near the penstocks and tunnel. You will be amazed by the sheer size of what you are about to see."

The group followed Riyad in two lines, with each camel following close to the rear end of the one in front of it. They had been trained for this, and rarely deviated from this type of procession.

"As I mentioned before we began," Riyad continued as the soft leathery webs of the camels' feet padded softly across the hard-packed, salt-encrusted earth below them, "construction of The Project required the excavation and construction of a large tunnel from the Mediterranean Sea. That tunnel funneled seawater through a series of hydroelectric penstocks, or enclosures, which generated electricity by releasing the water. That water then spread out from the release point across the basin, evaporating by solar influx. Due to the evaporative effect, water could constantly flow into the depression, creating a stable source of energy. Eventually, water flowing through The Project created a hyper-saline saltpan as the evaporating water left the salt it contained behind. That is what you have just been looking at, and what we are now walking across."

All eyes shifted downward.

"The only other comparable salt pan to the one on which you are crossing is the Bonneville Salt Flats near the Great Salt Lake in the United States.

"In 2034, just twelve short years after the completion of the Qattara Depression Project, a 7.1 magnitude earthquake destroyed the penstocks and release points and caused several large fissures along the length of the tunnel. The Project could not be repaired and was abandoned. While not necessarily as impressive as the Great Pyramids, what you are about to see will still engage your mind. The size of the tunnel and penstocks is truly remarkable."

"Why is it so far from the city?" a short man asked casually.

"That's a very good question, sir. Excavation for The Project required a series of small nuclear explosions. It was good to keep that away from the human population, of course. But also, this particular area was well-suited for this purpose due to the flatness of the terrain and being below sea level. The water from the sea flowed naturally downhill, and then was able to spread out and evaporate quickly to allow for more water to follow. This area, as you can see by looking around you, allowed for great quantities of water to evaporate at a fast pace."

"How much longer, Mr. Shafik?" Ms. Thompson whined, again.

Riyad couldn't believe this woman. He was surprised that anyone would sign up to go on a tour with her as their leader. "It is just around the corner of that hill in front of us. We should be there in less than five minutes. I hope that you can wait that long. You will also soon see a small pillar of sandstone in the shape of a snowman. Ahhh, there it is."

As the group neared the sandstone pillar, the full expanse of The Project opened up before them. It was massive! Every one of Riyad's guests stopped their camels to stare.

"How close can we get?" one man asked.

"You may approach it and walk within the tunnel if you would like. There are very few restrictions. The government of our country has stabilized the structure and torn down any part which could not be made safe. Feel free to wander about. Please check the time on your tech. I would like to begin our return trip in one hour in order to be back to El-Alamein before sunset. Your camels and a snack will be here for you when you return."

As the people dropped down from their camels and headed toward The Project, Riyad walked his camel over toward the snowman-shaped sandstone. The other animals followed, soon reaching the shade of the pillar of rock. Riyad had a favorite little nook on the rock in which he would sit and wait for his guests to return. To him, his seat appeared to be situated on the butt of the snowman, if a snowman could have a butt. Riyad had never actually seen a snowman, but he doubted that they were ever built with a rear end. Nevertheless, this snowman had a definite backside. A small, roundish protrusion stuck out from the bottom of the sandstone pillar on one side. It was always shaded at this time of day. And it was to that spot that Riyad prepared to climb, as he always did, to sit and watch the group wander around The Project in the distance.

Riyad climbed onto the snowman's rear end and settled in. A couple of small, black ants wandered about aimlessly nearby, but Riyad paid them no attention. He leaned back against the cool rock and adjusted his body to fit into the natural curves of the stone. A small fly ambled too near his left eye and Riyad reached up to swat it away, turning his head to the right in the process. Then he stopped, momentarily forgetting what he had been doing.

A swarm of flies, or some kind of flying insect, rose and fell on the breeze some 35 or 40 meters from his position, on the opposite side of the sandstone pillar from where the camels rested. It was the kind of swarm one might see around a dead animal, but Riyad knew it was unlikely there would be a dead camel, or any other animal that large, so far out in the desert. Riyad climbed down from his perch and walked toward the swarm. As he got nearer, he could tell that his vision would be impaired by the enormous volume of flies; and a strange, unpleasant smell wafted toward him on the breeze.

Riyad turned and walked back to the camels. In a bag on the side of each saddle was a full-face mask. On those occasions when the wind and dust blew, he and his tour groups would don the masks. Riyad pulled his mask from his camel's pack and placed it over his head. The mask, with its attached filter, completely covered his face, while still allowing him to breathe filtered air. An imbedded chip allowed him to communicate with those in his tour groups when they wore their masks.

With the mask securely fastened, Riyad turned and walked back toward the swarm of flies. As he approached, even with the mask, on instinct, he squinted his eyes to keep the insects from invading and blinding him. The closer he got, the worse the smell became. Despite the scent-dampening capabilities of the mask, his eyes watered and his stomach lurched. Through his tears, he saw a black object lying on, or in the sand. He moved toward it, his curiosity overpowering his revulsion.

Riyad stopped less than a meter from the object and crouched down, pulling the collars of his shirt together at the neck to keep the insects from entering his clothing. The movement of flies was kicking up dust along the surface of the sand, making it difficult to determine what it was he was looking at. Riyad squinted again as he peered through the swarm of flies and the accumulating dust. He could barely see the object. It was bigger than it had originally appeared.

Riyad moved his hand around over the top of the object, back and forth, trying to clear the flies enough that he could see what was there. *It must be a dead animal*, Riyad thought. *What else would cause so many flies to gather?*

And then he saw it. It was the head and shoulders of a man—the rest of the body buried beneath the sand.

Riyad jumped back to get away from the body of the dead man, tripped over his own feet, and landed hard on his rear. He looked around, frantically, trying to decide whether he was in danger. Riyad knew that his fear was irrational, but he had never seen a dead human body except at a funeral. As he moved his head from side-to-side, looking for danger, he saw another object in the sand about six meters away. He stood and approached cautiously. It only took a moment to identify the second object as the body of another dead man. But this one was different.

The body of this man had not been covered over by the blowing sands. The exterior of the body was dark, and perhaps bruised here and there, but it had not decayed much. *He must have just died!* Riyad thought. That terrified him. *Was he murdered? Is there someone out here killing people?* Riyad looked around again, his heart racing. Seeing nothing else unusual, he considered calling his group back and getting away from there. But something caught his eye.

Riyad bent down to take a closer look at what appeared to be a large hole in the second man's torso. His clothing had been ripped and there was dried blood on his clothes and skin, although not a large amount. Riyad peered closer, the smell so putrid that his stomach heaved in revolt. Several dung beetles scurried from under the man's body toward some unknown destination as Riyad's shadow crossed over the man.

Riyad pulled out his camera and zoomed in. It was the only way he would be able to see through the flies and dust without sticking his face right up next to the body. What he saw on his screen shocked him.

Through the large cut, or bite in the man's chest, Riyad could see that the body's interior contained little more than bones. His body cavity was nearly empty.

Riyad stood and considered what he was seeing. "Who would remove the man's organs and tissue?" he asked aloud. "How can this man be literally just skin and bones?"

Riyad knew there would be no answer, especially since his tour group was still out exploring The Project. He determined that it might be better if they didn't see the bodies. He quickly took several photographs of both bodies, not knowing what to do with them. But knowing the desert as he did, Riyad was certain that, if he didn't take pictures now, the bodies might be covered over, or blown away on the sand of the next great storm.

Soon, Riyad heard the voices of some of the members of his tour group. They were returning from the penstocks. Riyad quickly moved back to the stone pillar and removed his mask, placing it back into his saddle bag. He then climbed up onto the rock to wait, hoping the others would not see the marks around the edges of his face caused by the tightness of the mask against his skin. He had to keep the others from viewing the bodies, or the flies, or anything else that would give away the existence of something unusual.

Within minutes, the whole group had arrived, and he quickly steered them toward the camels, urging them to mount.

"Why are you rushing us?" Ms. Thompson asked.

"Unbelievable," Riyad replied under his breath. Then, calmly, he answered, "We need to get back before the sun sets, Ms. Thompson." Then, turning to the rest of the group, he said, "There is granola and raisins in the packs at your side. Please help yourself as we return to El-Alamein."

"How long will it take us to get back?"

"I would like to get back as quickly as possible," Riyad replied. "Let's get going please."

2

The Cuban sat alone in the dark room, sweat dripping down his spine. His white cotton shirt clung to his bulky midsection, even as his stomach grumbled in anticipation of his next meal. His third cigarette had burned down to its filter and he pressed it into the ash tray on the table beside him. The humidity and smoke in the small room was suffocating; but he had to tell the story. The world had to know what happened. The guilt was tearing him apart.

He considered how he would tell the reporters about his role in the tragedy. He knew for certain that Director Adal Jass, director of the South American or "South AM" Region of the IWO, had to be named. Jass' cold-blooded direction to shoot down Gortari II could not be forgiven. And, more importantly, if Director Jass would do this, what else would he do?

After several long minutes, the old intercom system crackled to life.

"Good morning sir, could you please verify your name?"

"No. I told you I wouldn't say who I am. My name stays out of this."

"That's fine," the voice replied.

"And don't turn on the lights," the Cuban added. "If my face is shown, I'm as good as dead."

"I understand. I also understand you have some information concerning the destruction of Gortari II yesterday. Is that correct?"

"I do. I know everything about it."

After a short pause, the voice coming through the intercom system said, *"Why don't you start from the beginning."*

"Okay. About two weeks ago, I was contacted by a high-ranking official within the IWO. He solicited my help with a project that would, as he said, help Cuba peacefully assimilate into the greater world society. He told me that my help would be invaluable. I asked him why he thought I would want Cuba to assimilate into the IWO. He said he had an extensive background portfolio on me and threatened that if I didn't cooperate, he would disclose my background to Cuban authorities."

"Did that worry you?"

"I'm not going to talk about that. My background has nothing to do with this. Anyway, I agreed to help and then didn't hear from him again until yesterday."

"What did you hear yesterday from this IWO official?" the voice asked.

"He asked me to help shoot down Gortari II. He said that . . ."

The Cuban stopped speaking as a quiet sound arose from the other side of the door to the small room. It sounded like a ticking clock, but he hadn't heard one of those since his childhood.

Suddenly, a violent crash filled the air and the heavy, metal door flew from its hinges, crashing against the table at which the Cuban sat. The table shattered, a sharp wooden edge cutting the Cuban's leg, the blood dripping to the floor.

Light poured into the room from the hallway. The light was so bright, and the man's senses were so dulled from the explosion, that he couldn't see anything more than the shape of a human figure standing in the doorway.

The figure approached the frightened man. As the figure neared, the Cuban could see that a mask covered the stranger's entire head.

The stranger lifted his arm and stuck the cold barrel of a gun to the Cuban's forehead.

"Wh-what are y-you d-doing?" the Cuban stammered.

"This is from our mutual friend," the man replied quietly. "He said you need to stop talking."

The stranger pulled the trigger and the Cuban fell to the floor, dead. A wisp of smoke rose from the barrel of the gun as the stranger fled.

JANUARY 28, 2093, LATER
HAVANA, CUBA

"It is done, Director," Miguel González said quietly.

"Are you certain that he's dead?" Director Adal Jass, director of the South AM Region of the IWO asked, his German accent clear.

"Yes sir. Any information he divulges in the future will have to come from the grave."

"Don't say things like that, man."

"Sir, my brothers and I need to escape Cuba, now. You promised you would help. What is the plan?"

"I will help," Director Jass replied. "In fact, I have another assignment for you that will get you out of Cuba *and* help me again."

"That was not part of the deal sir. You said one assignment, then you would pay us the money, save our family, and help us get away."

"Yes, and I intend to honor that deal. But you may be interested in this next assignment. It pays double."

"Double?"

"Yes, my friend. Double. And there are plenty of people who would be willing to help me for such a large sum. I'm offering it to you first, as a reward for your prompt and efficient help with that squealer."

"What is the assignment, Director?"

"I need you to find the Secretary General of the IWO and assassinate him."

"You want us to kill SEC-GEN Davis?" Miguel asked, incredulous. "Are you mad?"

"I may be," Director Jass replied calmly. "But his death is the only way to proceed with my plan. It must be done."

"If we do something like that . . . I do not know sir. That is a very big risk. I will need to speak with my brothers about it."

"There is no time for that. Accept the assignment now, or I will find someone else who will do it. And, I should add, if you don't help me, I might have a second, more urgent assignment to give to my next guys."

Miguel shook as he considered the veiled threat that he had just received from Director Jass. Jass had lied. He had told Miguel and his brothers that they would be rewarded for their help. Now Jass had just threatened their lives if they didn't continue to help Jass with whatever it was he was trying to accomplish.

It was easy to kill. The González brothers had done it many times. In Cuba, the laws, and enforcement of those laws, were a bit more lax than in the rest of the world. But this new assignment would require Miguel and his brothers to kill someone on foreign soil; and not just anyone. Jass wanted them to kill the Secretary General of the International World Order—the highest ranking governmental leader in the world. Miguel knew that he could not refuse this assignment. Surely the Director would find others who would kill SEC-GEN Davis. Then, they would find Miguel and his brothers too. And maybe even their families. He had no choice.

"Director Jass, I understand that you are offering us a great opportunity. We will do it."

"Excellent!" Jass said.

Jass' excitement over this assignment was frightening. Miguel knew there were men in the world who had no inhibitions about taking the lives of others. He had read about such men in history text books. People like Adolf Hitler and Joseph Stalin. Even some of the presidents of his own country. To Miguel, Jass appeared to be just like them.

"Where do we begin?" Miguel asked, the fear already building inside of him.

FEBRUARY 4, 2093
HAVANA, CUBA

"Sir, there are 3,000 people here now. How many more can we hold?"

"That's it. Cut it off."

"But there are hundreds, maybe even thousands more at the gate. What do we tell them?"

The general sighed. "I don't know. Tell them we are working on ways to get more in. Or tell them we're building more bunkers."

"But neither of those things is true, sir," Colonel Fonseca replied. He was very uncomfortable with this whole process.

After the destruction of Gortari II a few days earlier, by someone on their island, people began getting sick. There had only been a few cases of Anthrax E reported so far, but the numbers were increasing, and President Raul Acosta had ordered that his senior staff and their families be shut off from the world in an old bunker that was built during the Cold War more than a century earlier.

Colonel Anton Fonseca was one of the few people in Cuba who knew anything about this particular bunker. He and a handful of other soldiers had been assigned to keep it in working order, "just in case". He had always believed that "just in case" would never happen. Nobody fought wars any more. Cuba was still communist—a dictatorship—but the rest of the world wasn't. If anyone started a war involving Cuba, it would be Cuba.

Of course, Cuba *had* just started a war. The international backlash against his country was enormous. And Colonel Fonseca wasn't surprised. Thousands of people had died when Gortari II was destroyed, parts of the shuttle and the shuttle's human cargo raining down from the sky and landing all over the Caribbean. Of course the world was angry.

When the orders came from General Borrero to open up the compound and make it ready for habitation, Colonel Fonseca wasn't surprised about that either. But the numbers the General was talking about were outrageous. Sure, the bunker could hold that many people, but how long could they stay alive in there? The bunker hadn't been fitted with any of the modern food processors or oxygenation units. Instead, it was jam packed with canned goods, old government-grade ready to eat meals, spare batteries and water barrels. Colonel Fonseca was certain that, with 3,000 people inside, they wouldn't survive more than a couple of months.

But Colonel Fonseca wasn't in charge. He obeyed his orders. That was the way it worked in Cuba. Obey orders or be imprisoned, or worse, for insubordination. Another reason the world hated Cuba.

"I know it isn't true," General Borrero replied. "But what do you propose? Do you want to tell them that we're full and the rest of them should just hope for the best? If our enemies don't kill them, Anthrax E might. Good luck with that speech Colonel."

"I understand sir," Colonel Fonseca replied. "I hope I can be convincing."

"So do I. Before you go out there, I'll confer with President Acosta. Let's make sure all of his people are in here before we close it up."

Two hours later, Colonel Fonseca and his team heaved and pulled at the giant wheels that moved the massive iron doors into place. The wheels creaked and the doors groaned with the foreign movement. The doors hadn't been closed in a very long time. Outside, at the gates, thousands of people shouted curses against their government. The wrath of its citizens nearly equaled the international wrath Cuba now faced.

As the doors screeched to a halt, the remaining sliver of natural light vanishing as the crack between the iron doors disappeared, Colonel Fonseca felt a twinge of fear. He knew he would not be leaving this compound for a long time; but much more troubling to the Colonel was that *nobody* knew how long they would be isolated within the compound. The government officials still on the surface would make that call. Until President Acosta received an all-clear signal, the giant, impenetrable doors would not open. Anthrax E would not get in; their enemies would not get in; and Colonel Fonseca and 3,002 of his fellow countrymen and women would not get out.

3

"This is not your regular meeting schedule. What's going on?" the director's assistant asked.

"SEC-GEN Davis has called an emergency meeting," South AM Director Adal Jass replied. "I'm certain he wants to share his wisdom about how to deal with this 'global crisis', as he refers to it."

"Do you not think it's a global crisis? There are deaths reported in Mexico and Florida. There are indications, although not publicized, that it is spreading quickly throughout Central AM and it is likely spreading into both North AM and South AM."

IWO Secretary General Antonio Davis appeared on the holo at that moment, cutting off the conversation between Director Jass and his assistant.

"Is the holo on receive only?" Director Jass asked, using the opportunity to refocus his assistant's attention elsewhere. He really didn't want to answer that question.

"*Ladies and gentlemen,*" the SEC-GEN began, "*thank you for joining me on short notice . . .*"

"As if we had a choice," Director Jass grumbled to himself.

"*. . . the global crisis requires that I receive regular status updates from each of you so that we can focus our resources where they are needed most . . .*"

"Is the SEC-GEN sending troops to contaminated areas?" Director Jass' assistant asked.

"Humph," snorted the director. "Not bloody likely!"

"*. . . start with Africa North Region. Director Naser, what is your status?*"

"*No reports of sickness with the suspect symptoms. Is that what you want to know?*"

"*You have people at each of the hospitals, reporting to you?*"

"*Naturally.*"

The SEC-GEN moved on. "*Africa South?*"

"Not even a thank-you," Director Jass grumbled.

"*We look generally good everywhere,*" Director Pretorius replied.

"*What do you mean 'generally'?*"

"*Well,*" added Director Pretorius nervously, "*we have a report of some symptoms near the Johannesburg airport, but it appears to be just the flu.*"

"*Contain it!*" the SEC-GEN ordered.

"*What do you mean?*"

"*Just what I said. Contain it before it spreads!*"

"*But the only way to do that is with foam, as was done in El-Alamein. There are sixteen million people in Johannesburg and we don't even know what it is!*" Director Pretorius exclaimed in alarm.

"*You are in your bunker. You are safe. Do it before it spreads. NOW!*"

Murmuring was heard through the holo, followed by Director Pretorius turning his head to bark directions. Then Director Pretorius dropped off the holo.

The SEC-GEN continued through the regions until he got to Central AM.

"*Central AM, report.*"

No response.

"*Central AM?*"

Still no response.

"*Switch to my private frequency for Central AM,*" the SEC-GEN said to someone outside the holo view. He could not be heard, but he could be seen, first getting more agitated. Then the blood drained from his face. Soon, he gathered himself again and signaled to someone off to the side, at which time the audio returned.

"*It appears we've lost the Central AM regional office ... we will continue. North AM, report.*"

"*Sir, as you are aware, symptoms are spreading north and west from the Gulf Coast. We have shut down all major highways, rail and air transportation from the southeast. We ... *"

"*What have you done to contain it?*"

"*Contain it? Where would we start? We're not talking about an isolated city in northern Africa. This is a densely populated country ... *"

"*DIRECTOR! You are not telling me what I need to hear.*"

"*Wh ... ?*"

"*I want to see a containment plan on my holodesk before the end of the day or you will be dismissed. South AM, report.*"

There was stunned silence for several seconds. Then Director Jass motioned to his assistant to open the channel.

"South AM is clear," Director Jass said. "We drained the Panama Canal and stopped all traffic to and from Central AM and points beyond. We are in our state-of-the-art bunker and monitoring all airports and shipping terminals. That is our report."

"*Very good. Australia, report,*" SEC-GEN Davis continued.

Following the meeting with the SEC-GEN, Director Jass instructed his assistant to set up holos with Marcus and Latisha in North AM and to invite his deputies into the room. The assistant sent a com to the deputies to join the Director in the holo room and started to set up the holos. While they were waiting, his assistant finally spoke.

"You lied to the SEC-GEN. We haven't done any of those things."

"I told him what he wanted to hear," Director Jass replied. "To tell him we already have reports of illness here would just result in more questions that we don't have answers for. We need a cure and that is where I will focus my attention. Besides, we could still drain the canal and do the other things I said, if it would be of any use. And close your mouth before you start catching flies," the director said with a smile, the humor not reaching his eyes. "Let the others in on your way out."

The assistant shook himself out of a stunned silence, closed his mouth, completed setting up the holo through an encrypted line, and opened the door to leave, passing the two deputies on his way out. When the deputies were seated and two holo links had connected, Director Jass began.

"Latisha, Marcus, thank you for joining us on this com. It is encrypted, so feel free to discuss matters openly. Latisha, I've arranged for your placement in the bunker in North AM, near Boston, where some of the brightest minds, or so I'm told, are working to find a cure. I have a meeting with the SEC-GEN two hours from now to finalize our strategy for placing key additional resources in the bunkers. I'll let you know when I have more information for you."

"Okay, thank you sir," Dr. Latisha Bodily replied.

"Marcus, isn't it amazing how arrogant the SEC-GEN is? He treated you like you were a nobody. By the way, where are you now?"

"I'm used to his arrogance Adal," Director Marcus Dorian, Director of the North American or "North AM" Region of the IWO said. "As you suggested, we're headed northwest, away from the contamination. We're currently in Montana."

"Did the SEC-GEN know you weren't in your facility during that conference?"

"No, the link was relayed to us here in Montana. He had no idea."

"Excellent. Keep going northwest, clear to Alaska if necessary. Find a place to hide and continue to track USCAN and other websites. Who is 'we', by the way?"

"I brought Lin with me. She knows nothing, so she's good cover . . . and she's good company, if you understand me."

A chuckle from the director, then, "Clever."

FEBRUARY 23, 2093
RIO DE JANEIRO, BRAZIL

"CNN is saying that over 31,000 people have contracted Anthrax E in the western hemisphere," the director's assistant said.

"I know what they say," Director Adal Jass replied coldly.

"Is there anything we can do about it?"

"No. Please leave me."

"Sorry sir." Director Jass' assistant closed the door quietly as he left the office.

Director Jass sat at his desk for a few moments, his mind drifting between thoughts—the same thoughts that had plagued him for the past four weeks. He continued to act, outwardly, as though the Anthrax E epidemic was no big concern. He assured others that an end was near and that this plague would soon be put to rest. But in reality, he was terrified. Thoughts of his role in the spread of the disease disturbed his sleep night after night.

4

"Sir, your transport is here," SEC-GEN Davis' assistant said, opening the door only slightly to peek her head through.

Davis was seated at his desk in his office on the 70th floor of the IWO Center in Geneva, Switzerland. The room was opulent, as one would expect for an office housing someone as important as the Secretary General of the International World Order. Artwork from the greatest artists and sculptors of the world—Michelangelo, Titian, and Monet—adorned the walls and open spaces.

In the center of the 72nd floor—the top of the building—was an enormous terrarium full of exotic plants from across the globe. Its top was open to receive rainfall from the sky above. A glassed-in, marble-floored hallway surrounded the terrarium and led to the offices of important IWO staff and cabinet members along each side of the building. Every office on the floor had a view into the terrarium and a view of the city below, through massive, floor-to-ceiling windows. Plush Indian rugs adorned the office floors. While the whole building was luxurious, built with the tax dollars of all the nations of the world but Cuba, the 72nd floor was beautiful in the extreme. This is where SEC-GEN Antonio Davis spent his days. His nights were spent in other areas of the building.

The 71st floor housed large, luxury apartments for the cabinet members whose offices lined the floor immediately above. The 70th floor had an expensive, private restaurant and club, and a large pool and spa for use by IWO senior staff and their families only. While more than 15,000 people worked in the IWO Center, less than 200 had access to the 70th floor. Below the 70th floor, a spacious gym, lounges, restaurants, a movie theater and other unnecessary excesses were assembled to entertain the important and powerful women and men of the IWO. Many of these people never left the building.

As SEC-GEN of the IWO, Antonio Davis wielded more power than any other person on Earth—ever. Even his predecessors had not risen to this level of power. That supremacy granted him the right to interfere in international relations and to direct state governments the world over. He was all-powerful; almost a God. At least that's how *he* felt. But now he was afraid. Sitting in his office, he looked out over the vast city of Geneva and its more than two million residents and wondered how this would all play out.

He had been told that everyone on the moon was dead. Reported cases of Anthrax E in the western hemisphere were nearing 1.5 million. Of course, the population of the world was ten and a half billion now, and just a fraction of them were infected. But such a catastrophe, in this modern age, was unprecedented. So many people were dead and so many more would die. Davis did not intend to go down with them.

So far, the eastern hemisphere had been spared, but at the rate the disease was spreading, Davis was not confident that it could be contained.

"Did anyone ever find Director Jass?" the SEC-GEN asked.

"No sir, he still has not responded to coms."

Director Adal Jass was Davis' most-trusted ally. Jass had helped Davis win his first seat on the IWO Counsel in the early days. Since then, they had helped each other along the way. It was rumored that, when Davis' term was over, Jass could easily be elected the next Secretary General, if he could overcome certain violent tendencies. Davis intended to help Jass as far as he was able, but that was years away. In the meantime, Davis needed Jass' help to get through this crisis.

"Well, I need every available person to continue to hunt him down. If I haven't spoken to him beforehand, make sure he is on the next IWO conference call in two weeks."

"Understood, sir. We will track him down."

"Good. In the meantime, tell my driver that I'll be ready in a few minutes."

MARCH 6, 2093
VICTORY BASE, ANTARCTICA

As the small, modern ship touched down on the runway at Victory Base, Antarctica, formerly the American McMurdo Station, SEC-GEN Antonio Davis breathed a sigh of relief. He hated to fly. He rarely left his office in Geneva, for any reason. But two days earlier, he had made the decision to flee the mainland. Of course, he hadn't told anybody he was leaving. Only five people made the trip with him, and nobody else even knew they had left.

His staff had informed him that Victory Base, controlled by the Americans for more than 130 years, would likely be safe from Anthrax E, no matter what went down in the rest of the world. He had banked on it when he left his posh surroundings and the comfort of his apartment at the top of the IWO Center. And, since the American government was presently scrambling to remain viable, he believed there would be no opposition to his assumption of control of the Base.

"We're here, sir," Davis' assistant said.

"I know, thank you. Are the facilities ready for us?"

"We're checking on that now."

Antonio Davis unbuckled his lap belt and stood, stretching his legs. Looking out the window of the small jet, he could see piles of snow along the edge of the runway. En route, the pilot had told him that, normally, not much snow would fall this late in the winter season, but it would still be cold out there, probably below zero, and getting colder.

"While the base doesn't receive much actual snowfall," the pilot had said, "when it does snow, it stays. Only in the warmest winter months—December and January typically—does some of the snow melt, revealing solid, cold dirt. The little vegetation that grows in the area—Antarctic hair grass and pearl wort, some mosses, liverworts, lichens, and algae mostly—will likely be covered by snow soon, if it isn't already."

SEC-GEN Davis had spent a large portion of the flight reviewing the extensive notes his assistant had prepared for him concerning his soon-to-be new home. The first base on the site, he had learned, was only a small hut, was built in 1902 by British explorer Robert Falcon Scott. The United States officially opened its first station at McMurdo in 1956. Within a few years, the base, soon called McMurdo Station, became the center of scientific exploration in Antarctica.

Throughout most of its existence, McMurdo Station was Antarctica's largest community and a functional, modern science station. The Station included a harbor, three airfields, a heliport, a nuclear power station, and more than 100 buildings. McMurdo was previously home to more than 1,000 people during parts of the year. In the 2040's, it was enclosed by a retractable shield, capable of warding off nuclear radiation and other harmful agents. Davis was happy to learn that the shield had been opened for his arrival, but it would soon close again, and not be opened again until Anthrax E had been eradicated.

Less important, but equally exciting to the SEC-GEN was that fact that, while Victory Base was still capable of housing over 1,300 people at any given time, it now rarely housed more than ten or fifteen. Victory Base, he had learned, was rarely used for any purpose of real value these days. Only tourism kept the base open now.

In the warmest months, many brave tourists would come to watch the Adelie penguins and Weddell seals. Occasionally, a lucky traveler would see the Orcas stalk the ice edge, hunting their prey. But now, with the colder months approaching, there were likely to be only a handful of people on the base. Of course, SEC-GEN Davis knew that, with the travel bans in place, there would be no tourists.

When SEC-GEN Davis and his small staff landed on the only permanent airstrip inside the enclosed portion of the base, they were informed that a mere six people were on the premises. And, according to Davis' assistant, two of them were en route to the jet, across the frozen landing strip, to escort the small, but important party, to the Base's central hub.

MARCH 6, 2093, LATER
VICTORY BASE, ANTARCTICA

"Sir, we have confirmed reports of infection in Stansk, Siberia," the assistant said.

"Have the Russians done anything about it," SEC-GEN Davis asked.

"Yes sir. They have quarantined the area."

"We were right to leave Geneva, weren't we?" Davis asked, more to himself than to his assistant.

"Yes sir, I think it was the right choice."

SEC-GEN Davis, along with the four members of his personal staff, sat in a small, comfortable conference room just inside the main doors to the Base. They had been welcomed with open arms. Five of the six people on Base had come to welcome the small group. Most were enamored by SEC-GEN Davis. By popular opinion, he had done more to further the current good fortune of their world than any other person. In reality, SEC-GEN Davis had good people around him, most of whom served the people better than Davis did. But Davis was the face of the IWO. He held the power. He was an idol.

"Excuse me sir," an older man began, as he walked slowly into the small room where Davis and his team were talking quietly, "My name is Dr. Isaac Nelson. I'm sorry I missed your arrival. But we are so glad you are here. When we received the news yesterday that you would be joining us, we prepared special accommodations for you and your staff. Those accommodations are ready for you, at your pleasure."

"Thank you, Dr. Nelsen. I appreciate your concern," Davis replied.

"Dinner will be served in an hour. Thereafter, I would be most happy to take you and your staff on a tour of the facilities and answer any questions you may have. Although my legs don't work so well anymore, it would still be my pleasure, if you aren't in a hurry." The old man smiled and winked at a petite woman on Davis' staff.

"Dr. Nelsen, it would be our pleasure to have you as our guide." SEC-GEN Davis returned the smile.

"Wonderful. We don't have any staff here to prepare meals or tidy living quarters, but we take turns and get by wonderfully. Your stay will not be much like a vacation, I'm afraid, but if there's anything you need, it's available."

"Very good Doctor. My staff and I would like to talk, alone, for a few minutes more, before dinner. After that, we would be pleased to see the base. Thank you, again."

After Dr. Nelsen left the room, closing the door behind him, Davis spoke again. "So, where were we?"

"We were discussing how fortunate we are to be here since Anthrax E has now invaded Russia," his assistant replied.

"Oh yes, that. Well, we are fortunate. And, it seems this facility will happily cater to our needs. If we play our cards right, I'll be in charge here by bedtime."

"I don't think it will take that long, sir."

5

"Joe, we need to get out of here, now!" Diana practically yelled as she burst through the faded, wooden front door.

"Calm down Diana. What's got you so upset?"

Diana dropped her coat onto a kitchen chair, then rushed from the kitchen to the bedroom of the small fishing cabin the young couple had rented for the spring. She came back carrying two suitcases and dropped them on the round kitchen table.

"Don't you care about the reports?" Diana asked, trying to catch her breath. Her asthma was acting up again.

"Diana, you need to calm down. Your asthma, remember?"

"Of course I remember, I'm not stupid. But my lungs won't be worth anything if we get infected."

Diana's doctor had instructed her, just after the couple was married two months earlier, that if she continued to breathe the polluted air in Moscow, she could die. The medications weren't treating Diana's condition the way they did for most other people with similar ailments. Her doctors were baffled. None of the specialists had seen a case of asthma this bad in their lifetimes. Most cases were fully treatable, and often curable. Asthma hadn't been a major concern in any developed country for over 40 years. But Diana had a bad case, and the usual medications not only weren't curing Diana's asthma, but they weren't even effectively treating it. Her doctors finally instructed her to move to some place with cleaner, cooler air. While none of the specialists knew whether it would work, they had no other option to suggest. Diana and her new husband, Joseph, heeded the advice and moved to Stansk in mid-February.

"Okay, okay," Joe said, standing slowly. "Let's pack up. Where to you think we should go? I was just watching the news and they said to stay indoors with the windows and doors closed. That's the safest thing to do, they say."

Diana stopped and looked at the man she had married. "Joe, come on. You're not that naïve, are you?" Diana didn't know Joseph that well. They had met just six months earlier, and had dated for only three weeks before Joe proposed to her. She had been enamored by his chiseled chin, dark brown eyes and muscled physique. When she was honest, she admitted that she married him for his looks, and not much more. The physical aspects of their relationship were amazing!

They had now been married for two months; and during nearly four of the prior six months, Joe had stayed in Moscow to work while Diana saw specialists in London. Neither of them minded the separation at first—only seeing each other on the weekends; but now, having spent significant time together in this remote corner of the world, they were actually falling in love. To Diana, who had never been in love, that was not nearly as frightening as the thought of death by Anthrax E.

"I'm not naïve, but I am a practical man," Joe replied. "I heed the advice I'm given when it's given by people who know what they're talking about. That's why we moved here, remember? Your doctors told us to, so we did."

"That's not the same thing," Diana replied, rushing back to the bedroom. "This is advice we shouldn't follow." She came back out carrying a pile of clothing and stuffed it into her suitcase, not bothering to keep it folded.

"Why?"

"Because Irena just told me she heard that the IWO is going to do something about the problem here. She didn't know what they were going to do, but I'm worried about it."

"So, you're taking the advice of an 80-year-old hair dresser over the advice of the government?" Joe asked, the surprise clear in his voice.

"It's not just that, Joe. I overheard one of the other ladies there talking about a man someone found outside the police station. She said her husband saw the man and he was dead. Nobody knew who he was, but everyone was saying he had Anthrax E."

"Let me com someone. Hold on."

Joe picked up the old desktop phone sitting on the corner of the kitchen counter. The tech in this remote fishing outpost was a few decades behind that of Moscow and the rest of the world, and it was taking some getting used to. He punched eleven numbers on the keypad. As Joe waited for someone to pick up on the other end of the line, he twisted the spiral cord tethering the telephone's handset to the phone in his fingers. A few seconds later, Joe said, "Hey, this is Joe Ivanov . . . yeah, the new guy . . . yeah, I was wondering what you've heard about some guy with Anthrax E here in town . . . uh huh . . . and is it confirmed? . . . right . . . what are you going to do about it?" There was a long pause, then "Okay. Thanks."

Joe set the handset down and looked at his wife, the concern etched across his face. "Diana, it's time to go. I'm sorry I didn't listen to you."

"Do you hear that?" Joe asked as he zipped up his last bag. He and Diana had the hover packed except for this last bag. They both stopped moving and listened.

Moments later, Diana replied, "It sounds like a ship or a chopper."

"Yeah, it does." Joe hurried to the front window and pulled open the dark purple, velvet curtain. He looked up. "There's nothing out there. We need to get outside to see."

"Let's just go," Diana replied. "I don't really care what it is."

Joe picked up his final bag and the couple moved to the front door. Joe opened the door and was hit by a blast of air and snow, along with the loud hum of some automated machine. Lowering his head to shield his eyes, he moved out into the evening. Diana followed close behind. As they reached the hover, the sound became deafening. Diana braved a look upward as she opened her side door.

"What is that?" she yelled over the noise.

Joe looked up just as a blast of warm air engulfed them. Seconds later, the air stilled.

"I don't understand," Joe began. "What's going . . . ?" He stopped mid-sentence. Diana followed his gaze.

No more than 150 meters away, a large wall of white moved toward them. They watched for several seconds, hypnotized by whatever it was they were seeing. Suddenly, Diana screamed, the sound waking Joe from his thoughts.

"Get in the hover!" Joe yelled. Diana was already inside, slamming her door behind her.

Joe engaged the thrusters and backed out of the short driveway into the street. The rear of his hover struck an old truck parked on the opposite side of the narrow lane. The crash surprised him and he stopped moving, lost between the commotion of his wife's terrified screams and thoughts about what he had just done to his new hover.

"Go!" Diana screamed. "Go Joseph!"

Joe hit the thrusters, crushing the old truck further. He had not reversed the thrust. This time, he didn't panic. Reversing the thrust into the forward position, Joe slammed his thumb into the steering panel and the hover took off. The speed of their retreat, coupled with the sharp angle at which Joe turned the hover to get it facing down the street correctly, whipped Diana's head to the side. Her gaze landed outside the window on the wall of white. It was nearly upon them. She screamed again.

The abrupt noise startled Joe as he began to round the corner at the end of the narrow lane. He missed the turn and the rear of the hover slid around to the right, causing the front of the car to face the white wall. Droplets of thick foam splattered on the hood and windshield, drying almost upon impact. Moments later, it engulfed them.

Joe tried to get the hover moving again. The engines roared under the pressure of the thrust; but the hover was stuck.

"Try again," Diana said, her voice cracking.

Joe tried again. He kept the thruster engaged so long that a red light began to blink on the dashboard. Moments later, a quiet voice said, "Engine failure. Please wait. Engine failure. Please wait." The voice repeated the same two phrases over and over again as Joe and Diana stared straight ahead at the white front window.

"Can we get out?" Joe asked quietly. Diana didn't respond.

Joe tried to open his door, but it wouldn't open electronically. He pulled the manual release lever, but the door remained closed. He reached over and tried Diana's door. It was stuck too.

Joe and Diana sat in their car for several hours. Diana cried until her tears ran dry. Joe closed his eyes and prayed.

Nobody would ever see Joe and Diana Ivanov again. Their bodies, and those of hundreds of others—like the thousands of bodies in El-Alamein, Egypt just six weeks earlier—would be trapped forever under rigid, high-density, microcellular polyurethane ("HMP") foam.

MARCH 7, 2093
VICTORY BASE, ANTARCTICA

"Did it work?" SEC-GEN Antonio Davis asked his assistant. They were sitting in the small conference room on the Base. The assistant lounged in a reclining chair while the SEC-GEN sat straight upright on the edge of a hard, plastic chair. Davis was surprised by the calm demeanor of his assistant.

Davis' assistant took a sip from a steaming mug and looked at the SEC-GEN. "Yes. The foam was applied across the entire town. As far as we know, nobody escaped."

"Is anyone talking about it? I mean, do people know what we did to Stansk?"

"I'm sure they do, sir. I don't know how it could escape the public's eye with the amount of news centered on the town's plight over the past few days."

"We censored the media though, right?" Davis asked nervously.

SEC-GEN Davis couldn't hide his concern. This move was a decision that he had approved as soon as it had been suggested. The fear in the west had driven him to make a rash decision, hoping to curb the spread of Anthrax E in the east. He knew, as did the rest of them, that if the plague escaped Stansk, Siberia, the rest of the world would fall. The decision had not been hard. But the ramifications of the decision—the death of hundreds of innocent lives—had kept the SEC-GEN up all night.

"Sir, you can relax," Davis' assistant replied. "We issued a gag order; but whether it is followed is no matter."

"What do you mean?" Davis asked.

"I mean that it should not upset you so much. You are safe here. Your position as Secretary General of the IWO is safe. Who would take it from you now, when your leadership is more important than ever? But there's more to it than that, Antonio. The plague is going to consume the world, and no amount of foam, no matter where it is spread over this globe, will stop it now."

"How can you be so calm?" Davis asked. "You believe the world is going to end, yet you sit there in your chair, drinking whatever it is you're drinking, talking as though none of this matters." The SEC-GEN was getting more animated with every word. "Have you no concern for the value of human life? What gives us the right to choose who lives and who dies?" Davis slumped in his chair as his words faded out. "Who gave us the right?"

"Sir, I mean no disrespect to you—or to the human race. But unless someone develops a cure or a vaccination to Anthrax E, we can do nothing."

The SEC-GEN looked at the floor.

"Look at me, Antonio," the assistant said. Davis looked up and into the eyes of his assistant. The man's eyes were filled with tears, threatening to escape if the man were to blink.

"Sir, I care. I care more than I can tell you. My family is out there, just like yours. They are going to die too. There is nothing we can do. I am just trying to accept it. You need to accept it too. The decision to bury Stansk may be the last decision you ever have to make as Secretary General of the IWO. Your reign, and the IWO, will soon have no power and there is nothing you, or we, can do about it. Nobody will fault your decision, because nobody will care. Soon, nobody will be alive to care. And anybody who survives this will not even remember who you are. If you can accept that, you might just be able to sleep at night. If you can't accept that, then it might be time for you to leave Victory Base and go down with the ship. But Antonio, that would be the wrong decision. You cannot save the lives of the world by your own death."

When the assistant had finished, both men cried. Several minutes later, Antonio Davis looked up from the floor, wiping his eyes with the back of his hand. "This never happened," he said resolutely. Then he stood and walked to the door. "Never happened," he repeated as he opened the door and walked through, closing the door softly behind him.

MARCH 9, 2093—PRIVATE HOLO CONFERENCE

"You're where?" South AM Director, Adal Jass asked, incredulous.

"Antarctica," SEC-GEN Antonio Davis replied. Jass could see the SEC-GEN on the Holo, and Davis didn't even look bothered.

"Why didn't you tell me?"

"I'm telling you now."

"Obviously," Adal replied. "But why didn't you tell me you were going there?"

"Well, I guess I forgot that I had to report to you and get your permission," Antonio replied, the sarcasm evident.

"Don't start, Tony," Adal replied. "You know it's because of me that you sit on that throne in Geneva. I should be on your right hand."

"Adal, the way you're acting right now, it seems I have you *eating from* my right hand. Now, grow up. You're a Continental Director of the IWO. Perhaps you should start acting like it."

"I . . . I'm sorry, sir," Adal replied, realizing his mistake. He knew it would not do any good to squabble with this man. He needed to prove his value. "You're right. I am acting poorly. Please forgive me."

"Forgiven," Antonio replied, lifting his head slightly with an air of authority. "Anyway, there is a reason for my call, and it isn't to upset you. You are my friend, and my ally Adal. I called you to let you know of my whereabouts, so that we may maintain contact in the face of this crisis. It will take both of us to head it off."

"Sir, let me come to you at Victory Base, before it's too late."

"It's already too late Adal. You can't leave your rocky fortress. You'll become infected. Obviously, that will not do either of us any good."

"You're wrong Tony. I will find a way."

"The answer is 'no'. I need you to stay where you are. You told me you had your team working on a vaccine, and that you would complete it before the American team. If that's true, then I need you to stay where you are and make that happen. The world is counting on you to save it."

"I can save the world from any place on it. My team will create a vaccine whether I'm here or there, or whether I'm on the moon. Let me help from your side."

"No."

Adal Jass paused only a moment as the SEC-GEN's final word sank in.

"Then I hope you haven't placed too much faith in me, sir," Adal said with derision. "I wouldn't want to disappoint you." Adal Jass disconnected the com.

MARCH 9, 2093, LATER—HOLO CONFERENCE

"He's in Antarctica," Director Jass said.

"What? How did that happen? He has not left the IWO building. I am sure of it."

"I understand. You have been very patient, my friend. But I assure you, he is not where you think he is."

"How would you like us to proceed?" Miguel González asked.

Miguel, and his brothers, Carlito and Fancisco, had spent the last two months waiting for the SEC-GEN to appear in public. They had rented a small apartment near IWO headquarters in Geneva, Switzerland. Davis never left the building and security was much too tight for them to gain entrance. Plus, none of them thought it wise to attempt such a feat deep inside the most powerful organization the world had ever known.

Now, finally, they had news, albeit a bit shocking. Their assignment, thrust upon them by threat—to assassinate Secretary General Antonio Davis—had been hard to accept at first. Miguel's brothers had rebelled against the idea, until they learned that their family was safe inside the government bunker in Havana in early February. But thereafter, knowing that their family was safe from Director Jass even if they failed, they were ready to take on the task. The money offered by Jass was significant—more money than most people in their native Cuba earned in a lifetime.

"I will give you instructions later. I have yet to figure out how you will accomplish your task now. Perhaps you should just stay where you are. My people will pay for another month's rent. Enjoy your stay amigos."

Director Jass ended the com.

6

"Thank you for joining me by teleconference this morning, ladies and gentlemen," SEC-GEN Antonio Davis began. *"I'm sorry we aren't able to see one another on the holos as we have done at other times. IWO holo controllers in the Americas are currently inoperable. It appears the channels have been hacked following the mass exodus of governmental employees due to Anthrax E."*

That was a lie, and Director Jass knew it. The holos worked just fine. But SEC-GEN Davis apparently wanted his privacy. Nobody else, apart from Director Adal Jass, knew where Davis was—at least not yet. Jass was certain the SEC-GEN didn't want his colleagues to see the despair and hopelessness in his eyes.

"In any event, as you all know, Anthrax E is still spreading. We have confirmed that it is airborne. No one is safe unless they are in a bunker with a positive air pressure ventilation system. Our scientists around the globe are working day and night to find a cure, or to produce a vaccine, and our citizens on the moon have been directed to stay there."

"Sir . . . " someone started to say.

The voice was overridden. *"Questions later,"* the SEC-GEN said. *"Africa North, report."*

"No change. No sign of the virus. No suspicious deaths."

"Africa South, report."

Silence.

"Africa South?"

Silence.

"Get Africa South on their private line . . . if you can," the SEC-GEN said, not attempting to hide his remark.

After an uncomfortable wait, the SEC-GEN continued. *"You will all remember that our last report from Africa South, two weeks ago, was that people were sick in the bunker. As of today, several are dead and the rest are too sick to join the holo. The director reports that he has no idea concerning the condition of his region and there will be no more reports from him.*

"North AM, Director Robinson, thank you for joining us. Please report, starting with the whereabouts of former Director Dorian."

"Thank you, Mr. Secretary-General," the new director for North AM said in a no-nonsense voice. *"Mr. Marcus Dorian's whereabouts are unknown. Our attempts to locate him have been frustrated at every turn. Our attempts at containment, likewise, have not worked. We cannot get enough healthy volunteers to fly the aircraft. The military is in disarray as more and more soldiers leave their posts . . . "*

As the director of North AM concluded her report, Adal Jass turned to his assistant and gave instructions.

"Don't open a coms channel," Director Jass ordered.

"South AM, report."

Director Jass' assistant looked at him, his hand halfway to the controls. He turned to look at his controls as his hand continued to reach. A quiet hum sounded, causing the assistant to turn back to the director. Director Jass held a small gravity ray gun in his right hand, and it was pointed at his assistant's face.

"I said," the director breathed through clenched teeth, "Do not, open, the channel."

The assistant's hand dropped to the table. He was clearly worried and afraid. Director Jass wasn't surprised. Jass was certain his assistant had never seen him in this light. The assistant's fear was evident to the director, whose grim smile didn't reach his eyes.

"South AM, are you there? . . . Get South AM on their private line. There must to be a problem with the telecom."

The private line started to ring in the South AM control room. The assistant looked at the ringing phone, then at Director Jass, expectantly. The gun was still aimed at his face as the director shook his head once. The assistant laid his hands flat on the table and gulped reflexively.

"I regret to inform you that South AM is not responding," the SEC-GEN remarked, his voice shaky. "This is . . . unexpected."

A short pause followed as if the SEC-GEN were thinking of possibilities or gathering his thoughts. Then, taking a deep breath, he continued. "Let's move on."

In the bunker in Rio de Janeiro following the meeting, Director Adal Jass' assistant disconnected the com and turned toward his boss. The gun was no longer pointed at him, but hung loosely in the Director's hand at his side.

With a look of relief on his face, the assistant asked, "Why did you do that?"

"I want the SEC-GEN to think we are dead."

"I gathered that, but why?"

"I'm tired of taking directions from that imbecile," Director Jass replied. "This way, we control our own destiny. Do you not agree?"

"That much is clear. But why do we not want to work with them to solve the crisis?"

"The crisis is beyond their ability to resolve. I have resources in place to acquire the cure when it is available. I will control who has access, not that idiot SEC-GEN," the Director spat, venom in his voice.

The assistant shrank back in his chair in fear. Then, as the realization of what the Director meant settled over him, he reacted.

"You can't do that! The cure needs to be free to everyone. You can't decide who will live and who will die!"

"Actually, I can and I will . . . as soon as my team tells me there is a vaccine and acquires it for me."

"*What?* What team? Why am I just now hearing about this? I'm your assistant."

"That is no longer true," Director Jass replied quietly. He raised the ray gun and shot his assistant in the forehead. Nobody else in the bunker heard the silent, deadly shot. Two days later, when asked about his assistant, Director Jass informed his team that his assistant had left the bunker voluntarily during the night, and would not be returning.

MARCH 19, 2093—IWO TELECONFERENCE
VICTORY BASE, ANTARCTICA

"Sir, no response from South AM's private line," Ms. Bria Newton said quietly. Ms. Newton had been SEC-GEN Davis' clerk for several years. She thought herself fortunate to be able to accompany the Secretary General from Switzerland to Victory Base two weeks earlier when her boss became convinced that Anthrax E might not be contained. Now, like her boss, she was frightened. She had friends in South AM; and now the Director of South AM, Adal Jass, had not answered. This was very bad.

Acknowledging his clerk with a slight nod of his head, SEC-GEN Davis returned to the teleconference. "I regret to inform you that South AM is not responding," he said, his voice shaking with the news. "This is . . . unexpected."

When the teleconference concluded, and all other personnel had left the briefing room, SEC-GEN Davis dipped his head and closed his eyes. "I'm sorry Bria," he said quietly, not lifting his head.

She laid her small hand lightly on his forearm, sympathetically. "It's not your fault Antonio. What else can we do?"

"I don't know what else to do," Davis replied, resting his hand atop hers and smiling sadly. "The plague is sweeping across North and Central AM. Africa South has fallen, it is spreading from Russia, and now South AM may have succumbed too. It wasn't contained in the west. I don't think we can stop it."

"Are the scientists in the United States getting close to a vaccination?" Bria asked hopefully, standing and moving closer to Davis. When she was close enough, she placed both hands behind his head and moved his head to rest against her stomach.

He put his arms around her waist.

"Not yet. They don't appear to be progressing—not quickly enough, anyway."

"Are you going to bring more people here to Victory Base, now that the situation seems so dire?" Bria asked. "Like you wife?"

"Yes. We have a transport scheduled to arrive on March 25th with a few people, including my wife. The plan was to bring in only key people from areas not yet contaminated. But, with our current knowledge, we must begin, I think, to fill this place up to capacity. It may be all we can do."

Antonio couldn't see her eyes, but if he had looked, he would have seen tears running down Bria's cheeks.

7

Thomas Franconi waited by the holo on his airship. He had touched down on the now-deserted runway at Dunedin International Airport in New Zealand an hour earlier. Due to the international travel freeze, no aircraft were flying these days. But Thomas had an important mission, and permission from high up.

SEC-GEN Antonio Davis was supposed to contact him, imminently. Davis had said the mission would be simple, but all Thomas knew was that he was going to be transporting a team of important people across the sea from New Zealand to somewhere in Antarctica in the next day or two. Thomas was excited to finally learn the logistics. He couldn't believe his luck at being courted by both the SEC-GEN, and more recently, Director Adal Jass. Thomas had been attempting to assert himself into politics for several years, with little success—until recently. Certainly, his acquisition of the A-400 airship had helped. The recent turn of events had been fortuitous, to say the least.

Six days earlier, Thomas Franconi had walked onto the grounds at the Kennedy Space Center, unchecked. There was nobody around—no guards, no employees, and no tourists. He was wearing a basic hazmat suit which had been delivered to his home by an unknown benefactor a few weeks earlier. He had guessed it was arranged by his former business partner, Alan Stein, until he heard that the moon was ravaged by the plague. Stein was probably dead. But it didn't matter who had sent it. Thomas had been wearing the hazmat suit since its arrival, and he was alive and healthy, unlike most others from his hometown of Bridgeport, Connecticut. His trip of over 1100 miles from Bridgeport to the Kennedy Space Center was simple. The streets were virtually empty. Upon his arrival, the A-400 was just sitting there, its doors closed but unlocked, as if waiting for passengers or crew who never showed up. A note accompanying the hazmat suit had said that would be the case and provided specific instructions as to the date and time Thomas should arrive. Once inside the ship, he followed additional directions written in the note through a complete decontamination of himself and the ship. He'd felt free and alive ever since.

The A-400 was a modern flying craft, and the only one of its kind according to Thomas' research after his acquisition of the ship. It was so sophisticated that, had he not been a pilot, he was sure he would not have been able to fly it. Not only did it have a long-range capacity unequalled in the modern flying era, but it also had containment facilities with airlocks and decontamination facilities. Why the ship had been left on the tarmac at a time when its use would be most beneficial to whomever occupied it was unknown to Thomas. But again, just like the hazmat suit, he didn't care. It was now his, and he intended to make good use of it.

For the past six days, Thomas had been flying around the world, watching the progress of the plague from live satellite news feeds aboard the ship, and hoping that someone would take notice of his new acquisition and beg for his help. He had com'd a personal acquaintance at the office of the SEC-GEN to give them the news. He had also com'd the secretary for a political supporter in Brazil—South AM Director Adal Jass.

But a recent encrypted message from Director Jass was confusing. Jass had said that the SEC-GEN was going to cut Jass and all of the other Continental Directors out of the picture and establish some kind of terror-based government. Thomas was no genius, and he never proclaimed to be, but Jass made it sound like the SEC-GEN had gone wonky. If Jass was right, how could he possibly help the SEC-GEN and feel good about it? Jass was supposed to contact Thomas too, but he didn't know when. And he didn't know what he would say to either of the men.

As Thomas awaited his com with the SEC-GEN, he began to doubt whether he should be speaking with SEC-GEN Davis at all. As he waited, an incoming com caused the light on his console to flash. The number was encrypted. Thomas touched the receive button on his screen and waited.

"Thomas, is that you?" The voice was familiar and kind.

"Yes," Thomas replied. "Is that you Director Jass?"

"Yes Thomas, it's me. Please, call me Adal. Did you get the package I sent you?"

"You mean the hazmat suit? It was from you?"

"Yes."

"Yes I did Director, I mean Adal. Thank you."

"You're very welcome," Director Jass replied. "Where are you now?"

"I'm in New Zealand. SEC-GEN Davis sent me here. He's supposed to contact me right now."

"Don't pick up that com Thomas," Jass said quietly. "I don't know his plan, or what he's going to ask you to do, but I do know this: his motives are pure evil. I don't want you to be sucked into whatever he's got going on. It won't end well for you, or for any of us. We intercepted an encrypted com between Davis and the scientists in North AM a couple of hours ago. They intend to create a vaccine and keep it for themselves. That lunatic Davis wants everyone in the world to die from Anthrax E. Whatever he has planned for you to do cannot be good."

"Sir . . . Adal, it is hard to believe any of that," Thomas replied quietly.

"I need you to believe me Thomas. We can't let Davis have his way, or we're all going to die. I promise you that."

"Then what can we do?" Thomas asked. "What can I do?"

"What is Davis' plan?" Jass asked.

"Well," Thomas began, unsure how much he should say, "I don't know everything yet, but he is supposed to have me take some people to him, somewhere in Antarctica, in three days."

"Three days?" Jass wondered aloud. "Interesting. That can't happen Thomas. I need you to shut down coms to and from Antarctica—all of them."

"How? I don't know how to do that."

"It will be simple Thomas. It is convenient that you are in New Zealand. There is a small island off the south coast of New Zealand called Campbell Island. It has an enormous communications facility that was built 40 years ago or so. It is largely uninhabited. Its operations are highly automated. Only two or three people are there most of the year. You have your ship, right?"

"Yes, I'm on it now, at the airport in Dunedin. And thank you for *that* too."

"You're welcome," Jass said. "I'll arrange for your clearance for takeoff within the hour and send you the coordinates for the island. All you need to do is blow the towers from the face of the Earth. Simple. That communications station is the only direct link with Antarctica. You can cut Davis off from the rest of the world with the simple push of a button."

"But won't I kill the people there?" Franconi asked, hesitantly.

"No Thomas, I will arrange for them to be gone within the hour. I wield a lot of influence you know."

"Are you sure Adal? I don't want to kill anybody."

"It will be taken care of. Wait for my signal, then fly on over and have a blast. Of course, make sure you're far away from the island. I wouldn't want you to be caught up in the discharge. I consider us friends and I hope you can join me in Brazil in the near future."

After a moment of hesitation, Thomas replied, "I'll do it Adal. I'll just wait for you to tell me when."

"Thank you Thomas. You are doing a great thing. I intend to reward you for it at the appropriate time. After you have completed the mission, return to Dunedin and wait for my com."

Director Jass had lied. There was no encrypted com between the SEC-GEN and the scientists in North AM. As far as he knew, SEC-GEN Davis was in Antarctica hiding from Anthrax E, not developing some plot to destroy mankind. Indeed, Jass knew that he was likely the only person plotting to rule the world, and that he, alone, was the only person likely to succeed. Of course, Jass wasn't about to tell Thomas Franconi any of that. He needed Franconi, and his ship. The idiot would do anything for a little recognition. That was the beauty of this situation. Jass intended to leave SEC-GEN Davis in Antarctica to die, or, if it could be arranged, to have his hired assassins delivered to Davis' doorstep. But it would take a bit of cooperation from the numbskull Thomas Franconi.

Adal Jass had said what needed to be said. He had no intention of warning or helping the two or three people on Campbell Island; nor did he ever want to see Franconi in the flesh.

MARCH 22, 2093, 10:07AM
DUNEDIN, NEW ZEALAND

"Mr. Franconi, I apologize for my delayed com. I hope you are still with us my friend."

"Of . . . of course, Mr. SEC-GEN. Whatever you need." Thomas Franconi was confused. He had just agreed to help Jass; and yet, SEC-GEN Davis still needed his help. He would have to choose. *Which one of them is more likely to follow through with his promises?*

"That's excellent. Where are you now?"

"I'm in New Zealand, just as you asked."

"Fantastic. As we discussed previously, I have arranged for you to bring a group of people, along with supplies, to me."

"But where are you?" Thomas Franconi asked, feigning ignorance. He needed to know whether what Jass had just told him was accurate.

"I'm in Antarctica, but I'm not going to tell you my exact location yet. I'll send the coordinates to you after you're in the air. And when you arrive, you will be welcome to stay with us, of course."

"Thank you, Mr. SEC-GEN. When do the people arrive?"

"They should be there in three days—March 25th—as we previously discussed. I will send you more details as we get closer. In the meantime, just stay where you are. Enjoy the weather. We will be in touch soon."

"I look forward to it." Thomas shut off the com. His decision had not been made for him. It should be so simple, but it was not. He could stick with Davis and be safe in Antarctica, or tie his hands to Jass and be safe in Brazil. But both of them were lying to him. He felt it in his gut.

But this he knew: he had a ship—the A-400. He could live in it, safely, until a vaccine was created. If one was never created, then living in Brazil with Jass *or* Antarctica with Davis were both depressing options. Perhaps he could leave both options open. Could he cut off Davis' communications as Jass wanted and still go to Antarctica if necessary? Perhaps Davis would never know it was Thomas who had done it. Certainly, if he failed to destroy Campbell Island, Jass would know, and then Jass would never let him in.

That was it. Thomas would have to destroy Campbell Island and take the chance that Davis would never find out. Then, both men would still be on his side and groveling for his services. The decision had been made.

MARCH 22, 2093, 10:53AM
VICTORY BASE

"Sir, communications are down," Coms Secretary, Jason Blunt said as SEC-GEN Davis entered the communication center.

"What do you mean?" SEC-GEN Davis asked, confused.

"I mean that we cannot communicate with anyone outside the Base. Everything is down."

"Well, fix it," Davis said, not reciprocating the urgency displayed by his Coms Secretary. "I need to place a call."

"Sir, we have tried to remedy the situation remotely, with no success. About five minutes ago, the computers registered a problem coming from the communication relay components on the perimeter of Victory Base. That system is necessary to relay coms between Victory and the outside."

"So, go fix it."

"A team is headed out now, sir. I'll let you know when they report in."

"What could have happened?" SEC-GEN Davis asked.

"We don't know that sir. There is no video surveillance of anything physical occurring outside. We've checked everything from twelve hours ago. There is no evidence of any vessel in the water, ship in the sky, or person on land anywhere near our location during that timeframe. So, physical damage to the relay components, here, seems unlikely. But . . ."

"Why do you hesitate?"

"Well, we lost coms, which is bad enough; but we also lost all satellite feeds. We have absolutely no link to the outside now. While we can certainly control coms from here, shutting them off or encrypting them, I think the problem lies outside the Base because we have absolutely no control now."

"This isn't good," Davis said quietly. "So, what if the system *is* physically damaged?"

"Well, without operational relay components, we can't communicate with anyone outside Victory. In order to reestablish coms, we would have to repair whatever went wrong, if the problem is here. And, if the problem is with the relay system here, we don't have those components. But again, I don't know whether the problem is here or elsewhere, physical or something else."

"We have people coming here in three days from New Zealand. Can't they bring us a new relay system, or whatever is needed, before they come in?"

"Sir, it's not that simple. Those people aren't going to be coming. You established the protocol. It's on your orders that the newcomers will only be authorized to travel here after we have received health records and confirmed the health for all persons one hour prior to their departure from Dunedin. We won't be receiving those records and won't be able to give them the green light to launch. Without our approval, they will never approach Antarctica. That would be a breach of your protocol, and unlikely. We are dead in the water, so to speak. And nobody out there even knows it. They'll just wait for our signal to proceed, which we can't give."

"So, you're telling me that we're stuck? No coms. No more arrivals. Nothing?"

"Yes, sir. I'm sorry. Of course, we could leave the Base and . . ."

"Absolutely not," SEC-GEN Davis said quickly. "That is out of the question."

"Then our only hope is that someone might come to us unannounced. If someone gets close enough to the Base, then our internal coms system might be able to pick them up through the shields. But the external system is gone. Sir, does anyone even know we're here? Does the team that was supposed to be coming even know where we are?"

"No. The pilot of the transport scheduled for three days from now would not have learned our exact location until the time of departure. There is only one person that knows exactly where we are."

"Who knows we're here?" Jason Blunt asked.

"Adal Jass." Davis sat down hard, leaned forward and put his face in his hands. He had forbidden Jass from coming to Antarctica. Jass would not come. Nobody would.

"What would you like me to do?"

"Pray for a miracle. We must hope that someone comes down here to find us."

MARCH 22, 2093, 10:57AM
RIO DE JANEIRO, BRAZIL

South AM Director Adal Jass sat in a straight-backed chair in a small office inside the bunker in Rio. The office, like the rest of the bunker, was small, but comfortable. The furniture, outdated by several decades, was functional, and left only a little to be desired.

Director Jass and a team of scientists, and others, had taken refuge inside the bunker to weather the storm. Anthrax E was devouring the whole country. Indeed, the whole world was in danger. And the speed at which the plague was progressing was frightening.

But on this occasion, Anthrax E was far from the Director's mind.

"What's the status?" Director Jass asked.

"Franconi succeeded at destroying the coms center," the man replied.

"And what of communications with Victory Base?" Jass asked, sneering as he said the words.

Adal Jass had learned from contacts in Geneva that SEC-GEN Davis and a handful of technical personnel and staff had vanished about three weeks earlier. *That would be when they left for Victory Base,* he figured. The base was much more significant than Adal wanted to admit. He had wanted in. He knew, as the SEC-GEN did, that Anthrax E was going to be trouble. But Davis told him "no", and there was no way any ship carrying an unwanted passenger, like Adal, would ever safely land at Victory Base; and even if they could land, they would not be allowed inside. So, Adal would be forced to stay in Brazil.

It was Adal's resentment at this snubbing that had led him to rethink his plans a few days earlier. If Adal had his way, the IWO would be fractured until only he had any control; but accomplishing that objective would take a bit more work. And that work had just begun. Things were looking up.

"They are also down, permanently, sir. Both incoming and outgoing."

"What assurance can you give me that communications entering and leaving Victory Base are permanently disabled?" Director Jass asked, a smile turning up the corners of his mouth as the implications began to surface in his mind.

"Sir, all wireless links and satellite coms have been severed between the Base and Campbell Island, as a result of the explosion. Until now, the only communications access Victory Base had with the mainland was via relay uplinks with Campbell Island. I don't know why it was set up that way, but it certainly has worked to our advantage. They are stranded down there and wholly unable to communicate with the outside."

"Will they be able to reestablish a link with anyone?" Jass asked.

"It is highly unlikely. As I understand it, Victory Base has no way to reestablish communications from their position. They would have to leave Antarctica."

"Excellent. And they aren't likely to do that, are they?"

"I think not, sir; not with the progression of Anthrax E presently."

"But what about personal coms equipment? Is that still operational? I can't have Davis communicating with someone via his personal tech."

"Also blocked. Every form of com technology at Victory Base relies on broadcasts from Campbell Island. 50 years ago, more or less, the Americans covered Victory Base with a retractable, clear, impermeable, high-tech version of the old Faraday Shield. It's a form of electromagnetic shielding. They had two goals. They wanted to protect the Base from nuclear radiation, in case the Russians, North Korea, or some terrorist group ever started another world war. And they wanted to shield the Base from unfriendly communications with hostiles."

"How does that work?" Jass asked, genuinely interested.

"It's difficult to explain. But generally, the Shield isolates electrical devices from the 'outside world'. Electromagnetic radiation is reflected from the surface of the Shield keeping internal communications inside, and external communications outside. It's kind of like a big microwave oven. Coms can be controlled—opened and closed—only from inside the Base. And, by the way, the Shield will also, almost certainly, protect the Base and its occupants from Anthrax E."

"So, because of this electromagnetic shield, Victory Base can't receive or send coms unless *they* want to? *They* have to authorize the coms?"

"That's correct."

"Then why did we bother destroying Campbell Island if coms can't get in or out without approval from the Base?" Jass was perplexed. He was a politician, not a scientist.

"Well, even though coms can be controlled from the Base alone, they still rely on various communication components to make it work. It's only through the use of directional microwaves, pointed directly at Campbell Island, and vice versa, that the Base is, or was, able to communicate with the outside. That system could be shut off, if necessary, from the Base. But from the outside, the only way to stop communications running *to* the Base, is to destroy the system. That's why I suggested destroying Campbell Island. By destroying Campbell Island, we have shut off coms externally. That means nothing they do at the Base can restore the system."

"Clever. This is good news," Director Jass replied.

"There's more, sir," the man said, smiling. His knees were bouncing up and down as he watched Jass' face.

"What is it?" Jass asked, uncomfortable with the broad smile lighting up his technician's face.

"As a result of the actions of your man at Campbell Island, the moon colonies are also no longer able to communicate with Earth. In fact, it appears that the shells of the moon cannot even communicate with each other."

"That's interesting. How did that happen?" Jass asked.

"Well, it was a work of genius on my part, if I may say so," the man replied, standing up, obviously unable to control his excited energy. "Just prior to Franconi's actions at Campbell Island, I re-routed all Earth-Moon communications through the Campbell Island station. Because everyone on Earth is so focused on containing Anthrax E, or staying alive, nobody even noticed."

"I won't bother asking how you accomplished that," Jass replied. "But it sounds like excellent news."

"It is sir, but for more reasons than you might imagine. Of course, SEC-GEN Davis won't be able to communicate with the outside now. But also, there are only six people alive on the Moon, as far as we know, including your friend, Mr. Stein. Now Stein can't communicate with Earth. And I thought that shutting off coms between the shells might be a nice gesture too, as it appears Mr. Stein is alone presently. I thought you might enjoy the thought of Stein wallowing in self-pity and regret until he goes insane."

"Ah yes. I had forgotten about that imbecile Stein," Director Jass growled. "The man who wouldn't die. Will any of them be able to restore moon-to-Earth communications? I can't have Stein informing any of the Directors in the IWO of my plans—and he will if he can."

"Well, it's possible. They could certainly restore moon communications among the shells, if any of them have such knowledge and capability. But in order to restore moon-to-Earth coms, they would require assistance—from me. That is, unless Stein is a genius. It would take a significant amount of intelligence, and a lot of luck, to figure out what happened on Campbell Island, identify the problem as being one of re-routing rather than anything physical, trace the protocols and formulas I entered to reroute communications through Campbell Island, and then reverse the process. I don't think many people, let alone Stein, could figure it out."

"But someone on Earth could help Stein, if that someone knew how to do so, correct?" Jass asked.

"Sure, but SEC-GEN Davis' people at Victory Base won't be able to resolve the problem since they can't communicate with the outside world at all now. Plus, why would Davis even care? And, because all communications and actions of the IWO run through the SEC-GEN, it is probable that the IWO will fall apart, or at least, they will run around like their heads are cut off. I doubt that anyone here on Earth will continue to monitor the situation on the moon any longer, since there will be no way to communicate. And you, sir, are the only one who knows what is going on."

"Besides you, of course."

"Of course."

"But if the moon and the surface somehow do reestablish coms, will it be possible for Victory Base to link in and gain access?" Director Jass asked thoughtfully.

"No, I don't think so," the man replied. "Again, Victory Base is cut off down there. They would need help from the mainland to reestablish a link with anyone. As far as we know, the only person with any authority that has any knowledge of the SEC-GEN's presence at Victory Base is you. Not even Marcus Dorian knows the SEC-GEN is there. And, if your plan goes well, you will soon be the only Director left alive anyway."

"Thank you, my friend. You have done well." Director Jass said, standing.

As the man reached for the door to the small office, Director Jass said, "Wait a minute."

"Yes sir?" The man turned back around to face the Director.

"Give me a moment." Director Jass had just realized that his plan to assassinate the SEC-GEN may have just become a bit more difficult. There was some kind of shield around Victory. How would the Cubans get in? Attempting to sound casual, he asked, "If this shield surrounds Victory Base, can Davis even leave, if he wanted to, that is?"

"Yes sir," the man replied. "*If* Davis wanted to leave his protected enclosure, he could easily do so. But I don't think we need to worry about that."

"But he could, right?" Jass asked.

"Yes. The shield is a physical shield, with included electromagnetic components. It's a technology that even I don't understand fully. But even though it's a physical barrier, it has doors just like any other shell or containment facility. They won't likely want to open those doors for fear of contamination from the outside. But they can easily do so if necessary."

"Thank you. Are you positive that only you and I know this information?"

"Yes, sir. I'm positive."

"Does anyone else know of your assignment or your incredible success?" Jass smiled as he genuinely praised the man's efforts.

"No, sir." The man smiled back.

"And you are the only person who could possibly restore Earth to Moon coms, right?"

"That's correct."

"Excellent. Let me see you out." Director Adal Jass walked behind the man toward the door to his office. Before the man reached for the door handle, Davis pulled his small gravity ray gun from his pocket and shot the man in the back. The silent but incredible current killed the man instantly. Jass removed the body, as he had done just three days earlier with his assistant. The others in the facility would soon learn that this man had also defected and would not be returning, the secret of restoring communications with the moon and Victory Base gone with him.

8

"We are ready to proceed Director, whenever you are," Miguel González said, boldly. He sat with his brothers in a posh hotel room in Geneva, Switzerland. Several bottles from the minibar sat, empty, along the countertop of the small kitchenette, and the smell of microwave popcorn wafted slowly through the still air. They had been bored, awaiting further instructions from Adal Jass.

Secretly, before this latest com from the Director, Miguel and his brothers, Carlito and Francisco, hoped that Jass had forgotten about them. They didn't want to kill anymore. They certainly didn't want to help the man who had threatened their families. Jass was an animal; but they could do nothing to stop the events unfolding around them. Anthrax E had reached Asia. It was steadily creeping toward Europe according to scattered reports on the Web. If the González brothers wanted to live to see their family again, they would have to do this. Plus, the farther they could get from Europe, the better.

"It is time," Director Jass replied. "I have arranged for your transport from Geneva to New Zealand. Your driver will arrive at the front desk at 7:00 tomorrow morning to transport you to the airport. In New Zealand, you will board a small aircraft. The pilot of the craft will have directions necessary to get you to your destination. All you need to do is locate the SEC-GEN and kill him. Once that is complete, your pilot will take you back to New Zealand. From there, you will contact me and I will arrange for your safe passage to any place you would like to go."

"We would like to go home, sir. To Cuba."

"That would be a costly mistake. As you certainly know, your country has been decimated by Anthrax E. Why would you want to go there?"

"Sir, you said we could go anywhere. That is where we would like to go." Miguel knew that what Jass said was true. They had heard that Cuba had almost-entirely succumbed to Anthrax E. But Jass didn't know that their families were safe in a bunker there, along with thousands of others. And Jass wouldn't know. That was important.

"Alright," Director Adal Jass replied. "That is where you will go, but not until you have completed your mission."

"Understood," Miguel said. "We will talk soon."

"Why did you tell him we wanted to go home?" Francisco González asked his older brother Miguel when the com with Jass ended. "You should have just told him we wanted to come back here. There is no reason to give him any belief that our family is alive."

"You are right about that brother," Miguel replied. "But how do you propose we get from Geneva to Cuba when this is over? Do you know of some transportation facilities that are still operating?"

"Uh, no."

"That is why I do the negotiating," Miguel replied. "I do the thinking, and I make sure we get home safely."

"I never doubted you Miguel," Carlito said. "I knew you had a plan."

"Shut up," Francisco said, glaring at his younger brother.

"In any event, hermanos, we will proceed as we planned, according to *my* plan, not Jass' plan. He will get us to our destination, but *we* will decide what we do from there."

MARCH 24, 2093, LATER—HOLO CONFERENCE

"Thomas, you have done well," Director Adal Jass said through the holo. He watched as Franconi smiled at the compliment.

"Thank you Adal. What would you like me to do next?"

"You are expecting visitors tomorrow, no?"

"Yeah. The people Davis was going to have me take to Antarctica."

"Instead, Thomas, I would like you to pick up *my* team and take *them* to Antarctica."

"Who are they?"

"That doesn't matter. But they will arrive just after 2:30 tomorrow afternoon. I will send you detailed instructions as to how you are to proceed once they arrive."

"What do I do with Davis' people?"

"Well Thomas," Director Jass replied, frowning as he said the words, "you are going to have to kill them."

"But . . ." Thomas was cut off as the Director continued.

"Listen my friend, I know you are not a killer. That is one of the many qualities I appreciate about you. But desperate times, as these certainly are, require that we act for the greater good. The greater good, I assure you, will be to prevent SEC-GEN Davis from furthering his program. Remember what I told you? Davis wants to cut me and all of the other Continental Directors off. From his base in Antarctica, he intends to ride out the storm of Anthrax E and establish his own government to rule, as a dictator, over those who live. We can't let that happen. My people, who you will deliver to Antarctica tomorrow, will ensure that it doesn't happen."

"I'm not sure I understand why this is necessary, Adal. But I trust you. I will collect your people and take them to Davis. Just promise me that I won't be blamed for this. I'm not going to be liable, am I?"

"Thomas, my friend, you will not take the blame. If anything comes of this, I will take full responsibility. I promise you that."

"Okay, I'll do what you want," Thomas replied. He tried his best to hide his apprehension. Director Jass was asking him to do something he had never done before, at least not knowingly. Thomas wasn't a killer. He wanted power, and protection, but he wanted to do it the right way.

"Wait for my instructions. They will come in the next few minutes via an encrypted message to your tech. I am very pleased with your decision Thomas. Things are going to work out wonderfully. Thank you."

Director Jass closed the com. Thomas contemplated his next move. He knew that Jass was a dishonest man. How could he not be? He was a Regional Director in the IWO. As far as Thomas was concerned, they were all crooks and liars. But that meant that SEC-GEN Davis was rotten too. Could he really trust either of them? Both promised him power and protection, which is what he wanted, especially given the nature of the disease that was threatening to kill so many people. But to get protection from one, he had to stab the other in the back. If he made the wrong choice, he would be cut off from both. If he made the correct choice, if there *was* a correct choice, he may still be cut off. He didn't trust either of them. Perhaps it was time to make his own plan.

MARCH 25, 2093, 2:35PM
DUNEDIN, NEW ZEALAND

"Your ride to the sea terminal awaits you," the pilot of the small aircraft announced as the González brothers stood and stretched. The flight had been quiet and smooth, but the cramped space had been a nuisance. Of course, Miguel knew they were lucky to be flying in the first place. With travel restrictions in place worldwide, it was fortunate they weren't on horseback.

"Thank you Señorita," Miguel said, tipping his head toward the pilot in the front seat. "You have been a gracious host."

Carlito and Francisco exchanged sideways glances at this remark. The pilot had done nothing to make their ride more comfortable. They had nothing to eat or drink the entire ride. The craft was too small to have stewards waiting on them, but a small cooler, or anything, would have been nice.

"Sí, gracias," Francisco added as he walked behind the pilot and crouched down to exit the craft through the small door. Carlito followed silently.

As Carlito took the last step onto the tarmac, a small, black hovercar rounded a corner at the far end of the runway and sped toward them. The three brothers watched silently as the hover approached, the sun glaring off the clean, dark exterior.

"You don't think this is some kind of trick, do you?" Francisco asked. "Remember what Jass is capable of. He kills those he wants out of the way."

"That is true," Miguel replied, "but it would have been easier for him to have the aircraft crash into a mountain than to fly us all the way here only to have us kidnapped by a hover driver and driven off a cliff."

"Yeah, you're probably right."

"So, let us be on our way." Miguel stepped forward toward the hover that had just come to a stop in front of them. As he reached toward the rear door, it opened toward him. The front driver's side door opened at the same time, and a slight, unassuming man in a navy-blue suit and cap stepped out. He hurried around the car and pushed a button to open the rear hatch of the hover. He continued right past the hatch toward the small pieces of luggage the González brothers had taken off the plane. Before any of them could complain, the thin man heaved all three cases into the back and shut the hatch.

"We need those cases, señor," Miguel said calmly.

"They will be safe while you travel, sir," the man replied, looking at the brothers for the first time. "Please, get in. We are late."

Miguel stepped up to the open doorway of the waiting hover. It was dark inside. He looked back at his brothers standing behind him. He wouldn't let them see his fear, or his confusion. Turning back toward the open hover door, he stepped forward, crouched down, and entered the blackness. His brothers hesitated, briefly, then followed.

The moment they were all seated, the door closed and locked. They were alone in the hover. It began to move. The driver had stayed outside.

"It is a trick," Carlito said, reaching for the door handle. He grabbed it and yanked, even as Francisco reached toward the other side and tried to open the door there. Neither door opened. Instead, the hovercar accelerated as the windows blacked out.

"What do we do Miguel?" Francisco asked, his voice wavering.

"I do not know," Miguel replied, still trying to mask his own apprehension. It really didn't make any sense for Jass to attempt to kill them in this way. He still needed them to assassinate the SEC-GEN, didn't he? Plus, as he told his brothers moments earlier, why would Jass go to this trouble when he could have easily arranged for the plane to drop from the sky, obliterating any chance that anyone would learn of Jass' involvement? Something else was going on.

"Are we going to die?" Carlito asked, intense fear in his voice. He was only seventeen years old, and he was clearly frightened. Miguel could hear the despair in his youngest brother's voice, even though it appeared as though Carlito was attempting to hide it. Miguel was not ashamed of his brother, but he chose not to respond. Instead, he silently peered out the window as the hover sped away from the airport, hoping the opacity would diminish enough for them to see what was going on, or where they were going.

Several minutes later, Miguel turned back toward his brothers. "Hermanos, I am sorry I got you into this. I believed it was the only way our family could stay alive. I did not hold out hope that they would actually be let into the bunker in Havana. That was a long shot. But then they were accepted. Otherwise, I would not have agreed to this."

"Miguel, it is not your fault," Francisco replied. "If we had not taken this new assignment, we would be dead anyway. Jass told you this."

"I know, but I am still sorry I put you here. If there is any way out of this, I will find it. I promise you that."

Moments later, as Miguel, and probably his brothers too, silently contemplated their likely fate, the hover began to slow. It finally stopped and the three waited in tense silence for whatever would happen next.

"Well," Francisco began, "at least we did not drive off a cliff." He laughed nervously. Miguel smiled in response, but turned quickly as the left-side door began to open.

Moments later, after only a slight hesitation, Miguel moved toward the open door. It was bright outside, and his eyes took a few moments to adjust to the light. When his eyes finally focused, the reality of their situation hit him. They had not been driven off a cliff, but he certainly couldn't say this was any better.

Standing less than fifteen meters in front of the open door was a man holding a handgun of some kind. It was pointed at Miguel.

"Please exit the vehicle," the man said in English. "Your brothers too."

"What's going on?" Carlito asked in Spanish from inside. All three brothers understood and spoke English, but Carlito had not heard what was said.

Miguel answered quietly in Spanish, never taking his eyes off the man in front of him. "There is a man outside who would like us to exit the hover. He is holding a gun. We need to do what he says. Leave the rest to me."

"We are coming out, sir," Miguel replied in accented English. "We will come quietly. Please do not shoot."

"I don't intend to shoot you Mr. González. But I do need your cooperation."

"You have it, sir." Miguel had seen men like this before. The way this stranger held the gun and the way he stood with his feet close together told Miguel everything he needed to know about the experience of the man. He was no killer. He might not have even fired a gun before. But that kind of man was still dangerous. Miguel knew that one wrong move by him or his brothers, or any perceived threat by this stranger, could result in one or more of their deaths. They had to be careful.

"Thank you. Please step out, and have your brothers follow."

Miguel slowly stepped out and away from the hover, his eyes quickly darting around the area. Carlito and Francisco followed.

The hovercar had come to rest in a grassy field. Miguel could hear the sound of the ocean, not far away; but he couldn't see it. There was a small clump of trees perhaps 80 or 90 meters to his left. There were no structures or other places the men could take cover. Miguel wondered how the man had arrived.

"I see you looking around, Mr. González," the stranger said. "There's no place to go. I'm not an idiot. So, you might as well just play along here."

"Who are you?" Francisco asked.

"It doesn't matter. Now come along please." The stranger tilted his head to the right, clearly indicating the direction in which he would like the men to move.

Miguel waived his brothers on and the three of them turned to their left and began to walk. As they moved, Miguel whispered, "Just keep walking, but keep it slow. I'm going to get to the bottom of this."

Miguel fell back a step from his brothers.

"Señor, this is very strange to me. We were sent here by a very powerful man, and at his direction. We have a very important assignment."

"I know all of that Mr. González. I was sent to this island by that same man. But there's been a change of plan."

"What change?"

"We're now going to do this *my* way."

"Perhaps you can enlighten me a bit," Miguel said, slowing a bit more. He was trying his best to be civil and polite. He had a plan too, but it would only work if the stranger was as inexperienced as Miguel believed him to be.

"Look man, I'm not going to tell you what I'm doing, or where we're going, or anything else. It's very simple—you'll end up where you need to be."

"But who wants us to be . . . wherever it is we need to be?" Miguel slowed more. He was only two meters in front of the stranger.

"You'll figure it out all on your own in a few minutes. Let's just k—"

The man choked on his last words as Miguel spun and struck the stranger in the throat. The gun fell to the ground and Miguel swept it up, taking three large steps away from the man now holding his throat and trying to breath.

The stranger dropped to the ground, still clutching his throat; but his eyes moved upward to where Miguel now stood. The tables had been turned. Miguel had been correct. This man was no killer.

Francisco and Carlito jogged back to where Miguel stood. "What happened?" Carlito asked in Spanish.

"It should be obvious little brother," Miguel replied in the same language. *No need to let this stranger know what we are thinking.* "This man decided to give me his gun. I guess we're just too much trouble."

Francisco laughed, but it sounded forced.

"What are you going to do with him now?" Carlito asked.

"I do not know. What do you think?" Miguel said, switching to English. He didn't really care what Carlito thought, but he thought he knew what Carlito was going to say, and he wanted the stranger to hear it.

Carlito replied in English as Miguel had desired. "I . . . I guess . . . I mean, I guess we should probably kill him, right?"

The stranger looked up into Miguel's eyes and shook his head violently back and forth. He had tears streaming down his face and he had wet himself.

Miguel switched back to Spanish. *Let the stranger wonder,* he thought, a menacing look on his face. "I don't think I want to do that," Miguel replied. "Look at him. He's no threat. He was paid to do a job, just like we were. I believe I will leave him out here. Perhaps we will tie him to a tree and see if the animals will be as merciful."

"What animals?" Carlito asked.

"I do not know. The lizards or mosquitos, or whatever it is they have here."

"They probably have wild dogs," Francisco added, smiling.

"Help me brothers," Miguel said, bending down to lift the stranger from the ground. "Let's get him over to those trees. But I need something from my bag."

Francisco grabbed one arm and Miguel held the other as they headed back toward the hovercar. The man thrashed and twisted, trying unsuccessfully to escape their grasp. Miguel slapped his face. "Stop struggling. I do not plan to kill you, but you may change my mind."

The stranger wasn't hurt, except for his throat. It was as Miguel wished. The man could walk on his own, but he wouldn't be able to call for help.

As the group approached the hover in which they had so recently been imprisoned, Miguel reached over and pushed the rear trunk lock. He pulled out all three men's bags and dropped them on the ground. Opening his own, he felt around inside. Finding what he was looking for, he closed the bag and stood.

"Let's get moving," Miguel said, giving the man a small push to turn him back in the direction from which they had just come.

Two minutes later, the group arrived at a small stand of Kohekohe trees. The native trees, many with trunks up to a meter in diameter, had white flowers and new green fruit growing directly from the trunk and branches. The leaves were long and glossy, providing welcome shade as the men walked in under the canopy.

"Do you think we can eat that?" Francisco asked, reaching up to pluck a small ball from the trunk of the closest tree.

Nobody answered. Miguel led his brothers, still holding on to and pushing the stranger, over to a small tree and sat him on the ground against the trunk. Miguel pulled a small ball of carbon-laced rope from his pocket and tied the man's hands behind him around the tree. "You were polite to us, and that is why we will let you live," Miguel said. "But if we see you again, we will be the last people you see. Do you understand?"

The man nodded his head vigorously and tried to speak. His voice came out in a hoarse whisper. "I . . . understand. I will . . . not follow you."

"Very good. When you are finally asked by whomever it was that sent you, you will tell him that we are dead. Is that clear?"

"Yes . . . Mr. González. You are . . . dead."

"Thank you," Miguel replied. He didn't know whether he could trust the man; but he also didn't feel like he should kill him. A small green fruit fell from the tree and landed at Miguel's feet. He stared at it for a few moments, then looked back at the man tied to the tree at his feet. Despite Miguel's past, he did not enjoy the killing. He did what was necessary, but only *when* necessary. This man, who had no business performing this type of work, would live to see another day. Miguel hoped it wasn't a mistake.

"And now we leave you. But before we go, would you be so kind as to tell us your name?"

"I am Thomas."

9

"Why do you not just com Jass?" Carlito asked. They had left that sad man tied to a tree. He might never get free, but Carlito's brothers didn't seem to care. They left him, knowing that he would probably die. Carlito hadn't risen to that level of indifference. The man hadn't actually done anything to harm them; and Carlito felt ashamed.

"Think about that for a moment hermano," Miguel replied.

The brothers were retrieving their bags from the ground near the hover that was left sitting in the sun in the field. They had considered taking the hovercar, but decided it might be bugged or traceable; and they wanted to be invisible. As they began to walk away, Francisco bent down to look under the hover. He unzipped the backpack and pulled out a small knife.

"What are you doing?" Miguel asked.

"Making sure he does not follow us."

"Good thinking," Miguel said.

Francisco laid down on the grass and pulled himself under the hover. He reached up and cut some of the metallic hoses running under the hover.

"What did you do?" Carlito asked as Francisco rolled out from under the hover.

"I do not know; but I am sure those hoses I just cut do something."

Francisco stood up and, just as he turned to step away from the hover, it dropped to the ground.

"Well, I guess you are glad you did not stay down there looking for anything else to dismantle," Miguel said, smiling.

"Uh, sí. That was close."

"So, Carlito, did you figure out why we cannot com Jass?" Miguel asked, changing the subject.

"No. I stopped thinking about it," Carlito replied.

"It is very simple really. Jass promised us safety. He promised us that if we killed the SEC-GEN, he would take us home. Then, he sent someone here to kill *us*, or to leave us in the middle of nowhere. Is that a man you believe we should trust? Should we call him to say we are still alive?"

"No, obviously," Francisco replied before Carlito had a chance to respond.

"Right now," Miguel continued, "Jass thinks we are dead, or that we will be soon. He will move on to whatever he has planned without us. That gives us time to do what we need to do to survive."

"What if Jass finds out?" Carlito asked. "I mean, he is probably going to com that man we tied to the tree, yes? And when that man—Thomas—doesn't answer, Jass will get suspicious, won't he?"

"Yes, I am sure he will," Miguel replied. "But by then, I hope to be in Antarctica."

"Plus, Thomas said he would tell Jass that we were dead," Francisco added.

"Francisco, Thomas will not tell Jass we are dead. You can count on that."

"Then why did you let him live?" Francisco asked. "We should have killed him."

"Karma, hermano."

"Karma?"

"Yes," Miguel replied. "I let that man live so that Jesus will help us live. No other reason."

Francisco looked to the sky and crossed himself.

"Brothers, what are we going to do now?" Carlito asked.

"We find a way to Antarctica," Miguel replied.

MARCH 25, 2093, 5:35PM
NEAR DUNEDIN, NEW ZEALAND

Thomas Franconi sat in the shade of the Kohekohe tree. Every once in a while, another piece of fruit fell. Several minutes earlier, an animal of some kind had scampered through the leaves on the ground behind him. Thomas couldn't see what kind of animal it was, but he was certain it was small. He hoped there were no larger, or more dangerous animals also lurking nearby.

But even more important than that, he hoped his ship, the A-400, was still sitting on the tarmac at the Dunedin airport. He had no reason to believe the González brothers knew of its existence. He had failed to accomplish his own plan. He had first agreed to deliver Davis' team to Antarctica, but instead, had arranged for Jass' men—the González brothers—to be delivered to him. He had meant to leave all of them stranded on the island, tied up in these very trees, while he left for Antarctica alone. He would have told Davis that nobody showed up. Davis would never be the wiser because he had no communication with the outside. He would have told Jass the same thing. Jass would not be able to contact the brothers because Thomas had intended to leave them without any communication devices. That way, neither Jass nor Davis would ever know that he had been in league with the other. And, as a result, he would be safe with whichever of the men kept his promise. It might have worked, but Thomas underestimated Jass' men. Thinking about it now, however, Thomas realized that, if he only tied the people to a tree, as he had planned, they would have eventually escaped, and then told Jass everything. *Perhaps it is fortunate that I am the one tied to this tree*, he thought sullenly.

Sitting in the shade of the Kohekohe trees in the late afternoon, Thomas wondered why he had gone to the trouble of seeking either man's approval and protection. The A-400 had provided all the protection he needed. If it was still around when, or if, he got free, he would rethink his loyalties.

The day was beautiful. The sun shone and it was a bit humid, but Thomas was comfortable, even with his hands tied behind him. He figured, at one point or another, someone would come along and free him. He would just have to survive until then. But he needed food and water.

Just as the thought crossed his mind. A small piece of fruit dropped into his lap. Thomas wasn't very flexible, but eventually, he succeeded in retrieving the fruit from his lap with his teeth. It wasn't ripe, and was sour, but it would keep him alive just a bit longer. *One piece of fruit at a time*, he thought.

MARCH 25, 2093, EVENING
VICTORY BASE, ANTARCTICA

"Shouldn't they be here by now?" Bria Newton asked.

"I don't know exactly," SEC-GEN Antonio Davis replied. "They were supposed to arrive sometime today. But without communications, remember, we will be fortunate if they arrive at all. They never got clearance from us, and if they intend to follow protocol, they will not ever arrive."

"Just this once, I hope someone doesn't follow your directions," Bria said, smiling as she scooted closer to Antonio on the couch.

Antonio reached over and brushed a lock of blond hair out of Bria's eyes, and pushed it behind her ear. "Have I told you how great you look today?"

"No."

"Well, you look beautiful. And I'm glad you're here with me."

"Me too," Bria said, looking down at her lap.

"What's wrong Bria?" Antonio asked. Bria's body language did not emulate her words.

"I'm just scared, that's all." Once Bria started talking, the floodgates opened. "I mean, what if nobody ever comes here. If someone creates a vaccine, we'll never get it. Everyone here thinks we're safe from

Anthrax E, but I was watching the news—before we lost coms—and it doesn't look good. People are dying everywhere. Asia is getting hit right now and the western hemisphere is falling to pieces. Nobody is coming to rescue us and we'll probably all die. I don't want to die."

Antonio placed his finger on Bria's lips. "Shhh. Things will be okay." He placed his hands on either side of her face and looked into her eyes, smiling. He leaned in and kissed her softly on the lips. "Maybe the whole world won't fall apart anyway. And, no matter what happens, I am still in control of the IWO. I won't be left here. Someone will figure out what has happened and will come. I promise."

"I have a hard time believing that Antonio; although I don't know why. It's not that I don't trust you, because I do. Maybe I'm just being pessimistic."

"Well, in time, I think you'll learn to trust me more. Let's go to dinner. We can worry about this again tomorrow, after a good night's sleep."

The pair got up from the couch, hand-in-hand and SEC-GEN Davis led Bria across the room. Antonio let go just as they reached the door. He couldn't let others see him touching a woman who was not his wife. It didn't matter how powerful he was, that was a bad idea.

10

"There is our ride, brothers," Miguel whispered. They had just watched a small airship land on the tarmac. A person disembarked, but left the small craft running. Miguel couldn't tell whether anyone was still inside, but the ship looked like it couldn't hold more than about eight people. Airships were supposed to be grounded, by IWO orders. This craft was clearly violating orders, but so had the pilot of the ship that brought the González brothers to New Zealand earlier that day. Of course, that ship was directed by Jass. Maybe this one was too; but it didn't really matter. The brothers needed a ride to Antarctica. They had seen no other aircraft land or take off in hours.

"There must be people in there still," Francisco said. "They left it running."

"Yes, so let's hurry. They clearly do not intend to stick around."

Even before he had finished speaking, Miguel began to creep along the side of the small shed behind which they had been hiding. Reaching the front corner of the building, he knelt down in the weeds and peeked around the corner. There was nobody in sight. The man who walked off the ship had vanished.

Taking a quick look back to see that his brothers were still behind him, Miguel darted across the tarmac to the door of the small ship. A short set of stairs descended from the doorway to the ground. It was only six steps up into the craft. Miguel crept up them very slowly, stopping on each step to look both around him on the outside, and into the interior. As he reached the top step, he heard a voice, and froze.

"I'm sorry sir. We haven't received clearance for you to leave."

The female voice was coming from a dark building to the side of the tarmac, about 80 or 90 meters away. The only light giving any indication the building was even there was coming from the open doorway where a shadowy figure was perched on the bottom step. The woman's voice carried through the quiet, still air. With all air traffic grounded, there were no machines, aircraft or other noises to interfere with the conversation the man who had left the ship was having with a woman at the door to the small building.

"Well that doesn't make any sense," the man replied. *"The SEC-GEN summoned us. We're supposed to be delivering tech and supplies to him. Plus, someone very important to him is with us."*

"Again, I'm sorry. There's nothing I can do. You can wait here overnight to see if we get the clearance codes, but unless Victory Base contacts us, we won't be able to give you clearance codes and you won't be able to leave."

"Fine," the man replied. *"Is there some place we can sleep?"*

"Sure. Taxi your airship down to the far end of the runway. There's a bunkhouse down there. It's unlocked and nobody's using it. It might be a little stuffy. Nobody has been in there in weeks."

"Thanks."

With the conversation apparently ended, Miguel looked down at his brothers who had caught up to him at the stairs. Both were bouncing on their toes, anticipating Miguel's next move. They needed this airship, and they needed to take it now, before the man on the ground returned. There were obviously others on board, but they wouldn't be expecting this kind of surprise. Miguel made his move, pulling an old nine-millimiter Ruger from his waistband and stepping into the cabin of the ship.

"Who are you?" a thin woman asked as Miguel entered the cabin.

"It does not matter," Miguel replied. His brothers both moved inside as Miguel took two steps toward the center of the cabin. "Put your hands into the air."

"I will do no such thing. Do you know who I am?"

"No, and I do not particularly care. Hands up, now."

"You can't make me . . ."

The woman's voice was cut-off as Miguel stepped forward and struck the side of her face with the butt of his gun. She fell to the floor. Just then, a man stepped out into the cabin from the front of the ship. He looked around then quickly stepped back into the cockpit and slammed the door shut. A man who had been sitting a couple of rows back woke up at the sound of the slamming door. Before he could speak, Miguel stepped toward him and struck him as well. The man slumped over in his chair.

"What are you doing?" Francisco asked. "You should have killed them."

"Shut up little brother," Miguel replied. "There is no need for excess violence. Now, we need . . ."

Miguel stopped short as Francisco dropped to his knees. Two seconds later, he fell face forward onto the hard floor of the cabin. Miguel and Carlito stared at their fallen brother as blood first trickled, then spurted, and finally streamed onto the floor on both sides of his body.

Miguel was the first to move. He pushed Carlito back against the wall of the ship nearest the door and then crouched on the floor next to him. The shot had been silent. But it had clearly come from outside. It was probably the man they had seen talking with the woman. He was armed.

Miguel peeked around the edge of the doorway and pulled back just as another shot pinged off the outside doorframe.

"We need to get this door closed, now," Miguel whispered.

Carlito stood where he was. His face was ashen and he made no move to help his oldest brother. His eyes were glued to the still form of Francisco lying on the floor at his feet.

Miguel reached up and slapped his brother on the cheek. "Carlito! Snap out of it. We need to get this door closed!"

Carlito looked over at Miguel who was still crouched near the door. He bent down to touch his brother. A shot tore through Carlito's arm, severing tissue and bone, before lodging in his side. Blood sprayed from the open arm wounds, covering Miguel. Miguel tried to stand, but he slipped on the dark, crimson blood now flowing from Francisco's back and Carlito's wound. Hitting the ground hard, he used the momentum from the fall to roll over to the far side of the open doorway.

Carlito didn't make a sound as he dropped to the floor. He knelt, holding his arm, tears welling up inside his eyes. "I'm sorry Miguel."

"Do not be sorry brother. You are going to be okay. I just need to get this door closed. Back up, over there." Miguel pointed to a spot behind where Carlito was kneeling. Carlito didn't move. Miguel would have to expose himself to the fire from outside in order to push his brother away from the door. He had no choice. A lump formed in his throat, but he pushed it down. He couldn't give in yet.

Miguel crouched again; then jumped across the open doorway, landing against Carlito who made no attempt to move or get up. Miguel looked down at his brother as he stood. There was a lot of blood and Carlito looked faint. Miguel grabbed a blanket that was sitting on the chair closest to him and tried to rip it. He needed to stop the flow of blood. He would worry about the obvious hole in Carlito's side later. The blanket was too strong. Then he remembered that Francisco had a knife. He reached over toward his fallen brother but pulled his hand back quickly when another shot pinged against the far inside wall of the cabin.

"Francisco," Miguel pleaded. "Francisco!" He was certainly dead. And Carlito would be too, soon, if Miguel didn't do something to stop the bleeding. Miguel's eyes searched frantically around the part of the ship he could see from where he currently crouched. There had to be something—a rope, a belt, anything—to stop the bleeding. But he couldn't cross the doorway or he would be next.

As he searched frantically, careful to stay away from the doorway, he heard a thud behind him. He turned around quickly and dropped to the floor as the sound of another bullet bounced around inside the small cabin. Looking up, Miguel saw Carlito, lying on his side, his eyes still wide open.

"No. Carlito?" Miguel whispered. "My baby brother. Do not die. You cannot die."

Miguel reached over to his brother's neck. There was no pulse. He placed his hand in front of Carlito's open mouth. There was no breath. Both of his brothers were dead. Miguel would avenge them.

Feeling courage he never knew he had, Miguel fished ammunition from a pocket of his backpack and reloaded. Then took a deep breath and took two steps toward the open door. He plunged out into the darkness. Jumping off the top step of the small staircase, he opened fire. He counted each shot, his mind working furiously to keep up with his fingers as he shot randomly in all directions. His gun held twenty-four rounds and he had used fourteen. Then he ran around to the back of the airship and dropped to the ground. No sounds followed. No gunshots hit near him.

Miguel didn't believe his random shooting could have actually been successful. He couldn't see very far in the dark, so he waited. After what seemed like several minutes, Miguel heard a voice. It sounded as though it was coming through a communication device of some kind.

"*Sam, where are you?*"

The voice came from somewhere off to Miguel's left.

"*Sam, come on buddy. Where are you? I think they're gone.*"

Miguel didn't recognize the slightly-higher pitched voice. It wasn't the same man speaking as he had heard speaking with the woman about clearance codes. This was someone else, and it was not coming from the ship. *It must be the man from the cockpit, talking through a mic.*

Miguel waited for several more minutes, with no response from 'Sam' and no further questions from the other man. Then the airship's engines roared to life. Miguel didn't know whether the ship had been shut down at some point or whether it was just getting louder as it was about to take off. Regardless, Miguel knew he had to get back on board before it took off. He looked around, desperately searching for their attacker. He could see no one.

As Miguel stood to creep back to the open door, a light flicked on in the distance. It came from the small building down the runway. A petite figure peeked out, then stepped out into the night air. She screamed—the sound of death. That was Miguel's signal. He may have actually hit the other man.

Miguel ran to the open doorway and climbed the steps, taking two at a time. Inside, his brothers still lay where he had left them. The man in the back was clearly unconscious, maybe dead. But the woman was stirring.

Miguel quickly searched for a means of closing the door. His eyes finally landed on a small electronic pad high on the wall on the left side of the door—right where Carlito had been standing. Miguel reached out toward it, but pulled his hand back as the door began to close on its own.

"What happened?" a shaky voice called. It was the woman he had hit. She was no threat now. The only person who could help her was the pilot, and he hadn't left the cockpit since the melee started. *Weak*, Miguel thought. It would be no trouble convincing the man to fly him to Antarctica. But the woman would have to be dealt with.

"There is no trouble, ma'am," Miguel replied in his best accented English. He wanted to sound like he was from Europe, where this craft had likely originated; but his accent failed him. The woman's eyes flew open and she stared at Miguel. Now she was scared, and that suited Miguel just fine.

"Listen Señorita," Miguel began, returning to his native accent, "Look around you. You and I are the only people alive in here." Just then, the airship began to move. Miguel wasn't sure what the pilot thought he was doing. He clearly didn't believe Miguel or his brothers were alive on the ship. Otherwise, he wouldn't attempt to take off and leave himself at the mercy of his attackers in the sky.

"Then who's flying the ship?" the woman asked. The aircraft was accelerating quickly. Miguel left the question unanswered as he felt the ship lift off the runway.

After they were in the air, Miguel smiled. "My comrade is flying the ship. I suggest you do as you are told."

The woman's face turned pale as she sat back in her seat. She buckled her seat belt, probably out of habit, and looked straight forward. She appeared to be in shock, or something; Miguel was no doctor. But he didn't believe it would last. The pilot would continue to fly, but they needed to be going southwest. So, Miguel didn't have much time. He needed the woman to not interfere.

Then he remembered his backpack. It had rope. He could have used the rope to stop, or at least slow Carlito's bleeding. But he had not remembered it. Guilt began to creep into his psyche. His legs buckled and he nearly fell to the floor. But Miguel was stronger than that. He forced his body upright. He would grieve later. For now, he needed to control this situation.

Reaching into his backpack, he pulled out the thin rope. He cut a piece larger than the one he had used to tie the man—Thomas—to the tree hours earlier. The woman didn't move or struggle as Miguel tied her to the seat. *If only the man in the cockpit could be so easy*, Miguel thought as he finished tying some kind of mutated knot behind the woman.

Having accomplished that task, Miguel stood and moved to check the man in the back. He placed his fingers on the man's throat, just under his jaw. He was still alive. Miguel tied him up as well then walked forward to the door separating the cabin from the cockpit. He rapped on the door three times with his knuckles. "Sir," he began, "it is only you and I on this ship now. I suggest you open the door so we can talk."

Silence.

"Sir," Miguel said again, this time louder, "you and I are all that is left on this airship. You need to open this door before I smash it in. But you need not worry. I won't hurt you if you behave. I am not a pilot.

I need your help. If you cooperate, we can survive together. If you do not, I will quickly learn how to fly the ship and you will be left learning to fly like the birds."

Still there was silence. Miguel began to wonder whether his veiled threat made sense. He replayed it in his mind. . . . *fly like the birds . . .* Yeah, it made sense. The man must be scared. Then Miguel heard the faint sound of a door unlocking. One eye peeked out from the small crack that appeared between the door and its frame.

"You will not hurt me, yes?" the man asked in heavily accented English.

"That is what I said—if you will cooperate," Miguel replied, lifting his gun into position so that the man in the cockpit could see it.

"Please don't shoot me Monsieur. I will cooperate."

French? Miguel wondered. *That makes sense.*

"Please open the door the rest of the way and come on back here. Have a seat," Miguel said. "I assume the ship will fly itself for the time being?"

"Yes Monsieur. The ship will fly."

The scared man opened the door slowly and peeked out. His breath caught as he viewed the carnage in the cabin. "You said I would be safe . . ." he said as started to back up into the cockpit.

Miguel grabbed his shirt and pulled him back out. "Sit down," he said, pushing the man toward the nearest seat. "I didn't do this. Your comrade did it. These are my brothers. He killed them, before I killed him."

The man's face turned ashen and he looked around frantically. Then his eyes landed on the woman tied to the seat a few rows back. "Is Mrs. Davis okay?" He asked quietly.

"What did you call her?" Miguel questioned.

"Mrs. Davis."

"You mean that she is the SEC-GEN's wife?"

"Yes, Monsieur. That is who she is. Is she okay? Where are the others?"

"Sure. I think she's okay. Why don't you ask her?" Miguel looked back at Mrs. Davis, who had apparently passed out again.

"Well, she does not look so good," Miguel said, shrugging. "I hit her in the head; but she will live, just like you will if this all works out. As for the other man, he is back there, maybe dead." His casual attitude about all of this surprised even him.

"I am at your mercy. What would you like me to do?" The pilot asked.

"I need to get to Antarctica."

"I can't take you there. I don't have clearance codes."

"I do not care about codes. Take me to Antarctica."

"But without codes, I can't input coordinates into the flight deck. We'll never make it. It's too dark outside to see, and I've never been to Victory Base."

"So that is where the SEC-GEN is? Victory Base. Here is our new plan, my friend. You will take me to the nearest airport where you have clearance codes, and we will wait for first light. Then you will take me to Victory Base. We will find it by sight."

"That may not be as easy as you think Monsieur; but you are the boss. I will get us on the ground soon."

"And not the same place we just left. I will be sitting next to you the whole way. You will not contact anybody. Is that clear?"

"Yes. I am not beholden to anybody," he began, then, "at least not anybody still healthy enough to live for long. You let me live, and I will get you to Victory Base."

It was just as Miguel thought. The pilot was soft. *Too many people,* he thought, *living life in the moment, no care for the future.* But Miguel had a plan. He would see his family again, whatever it took. And he would see that his brothers received a proper burial too. But first, the woman—Mrs. Davis—would need to be disposed of.

11

Thomas Franconi was startled from his torpor as another small, white fruit dropped onto his head. The wind had picked up overnight while he tried to sleep. With the wind came a deep chill that settled into Thomas' bones, making sleep a very difficult proposition. Being tied to a tree had made it all the harder, his arms cramping and growing numb from poor blood-flow. Now, as the sun made itself known on the horizon, sleep was the last thing on his mind. He had to pee.

He had already wet himself earlier when the rotten González brothers had first accosted him. But at least they had treated him fairly. It was he, of course, that had started that chain of events when he decided to take matters into his own hands.

In any event, his pants had dried, and the stink was bearable. He didn't want to change that. So he had held it, all night. Now, however, his bladder screamed in protest. He had to do something.

Thomas looked around again, as he had done a hundred times already, searching for something, or some way to help himself out of this mess. He was just about to give up again, and suffer the consequences of his weak bladder, when he heard the faint sound of a motor. The trees were thick behind him, but the González brothers had tied him to a tree near the edge of the small forest. If anyone approached in front of him, he would see them before they saw him. But if someone, or something approached from behind, Thomas wasn't sure he would have the guts to call out. If he couldn't see who, or what he was calling to, he was sure it would end poorly.

Thankfully, moments later, a small object appeared on the horizon. The sound got steadily louder as the object grew in size. It was heading for him, or at least, toward the grove of trees.

Thomas sat up straighter, trying to get a better view. He had tried to stand several times, but knots or branches in the tree behind him had prevented the rope from sliding up the tree. Thomas strained his eyes. The sound was not made by a hover—it was too deep and gravely. But it certainly sounded like a machine of some kind, and it was approaching rather quickly.

Within seconds, Thomas could tell that it was something on wheels. Two wheels to be exact. It was some kind of old motor bike, with two people riding, one behind the other. Thomas had never been on a motor bike, and he couldn't remember whether he'd even seen one before, except in pictures. But he was sure that was what was approaching.

When he believed the bike was close enough, Thomas called out. "Hello over there!" There was no response, so he tried again, repeating the phrase three more times. Then the bike slowed. It veered to the right, changing course to head directly toward Thomas. They had seen him!

The bike slowed further as it approached Thomas. The two figures on the bike wore helmets. Thomas couldn't see their eyes. But he imagined their shock at finding a man tied to a tree in the middle of a field. He began to fear a bit that they wouldn't be friendly—or that they might be so concerned or afraid that they would speed away. So he spoke quickly, with as kind a voice as he could muster.

"I am so glad you found me. I've been tied to this tree for hours. Please help me."

The people on the bike sat still for several moments. Then the one in the front turned off the machine and removed her helmet. She was beautiful! Her skin was bronze, framed by dark, almost black hair cut just below her jaw line. She stood without speaking, lifted her right leg over the bike and stood next to it. Her companion then stood, lifted her left leg over the bike and stood on the other side. The companion gently set the bike down on its side on the grass then removed her helmet too. The second woman was not as pretty as the first, but she had a unique beauty with the same dark skin and hair. Thomas was mesmerized.

The women stared at Thomas and he stared back. Nobody spoke. Thomas was aroused from his trance when another fruit from the Kohekohe tree landed in the grass next to him. Shaking his head from side to side, as if waking from a dream, Thomas looked down at the fruit, then back up at his visitors.

He must have been making a face as the two women began to giggle. *That's strange*, he thought. Thomas looked closer, soon realizing that these weren't women at all. They were just girls—maybe fourteen or fifteen years old. *That would explain the giggling*, he thought.

"Why are you tied to a tree?" the first girl asked. "That is not normal here."

"Uh, okay, that's a great question. And, by the way, it's not normal where I come from either."

The girls giggled again, this time looking at each other as they did so. "Well then, if it is not normal for you to be tied to a tree, how did you end up that way?"

"Well, you see, I was . . . it's a very long story. Will you please just untie me? I really need to . . ." Thomas stopped. It wasn't their business. But time was running out.

"You need to what?" the first girl asked. The second girl hadn't spoken yet.

"Look, I've been tied to a tree for eighteen hours. You can probably guess what I need to do."

More giggling. "I think I understand," the first girl replied, attempting to stifle her laughter. "I will untie you. But first, you must promise me that you are not a bad man."

"I promise. I promise. I've never hurt anyone in my life. Please untie me." The desperation in Thomas' voice was clear. The girls stopped giggling. Clearly, the man had something he needed to do. The first girl understood, and she was impressed by his decision to be modest about it. That was rare, even in her village.

The girl walked behind Thomas' tree and tried to untie the rope. "Bring me the knife, Kaia," she called out a few seconds later. The second girl reached into a pack strapped to the side of the motor bike and produced a small hunting knife. She walked over to her companion and within moments, the ropes fell from Thomas' wrists.

"Thank you," Thomas said as he stood and ran into the forest.

The girls looked at each other and then laughed again. Their twittering continued until Thomas returned from the forest.

"You look better," the girl—Kaia—said.

"Yes, Kaia, I feel better. Thank you both so much." Thomas bowed slightly, in a friendly gesture. He wasn't sure about the customs of the Māori, but he reasoned that a slight bow couldn't be perceived as anything but a symbol of gratitude.

In response, the first girl, whose name had not yet been said, held out her hand with the palm facing upward. Thomas went to shake her hand, but she pulled it away. When Thomas lowered his hand, the girl lifted hers again, palm upward.

"I don't understand what you're doing," Thomas said quietly, embarrassed by his lack of knowledge of the girls' culture.

"Where is my gift?" the girl asked.

"I don't have a gift for you. Should I have one?"

"Of course. Do you live in a hole under the Kohekohe tree?" Kaia laughed, which started her companion laughing again. Thomas didn't understand the joke.

Seeing the look of confusion on Thomas' face, the first girl asked, "What is your name?"

"Thomas. What is yours?"

"I am Tia."

"Tia? That's beautiful. What kind of gift should I give you?" Thomas asked.

"One of your most treasured possessions, of course. That is what we do when someone performs a kind act. We reward them. It is called Koha. Koha helps us understand and trust one another. It is a sign of respect and gratitude."

"I see," Thomas replied. "Unfortunately, I don't have any possessions with me, let alone treasured possessions. I was abducted. The only thing I have is my hover, over . . ." Thomas stopped short as he looked across the field to where his hover had sat the night before. "Well, I *used* to have a hover sitting right over there. I can't see it anymore. So, I have nothing except the clothes on my back. As you can see, they are not worth giving as a gift."

"That is sad," Kaia said before Tia could respond. "Very sad that you do not have any possessions. I would like to give you something instead."

"But you already untied me. You shouldn't give me anything more. You don't even know me."

"We don't need to know you to understand that you are in need," Kaia replied. "Come to our village. We will give you a gift. In exchange, you can tell us your story. Maybe one day, you can give us a gift."

"That's very generous," Thomas replied. Tears began to form in the corners of his eyes. These girls had given him freedom; but more than that, they offered him a way out of this mess. He couldn't pass it up; and he vowed to return their kindness. He just had to get back to his ship first.

"Come with us," Tia said as she picked up the bike and straddled it. "But you will need to walk. You are too fat to fit with us." The girls giggled again as Kaia joined her friend on the bike before slowly driving away. "Besides," Tia called out over her shoulder, "you will find your transport at our village. Our hunters found it and brought it there last night."

Thomas jogged after them. *Such nice girls*, he thought, *and then they called me 'fat'.*

MARCH 26, 2093, 9:40AM—ANTARCTICA

"I still do not see anything resembling what I know of Victory Base, Monsieur González," the pilot said as he continued to peer out the window at the ground below. Light snow was falling, but a dizzying wind was causing the current snowfall and snow on the ground to swirl and spiral a hundred meters into the air. It was difficult to see the ground at all much of the time.

"We will search until we find it," Miguel replied. "Tell me what we are looking for."

"I have been informed that it is a large complex—many buildings. Most of them are no longer in use and may appear run down. But I don't know that for sure. There should be an airstrip just long enough for aircraft like this one to touch down. It is not very long. But mostly, what you should be looking for is some kind of shield. Unfortunately, the shield is clear. But it may reflect the sun—that is what I had hoped for. I only wish that the sun was not obscured by the snow."

"Well, keep looking."

"Thank you, Monsieur."

Miguel was getting frustrated. He hadn't slept well on the ship. The wretched old woman married to the SEC-GEN talked all night in her sleep. Whatever she was dreaming about clearly involved treachery and deceit. Miguel was pretty sure she was dreaming of a cheating husband. Miguel wouldn't be surprised. Who knew, really, what went on behind the closed doors of the government? He barely felt any remorse when he pushed her out the door onto the tarmac before they left the ground that morning. Had he been smarter, he would have killed her eight hours earlier. At least then he might have gotten some sleep. Now, she would probably die from Anthrax E, sooner or later. The other man had never regained consciousness. He was left on the ground next to Mrs. Davis.

But even if Miguel had been able to sleep through the woman's cursing and moaning, it was difficult to sleep sitting in a chair, and he could not curb his sorrow at the loss of his brothers. All around the world, people were dying from some unholy disease. But the

González family had been blessed. Most of them were safe inside the government bunker in Havana. But now, Francisco and Carlito would not be with him when he returned to Cuba. He would have to explain to his mother and father, and to their sisters and cousins, why they didn't return. What would he say? That they were shot in the back by bad men? Wasn't Miguel one of those bad men now? *What a hypocrite I am*, he had thought during the early morning hours before the sun rose. *We chose to kill and that meant we might be killed. My brothers knew that. I knew that. It is time I stop grieving for them.*

By the time morning arrived, Miguel had determined that his grief would not slow him down. He was tired now, but he would survive for his brothers and for his family. He would win. He had always been a winner. In this new world, he would remain a winner.

"I think I see it," the pilot said. "Look over there."

Miguel's eyes followed the man's outstretched arm. Through the swirling snow, Miguel could see what appeared to be a large compound, and there appeared to be a short runway running down the middle. But he couldn't see a shield. Miguel was sure there must be other locations like this one all over Antarctica.

"I cannot see any shield," Miguel said. "This is no different than any other village or base on this island."

"It is funny that you call it an island. I mean no disrespect, of course. But it is a very large island to be sure."

"Who cares what it is?" Miguel said, his anger bubbling to the surface. "Find the base before I change my mind about our deal."

The pilot gulped reflexively. "I will. I am sorry Monsieur. I will keep looking. I didn't mean . . . ahh, there it is. Look at the shimmer over the tower there."

Again, Miguel looked where the man was pointing. It was true. Miguel had thought he might see a sparkle as though the sun were reflecting off a glass skyscraper. But that was not what he saw. He wasn't surprised, since the sun wasn't shining. What he saw instead was only a faint shimmer—barely visible. It looked more like a reflection of dim light through a piece of broken glass. But it was certainly there. A light from a tower of some kind was blinking, and with each flash, a tiny shimmer reflected off something hovering over the tower in the air.

"We have found it. Now, we need to get down there without being noticed. Can you do that?" Miguel was hopeful, but not naïve enough to believe the pilot could perform such a miracle.

"I can do that Monsieur. Remember that communications with the base have been cut off. That is why I could not get clearance codes last night, as I explained. That means . . ."

Miguel finished the sentence, ". . . that they have no way to track aircraft."

"That is likely correct," the pilot replied. "But they may have cameras. Of course, if they see us with their eyes, we cannot avoid that."

"Then perhaps I am glad the snow obscures our vision. Let's circle around for a minute and see if anyone comes outside," Miguel said. Then thinking, he continued, "Wait a minute. How are we supposed to land with that shield in place? You tricked me."

Miguel rose from his seat and clenched his hand. He would show this man no more leniency. He rose his arm to strike, but the man called out. "Wait, there is a way. I did not trick you."

Miguel lowered his arm. "Tell me how this will work, and I won't punish you. But if you deceive me, you will be fish food. Do not doubt this."

"There is a way. I promise. But it will require landing a distance away and walking. There is small village or something—maybe twenty kilometers from Victory Base. There are roads. I can land there."

"How do you know?" Miguel asked quietly, purposefully keeping an edge to his voice. "You have never been here."

"I saw it a few minutes ago. We flew over it. But it was not what we were looking for. So I did not point it out to you."

"Well then, this is your chance to prove your worth. I will not be tricked. You will take us down safely. Do you understand?"

"I do. It will work."

The pilot banked sharply and flew in the direction from which they had just come. Within moments, Miguel spotted what looked like a small town on the horizon. He would not have been able to see it, but the sun broke through the clouds momentarily, just enough to light the ground in the distance. The pilot was right. It looked to be about twenty kilometers from the main base. But could the pilot land there? That remained to be seen. And if he could, how would they get to Victory Base?

12

"Careful!" Miguel yelled to be heard over the roar of the craft as it slowed for its descent. The narrow hull, easily 45 or 50 years old, could not keep the sound of the engines, or the howling wind, from piercing the interior. As the ship approached the small, nearly-forgotten settlement from the northeast, the wind strengthened.

"I am sorry Monsieur. The wind at this altitude is stronger than before. The gusts must be rushing across the land below us. This will be bumpy as we descend. You should probably fasten your safety belt."

Without further warning, as if to prove the pilot correct, a strong gust rocked the aircraft from the bottom right, nearly turning it onto its side. Miguel was thrown from his seat, landing on the pilot's lap. His elbow crashed into the side of the pilot's face as they both fell forward onto the control panel. Miguel struggled to get off the pilot—"Paul" he had called himself—as the nose of the ship dipped toward the settlement on the ground below.

Just as Miguel slipped off the pilot's lap, another gust from the opposite direction hit the craft, turning it back to horizontal. Miguel couldn't understand why they were still diving. He looked at Paul. The pilot's eyes were closed and blood dripped from his right ear. Miguel reached over and grasped the control stick that the pilot had been using to maneuver the ship, but he didn't know what to do with it. He wished he had paid more attention.

"Paul! Paul!" Miguel's shouting did nothing to rouse the pilot. Miguel pulled back, hard, on the control stick, causing the ship to change direction. Instead of going down, they had now started an upward climb. They were quickly gaining altitude, the wind still buffeting them from below and from the sides. But that was the wrong direction. Miguel needed to get on the ground.

Miguel gently pushed the stick forward and the aircraft leveled out. He looked out the window. The settlement was no longer in front of them or below them. They had probably passed it by. Or maybe they had just changed course in the wind. Either way, Miguel knew he had to turn the ship around, and descend. He had the control stick figured out, but otherwise, Miguel had no idea how to land.

"Paul!" Miguel tried again. Still no sound and no movement. Keeping his right hand on the control stick, he reached his left hand down the side of the pilot's body and pressed the seat belt release button. The seatbelt retracted into the wall. Miguel pulled the pilot from his seat and onto the floor between the pilot and the co-pilot's seats. Paul groaned as his head hit the floor, and his eyes blinked open.

"What happened?" the pilot asked.

"Señor, I need you to fly the ship. We are in serious trouble," Miguel replied, the urgency of his words betraying what he hoped would be a calm response. He had to remain in control.

"Help me up then."

Miguel reached his hand down to help the pilot off the ground. "Here, give me your hand," he said as another gust of wind pushed them from the right. The movement caused Miguel to fall back into the seat so recently vacated by the pilot. As he fell, he pulled on the control stick, causing the ship to sweep to the left. Miguel's gun, previously stuck into his waistband, caught on the seat belt latch as his body slid across the seat. The gun fell to the floor. Another gust of wind hit them from underneath, causing the ship to rapidly tip up and to the left. The movement propelled the pilot off the floor, and brought him back to his feet. He reached out and grabbed the back of the pilot's seat for balance.

As the pilot gained his balance, Miguel tried to get back up. Before Miguel could sit up, the pilot clenched his fist and struck Miguel. Miguel's head flew backward, hitting the wall with a thud.

"Curse you," Miguel said under his breath as he tried to rise, only to fall back against the door as the wind continued to buffet the exterior of the small craft.

"This is it for you," the pilot said quietly, reaching down to pick up Miguel's gun from off the floor. It had slid under the seat during the turbulence. The pilot reached around under the seat, sweeping his hand back and forth until he felt the cold metal of the gun's barrel. He tugged and twisted, but the gun was wedged under the chair. The pilot leaned backward, putting his weight into his attempt to free the gun. A moment later, the gun popped free, and the pilot fell backward, his momentum carrying him back to the floor.

Miguel had not seen what the pilot was doing. His head was spinning and he was fighting to remain conscious. But now that the pilot was on the ground, Miguel could see what he was holding.

"Listen to me," Miguel said, looking straight into the eyes of the pilot, "this is not how it will end for either of us. We have a destiny. You and I will land and . . ." Miguel's words were cut off as the airship smashed into the ground. Miguel's body flew into the front windshield, his head striking the glass. His body remained on the console as his breathing slowed. The pilot, previously lying on the floor, was thrown into the back of the co-pilot's seat, his neck snapping as the ship sped across the frozen surface of Antarctica.

The airship continued to slide across the solid, snow and ice-packed terrain southwest of the remote village for several seconds. Hills and smaller mounds of granite escaped from the surface of the unyielding ice sheets around the ship as it bumped and rocked across jagged protrusions in the ice shelf. A small fire broke out in the nose, but it was quickly extinguished by the snow cascading up and over the craft as it plowed a track across the solid surface. When the ship finally came to rest, the only sound was Miguel's shallow breathing.

Moments later, Miguel's eyes fluttered open. Pain immediately engulfed his body as he tried to move. His vision was obscured, but his head was so foggy that he wasn't sure he could see anyway. He fought the urge to retch as he slowly lifted his head. Turning to the right, he nearly lost his balance. He looked around, his vision no longer obscured, and found himself lying on the ship's console, up against the front window.

He tried to sit up, placing his hand on the console below him. He had placed his hand in something warm and sticky. He looked down, certain he knew what he would see: blood, and lots of it. Pressing his weight against his hand, he finally pushed himself into a sitting position. He began to look himself over as a violent surge erupted from his insides. He could not contain the bile as his body shook from the nausea. Much of his vomit landed in his own lap, covering his legs and feet and then dripping onto the floor.

Miguel watched as his bile continued to drip, drip, drip onto the hard laminate floor below him. As he watched, his eyes roamed further away from the foul pool forming beneath him. Then he saw the pilot— or what was left of him. His body was lying on the floor behind the co-pilot's seat, bent into an L shape at the waist. His head was twisted around so that he looked as though he were peering behind himself. Blood ran from his ear and his mouth. He wasn't breathing. He was obviously dead.

Miguel gazed at Paul's grotesque form for several minutes, until he finally realized where he was and what had happened. He tried to jump down from the console, but the pain in his head and back nearly immobilized him. Nothing felt broken, but he couldn't be sure. He slowly slid off the console, careful to avoid the gadgets and dials between him and the floor. As he placed his feet onto the floor, his left ankle buckled, a quiet popping sound barely reaching Miguel's ears. *That isn't good*, he thought, while also wondering why the buckling and snapping of his ankle didn't seem to hurt. *I wonder if I severed some nerve, or something?*

"I must get some help," Miguel said aloud as he tried to twist his ankle. It moved, but only a little. Another wave of nausea hit him as he tried to put weight on his left leg. He fought the urge to throw up again, swallowing back the bile. Looking around, Miguel saw his gun on the floor. He would need that, along with the others in his backpack, sitting back in the cabin. But more importantly, he needed something to use as a crutch. He knew that would be difficult to come by.

Using the back of the two pilot seats for balance, Miguel slowly moved his left foot forward. He followed that with his right foot, which, he noted, worked just fine. He slid his left foot forward again, afraid to put weight on it, then his right. He gathered his balance and moved his hands from the backs of the chairs to the walls on either side of the door leading from the cockpit into the cabin. The gun lay at his feet. Carefully, bending at the knees, with his weight on his right leg, Miguel bent down and scooped up his gun, returning it to its former place at his back, tucked into his waistband.

Standing, Miguel turned his head and the upper half of his body back to look behind him. He didn't believe there would be anything of use to him in the cockpit, but he might as well be sure. It was too hard to move; he wouldn't be coming back. As he scanned the tight cockpit, his eyes passed the window. It was pure white. He hadn't paid any attention before, but the fact that he was able to see at all was a tribute to the sturdy construction of the small airship. The electricity was still on. There was no light coming in from the front window. For all Miguel knew, they were buried in a snowdrift. *I may not even be able to get out.* A shudder ran up and down his spine as the thought drifted across his consciousness.

That problem would have to wait. For now, Miguel needed some crutches. He continued to move slowly through the doorway from the cockpit until the walls gave way to the open air of the cabin. The first row of seats was three meters away. He would need to crawl. He began to bend his knees, but then he remembered something. Francisco's backpack. While in Geneva, Francisco had a folding rifle. Miguel had not seen it since they left Switzerland, but he assumed his brother had packed it.

Miguel looked around the cabin, certain the backpack was still here. He hadn't moved it last night when he carried his brothers' bodies, and the body of the unknown passenger to the cargo area in the back of the ship. Eventually, he realized he would need to move back into the seating area. The backpack wasn't visible from his current position. So again, Miguel stooped, this time, moving into position to crawl. Pain shot up his left leg as he moved slowly across the floor, dragging his injured ankle behind him. Several agonizing seconds later, Miguel reached the first row of seats. Placing his hands on the seat cushions on either side of him, he slowly lifted his body off the hard surface. He was thankful that his arms hadn't been injured. His head, of course, continued to pound, as though he were repeatedly hitting it against the wall.

Miguel moved slowly back toward the rear of the cabin, his hope slowly fading as he neared the last row of seating. Then he saw it. It must have slid under the seats, or flown through the air during the storm. Now, he could only hope the folding rifle was in the pack. He sat down in the aisle seat on the right, breathing heavily from the exertion. The pack was near his feet below the seat adjacent to him. He reached down, but his arm wasn't quite long enough. He would have to change seats.

He shuffled sideways and into the adjacent seat. As he settled in to relax for a moment, the aircraft shook violently, shifting to the left and tilting downward at the front. *What the . . . ?* Miguel thought. *Why is the ship moving?*

Miguel reached down and grabbed the pack that was now easily in his reach. He set it on his lap just as the craft shook again, but not so violently this time. Miguel could feel another slight movement forward and to the left. The ship was definitely moving. It was time to leave. He opened the pack and was relieved to see the rifle case. It wasn't heavy, thankfully. He pulled the case from the backpack and snapped open the latch, quickly removing the gun. He twisted the lock on the stock and shifted the lever to the right. The barrel was free and Miguel swung it around, latching it into place. In this position, it would be barely long enough to serve as a cane. Just before moving, Miguel pulled a light jacket from his brother's pack and slid one arm through a sleeve. The rest would have to wait.

Miguel slid back over to the aisle seat and moved to stand. The ship shook again and shifted several more feet to the left. Miguel lost his balance as the craft tipped forward several degrees. He barely caught hold of the seat back in front of him with his left hand; his right hand clutching the rifle he had worked so hard to acquire. When the ship stopped moving, Miguel started. He realized that he was probably doing further damage to his ankle, but he felt as though he had no choice.

Using the rifle as a cane, he moved along the aisle to the first row of seats, then over to the door to the outside. He reached up and swiped his hand across the electronic pad to the left of the hatch, swiping upward in the direction the door would move. The metal wall began its ascent into the upper casing around the hatch. Miguel had hoped the six-step staircase would automatically descend, but he couldn't see it.

As the door opened, snow swirled inside the cabin. The wind was howling and Miguel could barely see anything outside the doors. He peered out and down, the snow making his eyes sting. He was several meters off the ground. He would have to jump. He lowered himself to a seated position, his legs dangling outside the cabin door. He hadn't dressed for this kind of weather, and Francisco's jacket would barely provide any warmth, but that was the least of his concerns as the airship shifted once again. This time, it didn't stop. It began to slide. Miguel pushed off and fell forward.

"Do you think they made it?" the dark-haired man asked as he strapped on his helmet.

"How should I know," his female companion replied. "And it doesn't really matter. Davis wants us to find the ship. Whether anyone is alive is of no concern. He just wants transportation, if possible."

"Sounds pretty harsh to me," the man said.

"Well, SEC-GEN Davis is not a very nice guy," the woman replied.

They climbed onto identical snowmobiles in the large room next to the hangar as the thick overhead door began to open. It was snowing outside, but it was the wind that concerned the woman most. She had been out in these freakish spring storms before. They were never pleasant. Her companion, a rookie really, would understand soon enough.

"Let's get going," the woman said through the com chip embedded into her helmet.

"Roger that."

As soon as the door had opened enough, the woman sped through the hangar door and out into the cold day. The man followed close behind. They knew the direction they needed to travel, but without operational coms or targeting equipment, they hadn't been able to track the airship's movement. The cameras lost the craft moments after it flew overhead.

The pair glided across the flat ground alongside the perimeter of the compound. The hangar they had just exited had one door opening into the shielded compound and one door exiting to the outside of the shield. They had exited outside the shield and felt the cold air blast them as they followed the curved shield to the west. Inside the shield, the temperature was certainly cold, but some ambient and radiant heat was always trapped inside. But outside, the storm raged and the woman didn't really believe they would ever find the ship—not unless the squall died down.

The airship had flown southwest, at a fairly low altitude, away from Victory Base, across the snow and ice of the Ross Ice Shelf which separated Victory Base from Brown Peninsula. According to the camera operator, it appeared to be descending. If the pilot knew what he was doing, it would seem he was trying to land at the small, abandoned settlement on Brown Peninsula a few kilometers away. That was where the snowmobiles were headed. It would take them over an hour with the storm. Their instructions, if the ship wasn't in the settlement, was to keep looking until dark. They would search again the next day if they had no luck today.

Just over an hour after they exited the hangar, the pair approached the settlement. It had once been an offshoot of Victory Base, but had been closed down years earlier. In the warmer seasons, the section of the Ross Ice Shelf separating the two stations was often too soft to cross, making travel to and from Victory Base difficult at best. But more importantly, the settlement had become redundant. There wasn't much exploration or scientific experimentation occurring in Antarctica anymore. The buildings had been abandoned, all personnel being reassigned to Victory.

As they approached the outskirts of the settlement, the woman slowed her snowmobile. The man sidled up next to her as they slowly moved down the main thoroughfare. Eventually, as they neared the end of the street, it became obvious that the ship hadn't landed there. The only place it could have touched down was the main street. No other place was suitable within the settlement; and even the main street was covered by ice and snow at this time of the year.

"So," the man began, "it looks like we keep going?" His statement was more of a question.

"Yes." The response was curt. The woman looked to her right, nodded her head at her companion, and then sped off.

"Should we split up?" the man asked through his com chip.

"If you want to be lost out here alone, by all means."

"I don't. Sorry Tal. I'll just follow you then."

Tal was having a bad day. Her companion hadn't done anything wrong. She felt bad. "No. I'm sorry Mark. I shouldn't take my frustration out on you."

"Oh, that's okay."

"So," Tal continued, feeling a bit guilty at her treatment of her companion, "we'll keep going southwest. I actually do think we should split up just a bit. Why don't you move about a hundred meters away to the right? But stay in sight. If you can't see me, you've gone too far. We've got another seven hours of daylight, but we don't want to get lost in the canyons during a storm."

"Got it." Mark moved away to the right. Tal kept him in her peripheral line of site, knowing he'd never been out this far from the Base.

Nearly half an hour later, Tal finally spoke.

"I found it Mark. Follow my beacon."

Before long, Mark reached Tal. The snowstorm had abated over the last few minutes, the clouds sailing away on a stiff wind. The sun was shining. It was as if they'd entered some alternate reality as the sun's rays lit up the freshly-fallen icy crystals like white Christmas lights.

Tal had stopped at the edge of a deep crevice along the eastern edge of the Royal Society Mountain Range and was standing next to her snowmobile. Mark got off his machine and moved to stand next to her.

"Down there," Tal said, pointing.

The ship lay at the bottom of a steep, rocky cliff, perhaps 100 or 150 meters below them, surrounded by granite cliffs that formed a deep gorge in the earth. At the far end of the gorge, small waves from an inland lake lapped at the rocky cliffs. Smoke billowed from the craft. The hull appeared to be split in half, a rocky outcropping sitting between the two halves.

"I didn't know we had any hot springs around here," Mark said, staring at the steaming water in the distance.

"Yeah, this whole area is volcanic. There was an earthquake here about thirty years ago. It wasn't very powerful, but the land shifted just enough to open a couple of the vents that had been dormant for fifteen million years. One of those vents sits down there in the middle of that lake."

"So I shouldn't go swimming?" Mark's eyebrows rose as he asked the question, apparently attempting humor.

"No, you shouldn't."

"I was kidding, of course."

"Whoever was on that ship is likely dead," Tal said, quickly returning to the task at hand.

"I'm sure. But we should look anyway, right?"

"I guess."

Tal looked around. If there was an easy way down, she would do it, for Mark's sake. He seemed so innocent and willing to help. If not, it was probably a lost cause. Tal took several steps to the right to see if she could get a better line of site, watching the snow-covered ground carefully as she walked. Mark slowly moved left at the same time. One misstep, Tal knew, and they would end up at the bottom too.

"Tal! Look!"

Tal walked over to where Mark was standing, pointing down to the snow at his feet. There were footprints, pointed northeast, back in the direction from which they had just come. They were still deep and appeared fresh.

"Whoever was on that ship is walking," Mark said. "That's a long walk."

"And maybe dragging something?" Tal added, bending lower to look more closely at the prints. "Actually, it looks like the person is dragging one of his own feet."

Mark bent down too. "Yeah. He, or she, is probably hurt. Let's go."

The duo rushed back to their snowmobiles and jumped on. Mark fired up first and was already moving before Tal put her machine into gear. They moved slowly, trying to follow the tracks. Many of them had been obscured by the wind of the storm that had now passed. Before long, Mark slowed down and stopped. Tal pulled up next to him.

"There he is," Mark said, pointing into the distance. "Maybe we should go around him and approach from the front so he sees us before we get there. If he's injured, we don't want to risk further damage if we surprise him."

"Good idea," Tal replied. Mark was a doctor, after all. While he was shy and quiet, Tal knew that Mark was brilliant. This wasn't necessarily a medical call, but she wouldn't argue against this decision.

They drove off to the left. The sound of the machines likely being carried off into the air away from the crash survivor. Eventually, they came around in front of the person, approaching slowly. Several moments later, the person stopped moving. He or she must have seen them, and likely didn't know what to do.

Mark and Tal continued to move toward the person slowly. When Tal thought the person would be able to discern more distinct movement, she raised her hand and waved it back and forth. She couldn't think of any other gesture to show they were friendly. Mark followed Tal's lead as she continued forward. When they were within ten or twelve meters of the person—a man—Mark stopped. Tal stopped next to him. Mark lifted his leg over the seat and stood in the deep snow next to his snowmobile.

Even though the air was bitter cold, Mark removed his helmet and placed it on the seat next to him.

"Hello there sir. My name is Mark. Are you okay?"

The man remained silent, shivering and looking back and forth between the two people in front of him.

"Tal, take off your helmet too," Mark said.

Tal removed her helmet and smiled. Then she reached into a compartment on the back of her snowmobile and produced a thick winter coat with a faux-fur lining. The man jumped, as though startled, as Tal turned to face him, holding the coat out in front of her.

"Sir, we are here to help you," Tal said. "We saw your ship. It looks like you're lucky to be alive."

The man took a shaky step, then another, moving slowly toward the couple. It appeared as though his shivering was making it difficult to walk. He reached behind his back, but soon brought his hand back to the front. It appeared to Tal as though the stranger was holding something, but it was hidden from their view. When he was no more than five meters from the pair, he finally spoke. "Hel-lo a-amigos, my, my name is Miguel." He stuttered as a chill ripped through his body. "Ye-e-es, I believe I am for-fortunate to be alive." Miguel's voice was as shaky as his body. With his accent, it was difficult to understand his words.

"Are you sick?" Tal asked.

"No. I, I am injured, a-and f-f-freezing, but I do n-not have Anthrax E, if-if that is what y-you are asking."

"Let me help you Miguel," Mark said, taking the coat from Tal and walking over to the man. He was limping pretty badly, using something short for a cane.

"Th-thank you amigo," Miguel replied, taking the coat from Mark and slipping his arms through the sleeves. With shaking hands, he zipped up the coat and pulled the hood over his head.

"N-now, the be-best way you c-can help me is to, t-to r-raise your h-hands into the air." Miguel opened his hand, revealing the gun he had been hiding, and pointed it at Mark. His hand was not steady, but at this close range, there was no doubt in Tal's mind that he was dangerous.

"What's going on?" Mark asked, slowly raising his arms above his head. "We're just trying to help."

"Oh, y-you are helping a-amigo. Y-you too Señorita—h-hands in the air."

Tal raised her hands in the air, her mind racing. "I think you're making a mistake," she said. "My friend here is a doctor. He can help fix you up. I promise you, we mean you no harm."

"Thank y-you for your k-kind offer. I, I am s-sure I will take y-you up on that. But for now . . ." Miguel paused. "For n-now, we w-will be taking these m-ma-machines somewhere a bit w-warmer, yes?"

"I'm happy to take you to the base," Mark said. "But I'll have to lower my hands to do that."

"Of c-course you will," Miguel replied. "H-here is what we will d-do. Y-you will sit on your m-machine and lead the way. I-I will j-join your pretty fr-friend on the other machine, with my g-gun resting in the small of her b-back. If you l-leave us, she will die. If y-you try anything fun-funny, she will d-die. If I th-think you are trying, in any w-way, to tr-trick me or lead me away from the b-base, she will die. And, if you c-communic-cate with the base concerning our arrival, she will d-die. Am I clear, am-amigo?"

"Yes. Perfectly clear. Let's get going. You can trust us. I promise."

"I w-would-d like your h-helmet too."

Mark handed his helmet to the stranger and then climbed onto his snowmobile. Miguel placed Mark's helmet onto his head, and then, as promised, sat behind Tal. He reached one arm around her waist and with the other, held the gun to her back. It felt to Tal as though the man's shivering had subsided somewhat. She knew the electro-thermal layer was adding necessary warmth to the man's core. As she sat there with the gun in her back, she wished she hadn't brought the coat.

"Can y-you hear me?" Miguel asked.

"Yes, I can hear you," Tal replied quietly. She was angry. She knew they shouldn't have come out here looking for the airship. The SEC-GEN had made a mistake.

"Good. I hope you don't think y-you can make me fall off of this con-contraption. I have a very quick trigger f-finger. If I fall, you will be dead before I h-hit the ground."

Tal nodded her understanding and started the snowmobile. She followed Mark as he sped back toward Victory Base.

13

"I have to tell them we are coming in," Tal said through her helmet com link.

"You tell them that, but nothing more," Miguel replied.

Mark had slowed on his approach to the outside door to the hangar. Tal realized from the way Mark was hunched over his snowmobile that he was trying to make as low a profile as possible in the cold wind. Tal pulled her snowmobile, with Miguel seated behind her, up next to Mark. Mark's face was red, with patches of frosty white on the tip of his nose and his left cheek. He was shivering. They waited for a response to Tal's com. A few seconds later, the large hangar door began to open. Within moments, it was high enough for them to pull in.

"No funny business," Miguel warned as they entered a large room inside the dark hangar. As soon as they had pulled completely inside, the door shut behind them and a quiet swooshing noise rose in volume as a contraption circled around them. Mark and Tal both stood up and got off the snowmobiles as the movement continued. Miguel followed their lead.

"What is that?" Miguel asked.

"It's the scrubbers," Tal responded as she removed her helmet. "They're cleaning us and our gear so that Anthrax E doesn't get in. You need to remove the coat and helmet so it can get to the clothes you were wearing when you arrived. Are you sure you haven't been exposed?"

"I have not been exposed, that I promise you."

Moments later, the sounds and movement stopped and a door opposite to the one they had come through opened up. Mark and Tal walked forward, leaving the machines behind. Miguel cautiously followed, limping on the gun that served as his cane. He hurried to catch up as light appeared on the other side of the doorway. After the door closed behind them, Tal set her helmet on a table nearby. Miguel placed his coat and helmet next to Tal's. He kept his gun pointed at Tal's back as he moved his head back and forth, surveying their surroundings.

There were a few lights scattered along the ceiling of the hangar, but most were turned off. There was barely enough light, once the large door closed behind them, for the trio to see all the way to the far end of the building.

The hangar was approximately 40 meters wide, with an arching ceiling, lower on the sides and rising to a rounded point approximately twenty or twenty-five meters high at the apex. The smaller room through which they'd just passed was located on one end. The other end, some 60 or 65 meters away, had another door similar to the one that had just closed behind them. Various pieces of mining equipment sat along the right wall. The left wall housed several stalls holding automotive machines and vehicles of various kinds. The space was well-kept, but poorly-lit.

"Are there cameras in here?" Miguel asked, looking at Mark.

"I'm sure th-there are. But I d-doubt they're on. E-even if they're on, it's un-unlikely anyone is w-watching them. There are no threats h-here, especially give-given the current global crisis."

Before Miguel could reply, Tal gasped. "Mark, I think you have frostbite on your nose."

"I do," Mark replied, still shivering. "I can t-tell. But for now, I, I think we h-have more pressing matters to deal w-with." Mark nodded in Miguel's direction.

Tal turned away from Mark, concern etched into the lines around her eyes.

"This 'global crisis' as you said. You are referring to Anthrax E?" Miguel asked, clearly unconcerned for Mark's well-being.

"Yes," Mark replied. "But we're safe here."

Tal glared at Mark as he said those words. She couldn't say so, but she thought it unwise to say too much to the man who held her hostage. Certainly, they shouldn't help him believe he was safe here. She could see no reason to make him want to stay.

"I am glad to hear it," Miguel replied. "Now, how many people are on the compound, and who is in charge?" Again, Miguel looked at Mark, obviously expecting the man to answer him. It was clear to Tal that Mark didn't understand the unwritten rules of hostage situations. She knew that the stranger knew it too. Mark wasn't supposed to talk until his life was threatened, or his family's life was on the line. Mark was making this too easy.

"There are only eleven of us. M-more people were supposed to be coming yes-yesterday, but they never showed up."

"And who is in charge?"

"SEC-GEN Davis is in charge," Mark replied.

"But he has six armed bodyguards," Tal quickly added.

"No he . . ." Mark stopped his retort as he caught Tal's glaring eyes.

Tal knew that Miguel couldn't see her face, but apparently, he was no idiot.

"What were you about to say Mark? You were going to tell me that Davis does not have guards, right?"

"Um, no, I was going to t-tell you that he doesn't *always* have six. They are on sh-shifts . . . yeah. Sometimes he only has three around him."

"Oh Mark, it is clear that you do not know who you are speaking to. But that is not your fault. You barely know me. But trust me when I tell you that I am not as dumb as you think I am. And Tal, you should not be coaching Mark that way. He was doing so well. I do not know what I am going to do with the two of you."

Miguel still had his gun pointed at Tal's back. He took a step back and straightened his arm as though preparing to shoot her. "Since the Señorita is making this difficult, I will have to remove her. Then you will cooperate, yes?"

"No!" Mark yelled, jumping toward Miguel.

In the second it took for Mark to cover the distance to Miguel and Tal, Miguel lifted the gun away from Tal's back and pointed it over her shoulder at Mark. "Stop," he said. "Don't make me shoot you."

Mark paused for just a moment, then jumped toward Miguel and Tal.

Miguel pulled the trigger, hitting Mark in the forehead. Mark staggered and dropped, likely dead before he hit the ground.

Tal gasped, and moved toward her fallen friend. Miguel grabbed her around the waist and pulled her back toward him, spinning her around in the process so that only inches separated their faces. He fought back the bile the rose from his throat, straining to keep his face composed. Although he had killed many times before, this was different. Mark had been different, and not really a threat. Miguel pushed his feelings down. He had to get back to his family, whatever it took.

"Now, Tal, this is your chance to prove to me that there is some value to letting you live."

"Whh . . . what do you want?" Tal began to cry, her grief and fear causing her body to shake with each sobbing breath.

"There, there. No need to cry. Let's just get back to what we were doing, okay?"

Tal nodded, dropping her head down so that her chin rested on her chest. Miguel took one step back from her, reached out his hand, and, placing it under her chin, lifted her head.

"Look at me Señorita. How many armed guards are there here? The truth this time."

"None. But . . ."

"But what?"

"But several people have weapons. Davis' team all have them. They aren't guards though. I think it's just protocol. Even Davis usually carries."

"How many of the eleven people—er, ten people carry?" Miguel looked over at Mark's body as he corrected himself. Tal followed his gaze.

Sniffing, she replied, "I think only three, or four maybe."

"Are you carrying a weapon, Tal?"

"No."

"I think I better make sure." Miguel reached out his left hand and began patting Tal's body through her snow clothes. "This is not going to work. Remove your outer clothing please."

Tal did as she was asked. After she removed her heavy coat and one-piece jumpsuit, she replaced her boots and stood to face Miguel. She was wearing jeans and a hooded sweatshirt with the San Diego State University logo on the front.

Miguel looked at her, his eyes wandering up and down her body. Tal shuddered as his eyes rested too long on her chest. Then he reached out again and began to run his hand along her arm. He continued to probe, violating her private spaces, as he searched for weapons. Tal shuddered again as his hands brushed along her inner thigh.

"Miguel, please don't do this." Tal tried to speak with force, but her plea came out weak, as though she were begging for mercy.

Miguel pulled his hand back and shook his head.

"I am finished," Miguel said. "Thank you for being truthful with me. Now, it is time to go. I expect your cooperation, Tal. I do not want you to end up like your friend over there." Miguel pointed to Mark's still form with the barrel of his handgun as he leaned against the snowmobile to rest his injured leg.

"What do you want me to do?" Tal asked tearfully.

MARCH 26, 2093, 1:41PM
VICTORY BASE, ANTARCTICA

Miguel, still leaning on his rifle for support, followed Tal across the spacious hangar to the far side. There, Tal pulled a lever on the wall next to a metal door. A locking mechanism disengaged, then Tal pushed the door open. She walked out into the bright light of the compound, and Miguel followed, the gun resting lightly in Tal's back.

The air was cold, but there was no wind or snow inside the compound. Outside the shield, however, snow was still twisting and swirling in the wind. Patches of sunlight filtered through the clouds here and there, both inside and outside the shield. Tal and Miguel walked through a patch of sunlight on their way across the open space between the hangar and the airstrip in the distance. Miguel paused a moment in the warmth of the sun's rays.

Tal stopped walking when she realized that Miguel had stopped behind her. She was afraid to look back, not knowing whether Miguel would do something crazy.

"Are we changing plans?" Tal asked.

"No Señorita, I am just feeling the warmth of the sun. We will move shortly."

Tal realized that Miguel must still be cold from being outside. Even under the shield, the temperature couldn't have been higher than 45 degrees Fahrenheit. Perhaps he was even stronger than she had given him credit for. Certainly, even with his apparent leg injury, he was not weak.

Soon, Miguel began to walk again, catching up to Tal a moment later. He nudged her slightly and she started walking.

"Tal, you are still taking me to see Davis, right? I would hate to have to prematurely end this romantic walk we are having together."

"Yeah, that's where we're going. It's the big gray building over there." Tal pointed to the largest building on the compound, some 150 meters away. They would have to cross the airstrip and weave between a couple of smaller buildings to get there.

Four minutes later, Tal stopped in front of the double doors leading into the large building. Inscribed along a large metal beam at the top of the doors was the phrase "Victory is Ours." Below that, the word "Facilities" was painted in black lettering.

"This is the place then? Will everyone be in this building at this time?"

"Yes, they should be. It is where we eat." Tal hoped that wasn't true. If everyone was here now, this would be easy for Miguel; although she didn't really know what his plan was.

"Then let's go inside. It is a bit cold out here, don't you think?"

Tal pushed open the doors and walked in. Miguel trailed closely behind. Tal imagined his eyes darting back and forth as they entered a reception area. The darkness of the room relative to the outside was disorienting at first, even for her. But her eyes soon focused. There was nobody in this room.

Tal walked forward across a large, open foyer toward more doors at the back behind a reception desk. She reached the doors then paused. Miguel wouldn't know, but she was listening for the sound of people.

"What are you waiting for?" Miguel asked.

"Just making sure you were behind me," Tal said.

"I am here," Miguel replied. "I want you to open the door wide, but do not step inside. I will look inside, then push you in front of me. If you make any move to escape or scream or otherwise attract attention, that decision will cost you your life. Do you understand?"

Tal nodded and took a deep breath. Then she took a step forward and pushed the door open wide.

14

On the other side of the double doors of the Facilities Building, a few people stood around a large fire in a stone fireplace along the left-side wall or lounged in chairs nearby. Conversations were muted and reserved. There was an air of tension in the room.

In an adjacent room on the opposite side of the large meeting space, behind a closed door, SEC-GEN Davis and two of his advisors were engaged in a heated discussion, loudly enough to be heard through the door.

As the double doors opened, all six people in the room turned toward the sound. They all expected Tal and Mark to arrive, hopefully bearing good news of rescue or at least news from the outside. They had been in the dark for four days. It was disconcerting.

As Tal took two steps into the room, then stopped, two men stood from chairs nearby and began to walk toward her.

"Tal and Mark, what news do you have?" Dr. Isaac Nelson, one of the two men, asked. He and the other man stopped abruptly as Miguel stepped in behind Tal.

"Who's that, and where's Mark?" Dr. Nelson asked. Looking at Tal's eyes, he hesitated before continuing. "Um, sir, are you here to help us? Are you here from the IWO?"

Instead of responding, Miguel grabbed Tal around the neck and pulled her close. Everyone in the room froze. Nobody said a word as time seemed to stand still.

Miguel finally spoke: "Buenas Tardes. My name is Miguel González. I am here on *assignment*, so to speak. I will be requiring the company of Secretary General Antonio Davis. As I do not see him here, I ask, politely, for someone to tell me where he is."

The people in the room continued to stare at the man, seemingly frozen by a mixture of fear and surprise. The argument in the next room could still be heard, although the words were not clear.

"Did I not make myself clear?" Miguel asked. "I understand your concern. But I assure you that your concern will multiply if I do not become acquainted with the SEC-GEN in the next ten seconds." Miguel tightened his grip around Tal, clearly trying to make a show of it.

Several members of the group started talking at once. Dr. Nelson could be heard over the others. "What are you talking about? Where's Mark? What's going on?" With each question, Dr. Nelson became more agitated, taking steps toward Tal and Miguel.

Tal wondered whether she should speak. She truly believed that Miguel had no qualms about killing innocent people. But would he do it, here, where so many people were gathered and could possibly overwhelm him. She didn't want to find out. As she pondered her next move, she became aware of Miguel's voice.

"... nine ... ten. This is unfortunate."

Miguel raised his gun from Tal's back and pointed it at Dr. Nelson, now only nine or ten meters away. "I insist that you stop, now," Miguel said. "I have killed before, and will do so again, if I must."

Dr. Nelson stopped and raised his hands into the air.

"Why? What do you want?" Dr. Nelson asked.

"I already told you that. Where is Davis?" Miguel's voice rose as he became more agitated.

Tal could feel Miguel's body shaking, but not from cold. Was he scared? Could he be stopped? She wanted to intervene, but the gun in the small of her back frightened her. One wrong word and it could be her on the ground next.

Dr. Nelson took another step forward. "Please sir, remove Tal and we can talk." Then he took another step forward.

Miguel pulled the trigger, and Dr. Isaac Nelson, the old man who had operated Victory Base for several years prior to the arrival of SEC-GEN Antonio Davis, fell backward against a table. People gasped and one woman screamed. Another fainted and fell to the floor, hitting her head against the cold concrete. Blood began to pool around her head.

As Dr. Nelson's precarious grasp on the edge of the table failed, his body slowly crumpled to the floor. Blood spilled from a hole in his abdomen, spurting in rhythm with his heartbeat as he fell. Miguel released Tal and turned, retching. His vomit plastered the floor at Tal's feet. She made to move, but was stopped as Miguel reached out and grabbed her wrist. He pulled her close again as he stood.

From behind the windows of the adjacent office, SEC-GEN Antonio Davis noticed the strange behavior of the people outside in the lounge. All eyes were turned in one direction, and nobody was moving. Something was wrong. He stood slowly and walked over the windows. His advisors stared after him. He slowly turned a small disc on the side of the window to open the blinds imbedded within the pane of glass. Leaving the blinds only slightly open, the SEC-GEN peered through. Whatever the people were looking at was too far to his left to see. He waited as his advisors peeked over his shoulder.

From behind the shaded window, Davis and his assistants heard the report of a small firearm and saw the body of Dr. Nelson fall. They didn't speak for a moment as they continued to peer out the window.

"Now see what you made me do?" Miguel said, his voice shaking. "I did not want to do that. That is not what . . . not what was supposed to happen. I just wanted to speak with the SEC-GEN. Please, somebody take me to SEC-GEN Davis."

The others began to slowly scoot back, away from Dr. Nelson and Miguel as he put the gun back down into the small of Tal's back. Tal began to cry.

Miguel began to relax, taking several deep breaths. This was necessary, he reminded himself. It was the only way to get back to his family. In a calm voice, not one that betrayed a weakness he had not known was buried within him, he continued: "You see amigos, that I can be reasonable. Only one of you has to die today. I only have the one request. Where is Davis?" Miguel's voice, which had been trying to control, became hard and demanding as he asked the question.

Near the back of the room, a short man raised his hand over his head, as though seeking permission to speak.

"Yes, you in the back?" Miguel began, "do you have something you would like to say to me?"

The man didn't speak. Instead, he moved his hand to his left and stretched out his finger to point. Miguel turned his head to follow the man's finger toward a lone door on his right. The door was closed and an adjacent window was mostly blacked out. A small amount of light shone through small horizontal slits in the window. Tal could see movement through those slits and knew that Miguel would see it too.

"Thank you señor," Miguel said, as he pushed Tal toward the closed door. He followed her as she walked slowly to the right, walking sideways, keeping an eye on the group. He wasn't foolish enough to believe that he could just walk into the room safely. He was certain someone would try to protect the SEC-GEN, and he didn't want more violence.

When Tal reached the door, Miguel reached over her shoulder to knock. He nearly lost his balance as he strained to cross the distance, keeping his weight off his injured left leg. He rapped on the door and then quickly regained his balance just as a quiet scraping sound came from behind the wooden door. Miguel pulled Tal back two paces. In his peripheral vision, Miguel could see that not a single person had made a move to stop him, yet. They hadn't even moved toward him.

Cowards, he thought disdainfully. Then, *would I be any different?* He shook his head to clear away the pathetic thoughts.

A voice from behind the door said, "Yes? How may I help you?"

"My name is Miguel González. I am here to speak with Secretary General Antonio Davis. I understand he is in this room."

"Yes, he is," the voice replied. "And he is armed. Please place your weapon on the floor and kick it away. Then the SEC-GEN will invite you in to speak with him."

Miguel laughed, nervously. "Instead, how about I shoot another one of your comrades out here if this door is not opened immediately."

"We will not negotiate with terrorists, Mr. González," the voice replied. "If you shoot another of our people, things will not end well for you."

Miguel laughed again, but this time, a more crazed sound escaped from his lips. "You threaten me from behind a closed door. That is *so* brave. Your people out here should be very grateful for your service and your heroism." Then he turned, pointed near a woman closest to his side of the room, and pulled the trigger. His bullet missed, just as he had planned, but the fear in her eyes was enough to make everyone outside the small room believe he was serious. He only hoped those inside the room with the SEC-GEN would believe as well.

Again, people in the room gasped as they began to back farther away from the crazy man who had already taken one life, and nearly another.

"Wait!" a second voice called out from behind the closed door. "Nobody else needs to die. I will come out."

"Is that you Señor Davis?"

"Yes, please lower your gun. I am opening the door."

"You see, Señor Davis, I have no reason to lower my gun. Your amigo already told me you are armed. Do not mistake me for a fool."

"It was a bluff. I'm not armed. But I also don't want to die."

Miguel thought again about the people behind them in the room. There were only five of them still alive, and one of them was passed out on the floor. He knew that he didn't have any real need to fear anyone here. He was in control, and that was, apparently, how it would remain. The SEC-GEN was even more afraid than those standing behind Miguel, or so it would seem. Miguel was rather surprised. Davis, the elected leader of the world, was surrendering.

"Open the door Davis. Let me see the whites of your eyes. I may let you live so long as I do not feel threatened."

Three seconds after Miguel stopped speaking, the door slowly opened out toward where Miguel and Tal stood. They stepped back to let the door swing open. Just beyond the threshold, two men stood, side by side. Their hands were at their sides and they remained still.

"That was a wise decision," Miguel said. "Please take four steps backward so that I may join you."

The two men stepped backward until they ran into a small desk in the center of the room. Miguel pushed Tal into the room in front of him, then followed. A quiet sound reached Miguel's ears and he flicked his eyes to the right just as a third man stepped out from behind a small bookcase. Miguel twisted to his left, pulling Tal in front of him just as the man squeezed the trigger of a small handgun. The bullet ripped through Tal's shoulder and imbedded itself into the wall behind them. Miguel raised his gun and shot the man between the eyes. He rapidly turned back toward the other two men as Tal slumped to the floor, blood draining from her open wound.

"Which one of you is the SEC-GEN?" Miguel growled, no longer sorry for his actions. Miguel knew the face of the man he was looking for. It was plastered on screens and tech the world over. This was a test. Miguel was gauging how weak his adversary was.

The man on the right, Coms Secretary Jason Blunt, raised his arm slightly and said, "Me."

"You lie," Miguel replied quietly as he raised him arm to shoot again.

"Wait, it's me," the other man said quickly. "I'm the SEC-GEN."

"I know," Miguel replied angrily. Then he lowered his weapon and shot Blunt in the leg.

The SEC-GEN cried out as Jason hit the floor, his blood splattering across the plush rug on which he had stood. Blunt fainted, with Tal not far behind.

MARCH 26, 2093, 3:05PM
VICTORY BASE, ANTARCTICA

"This way," Miguel growled, waiving his gun toward the open door.

"They're bleeding," Davis said, looking back and forth between Tal and Jason Blunt, both lying motionless on the floor. "Can I help her?" he asked, pointing to Tal.

"No sudden moves," Miguel growled as he moved away from Tal. He kept his gun pointed at Davis.

Davis looked around, lifted a linen cloth from the table and knelt by Tal. He carefully undid the top button of her blouse and pulled the material away from the wound, lifting her shoulder in the process. Tal opened her eyes and looked at him, a moan escaping her lips.

"I'm sorry Tal," he said tearfully. Tal closed her eyes and winced as Davis used the linen cloth to wipe the blood off her shoulder, looking at both the entry and exit wounds. He nodded his head, as though coming to a conclusion about what to do, then draped the cloth over both and applied pressure, front and back, with both his hands. They stayed that way for a couple of minutes until Miguel spoke again.

"That is good Davis," Miguel said. He was beginning to get nervous about being away from those in the other room for so long. "Now let us go join your friends in the other room."

"What about him?" Davis asked, nodding in Jason's direction.

"His wound is superficial. When he awakens, we will see to his needs."

"Come on, Tal," Davis said as he helped her to her feet. Taking slow steps, Davis and Tal moved together toward the open door. They stopped just before passing through. Tal's shoulder was still bleeding and it appeared to Miguel that she was having trouble staying upright. Davis kept one hand on the cloth over her shoulder and placed an arm on her back as they stood waiting for Miguel's next order.

"Please, continue over toward your friends."

Miguel had quickly scooped up the gun that had recently been pointed in his direction, and then frisked Jason Blunt's motionless body, finding nothing of use. He now held both guns in front of him as he followed Davis and Tal toward the middle of the large room. Three men were crouched next to a petite blond woman no more than twenty-five or twenty-six years old. They had placed a wrapping of some kind around the woman's head and were talking softly to her. The other woman, whom Miguel had purposely missed, sat on a chair, rocking back and forth. Upon hearing the others walk in from the office, the men stopped talking and scooted closer to the young woman, as if they could protect her. Miguel had no intention of killing any more of them, but they certainly didn't know that. He hadn't wanted to kill *any* of them, but they forced his hand. Yet, he felt incredibly powerful as he gave the SEC-GEN a shove in the back. The most powerful man in the world was his hostage.

"Gentlemen," Miguel began as he watched the three men hover over the pretty blond, "you need not be so concerned. I have no desire or intention to hurt any more of you. Now that Davis has surrendered to me, I believe we can become friends. As a sign of trust, each of you please stand up so that I can check you for weapons."

The men slowly stood. Miguel began to walk toward them but stopped suddenly. "Actually, it seems I am in a bit of a bind. With just one of me and seven of you, I seem to have the lesser hand. So, instead, I am going to need all of you to remove your clothing so that I can see you have no weapons."

"Not going to happen," one of the men said. The others were shaking their heads.

"Mr. González, can't we do this another way?" Davis asked. "There's no need to make these people more concerned than they already are. You have me. That's what you wanted."

"Actually, Davis," Miguel replied, "it is not really *you* that I want at all. I need to get home to my family in Cuba. I do not have the means to do that. You are going to help me get there. But before we go any further, please remove your clothing. Once you show your friends how easy it is, I am sure they will comply."

The SEC-GEN paused, seemingly considering his options. Miguel had killed people in cold blood—people who probably didn't deserve to die. Miguel knew the SEC-GEN would make the right choice.

"I need to help Tal sit down, then I'll do as you ask," Davis said. Miguel nodded, so Davis settled Tal onto a couch and moved her hand to her shoulder to hold the cloth in place. Then Davis removed his shirt, then his shoes and socks. He unbuckled his belt and slid his trousers to the floor. He stood in his boxers and turned around slowly.

"Thank you, Davis. Please put your clothes back on. You see, everyone; that was not hard. Tal, it's your turn."

Tal hadn't said a word since entering the main lounge area with Miguel earlier. She didn't move. Her eyes were half closed, as if she were on the verge of passing out again. Miguel appreciated her defiance. She was strong-willed. That was something he could admire, no matter how foolish.

The pain in her shoulder was intense, but the bleeding had stopped. Tal didn't know whether the bullet was still lodged in her shoulder, but it didn't feel like it. She felt faint from the loss of blood, but as the blood flow eased up, she believed she would be okay. But now she was being asked to undress in front of a man who had already shown he had bad intentions. It hadn't even been an hour since he touched her in a way that made her worry for her safety. Miguel hadn't actually touched her inappropriately, but she didn't trust him.

She would not undress in front of this man. He seemed to thrive on the weakness of others—Mark, SEC-GEN Davis, Dr. Nelson. She would sit there, defiantly, even if it would cost her life.

"Now!" Miguel barked.

Tal slowly turned to face the man. "Mr. González, I don't think I will do that. I can't raise my arm. Plus, we've already been through this outside, remember?" Tal didn't believe Miguel would let it go, but if he did, it would show that he wasn't here for that reason. Perhaps she would only need to fear his gun, not his body.

"Ah yes, that is right Tal," Miguel replied, visibly softening. "You are exempt. Who is next then? You." Miguel pointed his gun at the man standing to the right of the blond woman, and Tal relaxed.

Miguel checked the others for weapons, along with the body of Dr. Nelson. There were no other weapons. Strangely, and comfortingly, at least to Tal, Miguel had not asked anyone to undress Bria. She was a beautiful woman. Seeing her nearly naked would be a new experience for all of the men in the room, as far as Tal knew. Tal felt the need to protect Bria from that. But she hadn't needed to. Miguel had not even asked.

"Now, three among us need medical care, and I do not want to stand in the way of that. So, Davis, where are the weapons kept on the grounds?"

"I don't know," Davis replied. He was lying, but Tal wouldn't say it aloud.

"Then who does?" Miguel looked around the room at the others.

"I do," Tal replied weakly. She was lightheaded, dizzy. "I'll show you. But please let Bria and Jason get to the medical facilities. They need help."

"Bria? That is a beautiful name. Of course. Let us all take a walk to the medical facilities so that Bria, Jason and Tal may receive proper treatment. Afterward, perhaps we can see about the armory."

"Help," a quiet voice called out from the office. Jason Blunt staggered into the main room moments later and stopped. His fear was palpable, but nobody made a move toward him.

"Someone please help Mr. Blunt," Miguel said.

Tal stood with Davis' help and together, they led the small group down halls and around corners toward the medical facilities. Two of the men carried Bria. The third walked by Jason's side as he limped along the corridor. The badly-shaken woman stumbled along just in front of Miguel as he brought up the rear. He now held the only two weapons apart from those in the armory. Mark had told him, before his untimely passing, that the people had no need for weapons. Mark had been honest, before Tal warned him. Tal knew that only three or four people were likely to be armed. As it turned out, only one man had carried a gun. Now Miguel held it. If he could control the armory, he would control the whole compound.

Tal saw the writing on the wall. A new leader had emerged.

15

"I really need to go now," Thomas Franconi said. The small group of Māori surrounding him were quiet. Some were crying, but most were just watching as he bent over to hug a small child who clung to his legs.

Thomas had spent the past two weeks living among the Māori after Kaia and Tia had rescued him from the Kohekohe grove. He had no place else he needed to be. After spending the first night in a warm bed in one of the modest homes in the village, he had asked whether he could stay for a while. A short man he later learned was a chief of some kind, had told him he could stay as long as he liked. Thomas thanked them, then explained that he needed to find his ship. The hover he had procured upon arriving in New Zealand had not been repaired, so one of the men from the village had given him a ride to the airport in an old two-door pick-up truck.

Several hours later, Thomas had walked back to the village. His ship was intact. He had no messages waiting for him from Director Jass or SEC-GEN Davis. He wasn't surprised. Davis couldn't contact him now, after what he had done to Campbell Island. And Jass wasn't likely to com at all. The plan had been for Thomas to deliver the González brothers to Antarctica. There were a thousand things that could go wrong. Jass just wanted a report when the assignment was finished.

Over the next two weeks, Thomas had visited his ship once, or sometimes twice a day. Not one message. He felt betrayed, but happy. He thought, on several occasions, that he could find happiness living with his new friends in this small village. But each time that thought crossed his mind, he remembered that the world was falling apart around them. The peace in New Zealand would not last. Anthrax E would find them.

As sad as it made Thomas to leave his new friends, he had no choice—if he wanted to live. He had not discussed with them the plague sweeping across Asia southward. Thomas didn't know whether they had any idea what was coming. A few members of the tribe had tech, but he hadn't seen them using it much. And not once, in fourteen days, had he heard or been a part of any conversation related to Anthrax E. Ignorance was bliss.

But Thomas was not wholly ignorant. Each day, from inside his ship, Thomas searched the Web for news. There wasn't much being reported, but yesterday, there was a report from Australia that Anthrax E had reached Sydney and Brisbane. It was too close. Thomas had to leave. But his sorrow threatened to overwhelm him as he bent low to hug the small child.

Thomas stood back up as the mother of the child scooped down to pick up her daughter. Kaia, Tia and their father were standing nearby and walked toward Thomas as he scanned the group of villagers.

"I will miss you Thomas," Kaia said as she reached over to hug the man she had met only two weeks earlier. Tia joined the hug as their father watched on, a proud look upon his face.

In a quiet moment the night before, Thomas had overheard the girls' father telling another man that he was proud of his daughters for rescuing Thomas, and proud of them for their benevolence toward a stranger. Thomas had been kind and gentle with all four of his children, the father had said, and he respected Thomas for that. Thomas would be missed. The other man agreed, and it had warmed Thomas' heart.

Thomas knew that Kaia and Tia's father, and most everyone else in the community, wondered why he was leaving. But when Thomas refused to say more than "it's time I leave", nobody questioned him. He didn't really belong after all. They must have known.

"I'm going to miss you too Kaia; and you too Tia. Thank you again for rescuing me from that tree. I'll never forget you."

"Well, you'll come back to visit, won't you?" Kaia asked, smiling.

"Of course I will. It may be a few months though. I just meant that I'll miss you and won't forget about you for the next little while, that's all." Thomas hated to lie to his new friends. But he knew that he would never see them again. Anthrax E was approaching, and there was no way he could save them—not without a vaccine. He had considered inviting a few of them to join him on his ship. They would see that he saved their lives, in time. But he was certain they would hate him for leaving the others behind when they saw what happened to the rest of the village. It would be better to leave them in their ignorant bliss. At least that is what he had convinced himself to believe. He wasn't sure he was right.

"Then we will see you when you return." Kaia replied. "We'll keep some rope and a Kohekohe tree around with your name on it."

Everyone around laughed as Thomas hugged Kaia and Tia one last time. Then he turned and walked away. A few minutes later, at the top of a small hill up the street from the village, Thomas turned around to wave. But nobody was watching. They had resumed their daily activities. It was planting season. The work never ended, but they were happy. And, for two short weeks, they had been able to share their happiness with a stranger.

APRIL 10, 2093
RIO DE JANEIRO, BRAZIL

"Sir, you need to see this," the man said, walking toward South AM Director, Adal Jass. The man was carrying a small tablet, holding it out in front of him as though it were hot.

"What is it?" Director Jass asked.

"It's an op-ed piece published in Germany's "Free People's News Corp. Press", dated today. Here, read it." The man handed his tablet to Director Jass, who immediately looked down and began reading.

"... *Clearly, some form of* Bacillus anthracis *was released in the Egyptian desert. Our leaders, and their puppet media have claimed that such release was 'accidental' and that Anthrax E was discovered in a 'hidden', 'unknown' cave during a sand storm. The truth, my friends and allies in our fight against governmental tyranny, is that our leaders, those to whom we have given our blind and ignorant respect and trust, have intentionally released against us the very agents that our ancestors fought so hard to defeat 150 years ago.*"

Director Jass scanned through the rest of the article, finally coming to the closing paragraphs.

"*Do not believe that we live in a safe and sophisticated world, and that the IWO labors on your behalf. The IWO and all of its political affiliates want power and control. They want to rule you. They want you to serve them.*

"*Indeed, you are a slave already; but you can throw off those shackles and be free now. The truth is out. You, the individual, are not required to be bound by their laws and their restrictions. You, the individual, have been pushed far beyond what is natural and moral. YOU, the individual, have the right to stand up and demand the release of the vaccine that your government developed long before the 'accidental' release of Anthrax E upon our world!*

"*The vaccine exists! Even now, your 'leaders', and those deemed worthy to continue to live in this world, are hunkered down in bunkers receiving vaccines. They are safe. Do not rest, satisfied that you may, yourself, be safe from Anthrax E. You are not. You are going to die from the horrible madness intentionally released upon our world unless we rise up together and demand, through whatever means necessary, that our governments release the vaccine to the public. Fight with me! Live with me! Or die trying!"*

When Director Jass finished reading, he gazed upward, toward the rocky ceiling above. The man standing next to him followed his gaze. Several second later, Director Jass lowered his eyes and stared at the man. "This is false, of course," Jass said.

"I'm am glad to hear you say that, Adal. It would worry me to believe that anyone in our government, you especially, would intentionally do this to the world."

"I appreciate your concern Nic. Believe me when I tell you that none of this is real. The discovery of what is now called Anthrax E was accidental, I assure you."

"Thank you Adal. I will think nothing more of it."

"That's good. And don't show that to anyone else either, okay. We don't need any false rumors turning us against each other. I'm sure the SEC-GEN will squash this little rumor before long. Thank you for bringing it to my attention."

APRIL 12, 2093
RIO DE JANEIRO, BRAZIL

"Turn on the recorder," Director Jass said to the man sitting at the desk in front of him. "I have a message to send to the world."

"Aren't world-wide proclamations supposed to come from the SEC-GEN?" the man asked.

"Yes, usually," Jass replied casually, "but he asked me to do this one. We spoke about it at length. Do not worry."

In truth, Jass knew what nobody else knew—that the SEC-GEN wouldn't be making any public statements for a long time. Perhaps never again. Jass had originally decided against issuing any public statement on behalf of the IWO. Everyone outside his little bunker was going to die, one way or the other, so why bother with any attempt to pacify whoever was left out there? But after two days, he changed his mind. To keep up the appearance of government control, and to keep the peace inside his safe haven for as long as possible, a short statement was probably a good idea.

"Okay boss," the man replied. "Put this on." He handed Director Jass a headset with a microphone extending from the right side down toward his mouth. After Jass had placed the headset over his head, the man touched the screen in front of him and pointed at Director Jass.

"Let it be known: the IWO wholly refutes the alleged conspiracies now being propagated by agitated and scared individuals in our society. Do not believe the stories. There is no truth to the theory that your government intentionally unleashed the plague that is now ravishing our brothers and sisters in all quarters of the world.

"While no vaccine is currently available, as has been stated from this venue multiple times in the past, dozens of facilities and teams, employing the brightest minds, have been organized throughout the world, working to find or create such a vaccine. When it is discovered, or created, it will be freely distributed to the masses.

"Please be calm and rational. This conspiracy theory is no different from those of the past which have been generated to promote fear and stir up hostility. Do not be led down that path. Let us strengthen one another and resolve to spend whatever days we may have left on this Earth making peace and loving our neighbors."

When Director Jass finished, he lifted the headset from his head and handed it back to the man seated in front of him.

"That was very nice, sir," the man said, taking the headset and placing it in a drawer below the desk.

"Thank you," Director Jass replied. "I'd like it to air now. Send it to every available news outlet with official IWO instructions that it be played every hour, on the hour, for the next twelve hours."

"Okay," the man replied. "But is all of that true?"

"Of course it is. I wouldn't say it otherwise."

16

"The animal testing is going well," Latisha Bodily said quietly into the microphone on her wristwatch. "Shevchuk said the animals are immune."

"That's good news Latisha," Director Jass replied. "You don't sound very happy about it."

"That man—Shevchuk—I hate him. I want him dead."

"Easy now. You can't go killing people who are trying to save your life, you know. If you kill Dr. Shevchuk now, no matter how badly you want it, you will put an end to any chance of creating a vaccine. That's not what you want, is it?" Director Jass spoke as though he were speaking to an unruly child. Latisha didn't seem to notice the condescension in his voice. "What did he do this time?"

"One of the morons here started talking about Anthrax E getting into bunkers and some backdraft theory and smoke being sucked into some building in Wyoming, and . . ."

"Slow down Latisha. I don't know what you're talking about."

"I'm sorry Adal. I'm really worked up. It doesn't matter anyway. But when I questioned why we hadn't been told about all of that stuff, Shevchuk snapped at me. He said, 'This is my lab, my facility, my operation. You'll listen when I talk and jump when I say so, and shut up when I tell you to' or some rubbish like that."

"Well, I can see why you're so upset. He doesn't seem like a very nice person," Jass replied casually. "Of course, I have met Dr. Shevchuk, you know. I found him to be very personable. But that was years ago. Perhaps he has suffered from a personality change over the past few years." Again, Jass was only humoring Latisha. She never seemed to understand when he was playing with her. Like a blind mouse following cheese, Latisha did exactly what Jass told her to do. He found it humorous that she was so upset over what Dr. Shevchuk had said. The reality was that Latisha always did what others said. People in power ruled Latisha Bodily. Shevchuk was the person with the power in that Bunker near Boston. Jass had no doubt that Latisha would do exactly what Shevchuk told her until her death—or until a vaccine was created allowing Latisha to finally escape her 'underground prison', as she called it.

"Well, I won't kill him now, of course," Latisha said, calming down. "I need him to get me out of here, so I can join you."

"Of course," Director Jass replied. "Smart girl. I knew you would make the right decision, and all on your own. Let me know how things progress."

Jass disconnected the com, smiling. Latisha really was a child. She had no idea that she was his pawn. He had only one need for her—to track the progress of a vaccine. When she had done her job, he would be through with her.

MAY 2, 2093—PRIVATE COM

"That's excellent news!" Director Jass said. He couldn't hide his excitement. Dr. Shevchuk, and the men and women in the bunker in North AM, had finally created a vaccine, or at least, that's what they believed. They were ready to test it.

"And I'm going to volunteer to be injected first," Latisha Bodily said. "The sooner I'm vaccinated, the sooner I can get out of here."

"And what will you do once you have been vaccinated?"

"I'm going to . . . well, it won't be pleasant, I assure you."

"I'd really like to know your plans Latisha," Jass said, as pleasantly as he could. He didn't need Latisha Bodily taking any action that could jeopardize his chances of outliving the disease. Once she told him the plan, he would approve it, or he would condemn it. Either way, she would do what he said. She always did.

"You don't need to worry about it, Adal. But some people are probably going to die."

"Latisha, I don't want any of those people to die, at least not yet. So, you're not going to take any action that will put their lives at risk, do you understand me?"

"I understand Adal. But this time, you're wrong. Don't you think I know how you like to play with my mind? How you treat me as a child. I'm not naïve. I see right through you. I've played you as much as you've played me. You got me into this bunker, and all I had to do was fake my loyalty to you. It is *you*, Adal, who is the fool."

"I don't know what you're talking about Bodily. But I assure you, if you go against my orders, you will not be welcome here. You will be left alone in the world. Your only friends will be whoever you let live from your little bunker. And they can't save you forever. I hope you understand the power I hold. This will not end well for you."

"You don't scare me Jass. In fact, it is you who should be scared. Once I have the vaccine, *I* will hold the power. I'll take those who are with me and you will die, slowly, rotting away in that cave of yours."

"Latisha, this is the last warning I will give you. My rules, or you will pay the price."

"Damn your rules Adal. The only price anyone will pay is the price *you* will pay for your arrogance. Goodbye—forever."

Latisha Bodily disconnected the phone, leaving Director Jass to wonder how he could have been so wrong.

MAY 4, 2093
RIO DE JANEIRO, BRAZIL

"They've done it!" Nic Heiberg said. He was nearly shouting. "They've created a vaccine!"

Others in the bunker gathered around Nic as he held up his tablet.

"Are you sure?" Director Jass asked.

"Yes, I'm sure."

"And . . . were there any troubles. I mean, did everyone live?" Director Jass had not stopped thinking of Latisha's threats from two days earlier. He thought, without much doubt, that she would try to kill someone, or maybe all of them. While he didn't really care whether any of them lived in the long run, he now knew that, without at least a few of them left alive, there was very little chance of the vaccine getting to Brazil. Latisha would not save them—*that* he knew for sure.

"As far as I know, according to Shevchuk's post to the database, they're all alive."

"What about that thing a couple of days ago?" another man asked.

"Oh, you mean that little scare they had?"

"What scare?" Jass asked.

"Well, I guess someone released Anthrax E into their bunker, so they vaccinated everyone just after starting the tests on their test subjects."

"You just said they had created a vaccine," Jass said, slowly. "It sounds to me like you're telling me they vaccinated everyone without knowing whether it actually works."

"Well, yeah, that is what happened," Nic replied. "But Shevchuk seems to think it will work. He may be the smartest man in the world, even before the plague. So I believe him."

"We shall see," Jass replied. "Keep me posted. I'd like to know when they have *actual* proof that the vaccine works."

Several people in the group, previously happy and smiling with the news, shook their heads as they walked away. They had no proof. There was no cause for merriment yet.

MAY 13, 2093
RIO DE JANEIRO, BRAZIL

"Adal," Nic called out excitedly. "Adal, come over here."

"I'm coming," Director Jass replied. He had barely spoken to Nic over the past few days. He had become more frustrated each time they talked. Nic believed they would be saved, but he never had any proof.

"They've finally announced a successful vaccine," Nic said as Adal approached.

"You mean, it actually worked? And they've posted their results?"

"Yes. That's what I mean." Nic smiled. "We're going to live."

"Yes, we are my friend," Adal replied. They shared a smile, but Adal's quickly faded. "Tell me Nic, is there any chance we can duplicate the formula and process here? Be candid with me."

"I've already told you that we can't. You know that. I'll re-check the final formulations posted by Dr. Shevchuk, but if things haven't changed significantly, we won't be able to do it—at least not from here. I'm sorry."

"That's okay, Nic. We'll get them down here somehow. We're going to be okay."

"Yeah, we are. We should celebrate. And maybe it's time we posted something into the Anthrax E database."

"I'll do that, Nic. In fact I would like to take over your operations. I'd like to be the one communicating with the rest of the bunkers from here on out. It's nothing personal, of course. Now that there is a real chance for survival, I think I should be on the front lines, leading. That's what I was elected to do."

"I have no problem with that Adal. I'm sure you'll do a great job." Nic smiled.

"Thanks Nic. If I need any help, I'll let you know."

"You got it boss. I'll go tell everyone the great news!"

As Nic Heiberg walked away, Jass logged into the central systems and changed the access passwords. His technical abilities were not as rudimentary as they seemed—not as he had led his associates to believe. He had sat through Nic's lessons, bored, but attempting to look interested. Nic thought he had taught Adal how to use much of the equipment, but Adal had just assigned out the work anyway, to keep the masquerade alive.

Adal smiled as he then restricted communications with the outside to him alone. He set up several encryption systems, including new algorithms he had secretly created himself over the past couple of months which would make it appear that communications were not coming through.

His technicians had finally broken into the USCAN system. Jass would let them keep running that system since it only allowed them to see what was going on outside. But actual communications, and information learned through those communications, would be strictly on a need-to-know basis moving forward. And as far as Adal Jass was concerned, he was the only one who needed to know.

17

"Run girls," Hasan Tabak yelled, as the monster dug her teeth into the soft flesh of his thigh. *"Run!"*

It was unclear how it had happened, but the Skins—that's what the Americans had called them during a hasty conference call a few days earlier—had found them. The small research team was secluded in an underground bunker in the hills on the western shore of Çamlıdere Baraj Gölü, a large man-made lake 90 kilometers north of Ankara, Turkey. Not only had the Skins located them underground, but they had actually found a way in. Now, the scientists and politicians that had hidden there for so long, believing they were safe from Anthrax E, were rapidly falling to the terrible ferocity of the monsters.

Only two weeks earlier, the people in the bunker had finally been vaccinated from Anthrax E. They had precisely followed the formula created by the scientists in the United States. But they all knew that a group of scientists in Toronto, Canada had made a mistake, which had caused those inoculated with the Toronto formula to turn into these creatures, whatever they were. While they appeared human from the satellite feeds the group had been watching, here, up close, it was not so clear. The blood on their skin and bits of clothing clinging to their bodies, along with the patchy hair and snarling teeth, made them appear more like beasts than humans.

"Dad!" Sena screamed as her father fell to the ground. Within moments, he stopped thrashing and became completely still. Then the woman, or whatever she was, lifted her head and stared at the two young girls. She cocked her head to the side, but made no further movements. They had heard reports from others around the world that the Skins attacked, unprovoked and without thought. They had also heard, however, that some of the women were less brutish. Now, in this place, this lone female hesitated.

Sena Tabak, the older of Hasan's two daughters, slowly reached over and grasped her sister's hand. Sena was mentally strong for her age. At only seveteen years old, she had experienced a great deal of tribulation in her life. Her father, Hasan, was a member of Turkey's oldest and most influential ruling party. But in Turkey, unlike most of the world, the political parties were not as peaceful as they appeared. On the surface, they worked harmoniously, within the mandates of the IWO. But secretly, underground resistance fighters continued to create havoc within the borders of the country. The Tabak family had seen their share of the action.

Dilan was only fourteen years old. She had celebrated her fourteenth birthday in the bunker on the day the Americans announced that they had created a vaccination. It was a birthday she would not forget. Although Sena had heard of, and experienced much of their father's political dealings, her young sister Dilan had not.

During the early stages of the epidemic, Hasan Tabak had taken a tremendous gamble, and risked his life and the life of his family, to procure a place for himself and his daughters within the safety of the bunker. He had broken numerous laws and even had others jailed in order to remove those that stood in the way of their placement in the bunker.

Now, their security was gone. Hasan was dead; and his daughters stood face to face with the monster who had just killed their father.

"Move slowly," Sena whispered, gently tugging the hand of her sister. "Very slowly. Don't lose eye contact. Whatever you do, keep your head up."

"Okay," Dilan whispered in reply, her voice shaking from fear.

The tears that had formed in Dilan's eyes almost instantly when their father was attacked moments earlier had already dried up. Sena could not believe that Dilan had already overcome the grief, but certainly, her fear was stronger than any sorrow she could possible feel at that moment. Sena knew, because she felt the same way.

The girls slowly backed away from the monster still staring at them. Behind the naked woman, others continued to tear down doors, hungrily seeking out the remaining humans. Sena did not point it out to her sister, but she could see some of their friends rise from the floor in the distance and join the pursuit. For now, however, only one Skin was paying them any attention.

Thankfully, when the attack began, Hasan had hidden with his girls in a closet close to the main entrance to the bunker. As his girls begged to move farther away, he assured them that this was the safest place as it would allow them to slip out after the monsters all came in from the outside. Sena hoped her father had been right.

The girls continued their slow, methodical retreat toward the main entrance to the bunker. Their progress was cut short when Sena ran into the sealed doorway to the decontamination chamber. She knew exactly where she was and slowly reached up to her left, just above her shoulder, and touched the keypad. Again, she silently thanked her father as the door whooshed open. She knew that he had already keyed in the opening sequence before they hid. That way, all it would take was a touch to the keypad to open the doors.

The sound from the doors opening awakened the Skin. In a mad rush, she screamed as she practically flew toward the girls. They jumped back into the chamber and Sena slammed her hand into the keypad on the other side just before the Skin reached them. The door closed on the woman's hand and wouldn't close the rest of the way. As Dilan cowered in a far corner of the chamber, the nearly-naked flesh of the bloody woman slammed into the outside wall of the chamber over and over again.

Sena looked around and grabbed the only weapon she could find, an oxygen tank used with the protective suits that were stored just inside the bunker from the decontamination chamber. With fear spiking her adrenaline, Sena beat at the hand of the screaming woman with the metal cylinder until the hand severed from the woman's wrist and fell to the floor. Sena gagged as she watched the fingers on the detached hand twitch thrice as the door closed the rest of the way. Then the machines began to swirl around the girls, decontaminating them before opening on the other side.

A long set of metal stairs led up from the decontamination chamber, lit by one fluorescent bulb half way up the incline. Sena barely remembered the staircase; they had arrived here in the night, fighting to stay awake from the fatigue of a long journey, many months earlier.

The girls ran up the stairs, Sena in the lead, and hesitated briefly at the top where an iron door kept them trapped in darkness. Sena tried the handle. It was unlocked. She vaguely recalled her father and another man, at some time in the past, discussing the locking mechanisms keeping the outside world out and them in. Something about an automatic locking system that worked in symmetry with the decontamination chamber. *Perhaps this door unlocks when the chamber opens on this side*, she thought. She spent no additional time considering the matter. She pushed the door open.

As the door opened to the outside, a rush of warm, humid air engulfed the girls. They hadn't been outside in many months, and the air and bright sunlight felt wonderful on Sena's bare arms and face. Outside, it was silent, and Sena forgot for a moment that their lives were in danger. She put her head back and stared up in to the sky, relishing the warmth and the sunshine that she had missed for so long.

"Sena!" Dilan said, grabbing onto her older sister's arm.

The call awakened Sena, reminding her of their precarious situation. A sudden chill swept over her body as she realized they were standing out in the open. She looked around quickly, trying to familiarize herself with their surroundings. They had just exited a small storage shed behind a large house. She had never been to this place before the epidemic. They needed to get away. But they couldn't just run. They needed transportation.

"This way!" Sena said, pulling her sister along by the hand.

The girls ran hard toward a large garage-type building on the far side of a small parking lot. Native Black Pine trees dotted the landscape surrounding the concrete pad. In the distance, to their right, sunlight sparkled on the small waves of Çamlıdere Baraj Gölü. The reservoir, Sena knew, would typically have had dozens of sailing craft and fishing vessels. But not now. It was empty. The only movement near the reservoir came from the birds.

They slowed their speed as they approached the large hanger. Its massive doors were closed and Sena could see no way to open them.

"There must be a side door somewhere," Sena said. "Stay with me."

Dilan nodded as she followed her older sister to the left around the side of the building. As they rounded the corner in back, a large crash sounded from the direction of the bunker.

"What was that?" Dilan asked.

"I think it was *them!* Go, go!" Sena whispered frantically as she pushed her sister from behind.

The girls continued around to the back of the building. There it was! Another door. Sena rushed to it and tried the handle. It opened. Sena grabbed Dilan's arm and pulled her inside, closing the door quietly behind them. The door had two locks. Sena twisted the smaller deadbolt lock until it clicked, then slid the bar on the edge of the door across the gap between the door and its frame, fitting it through three iron clasps fastened to the door casing. She didn't know how long that would hold. This safety was temporary.

The girls walked slowly, side-by-side, as their eyes adjusted to the darkened enclosure. Within moments, Sena could just make out the contours of what she believed would save their lives—hovercars. She crept toward the nearest shape, careful with her footing to ensure she didn't trip over something unseen in the darkness. Dilan followed close behind, holding onto the tail of Sena's shirt to avoid becoming separated.

As Sena approached the nearest shape, she reached out her hand. When her hand touched the cool metal in front of her, she was certain. It was a hover. The shapes in the distance looked to be more of the same. She wondered which one to choose. She had flown a couple in the months before isolation in the bunker and knew she could handle them. But that wasn't her fear. The unknown element here was whether the hover was operational or in need of repair. Would it work for a time and then let them down? Would it hold a charge for long enough? Sena didn't know enough about them to do anything more than operate one.

"We need a light," Sena said. "I want to find the one that looks the newest. I think that would be the one most likely to operate for us."

"All I have is my wrist transceiver," Dilan said."

"You have your tec? Why didn't you tell me that before?"

"When?" Dilan asked, scowling. "Did you want me to stop you outside to tell you I still had my tec?" Dilan was young, but she was obstinate, like their mother. Sena was often surprised by the intelligence she observed in her young sister. At fourteen years, she acted more mature—most of the time—than the majority of Sena's friends.

"No, I guess not," Sena replied. "May I see it?"

Dilan handed Sena her transceiver and Sena turned it on, quickly finding the button for the flashlight.

"Wait," Dilan said, urgently just before Sena flipped the light on. "What if there are windows in here. The monsters might see the light."

"There aren't any windows," Sena replied. "If there were, we wouldn't need your light."

"Oh yeah."

Sena turned on the light and moved it around, its beam shining across the exterior of the nearest hover. Its metallic surface reflected the light from the phone. Sena walked toward the front of the hover, her light reflecting off other vehicles in front of her. "Well, we can't take this one," she said.

"Why not? It looks nice."

"Yeah, but all of those hovers in front of it are blocking it. We need to find one at the front, or we'll never get out."

Sena didn't wait for a response from Dilan. Instead, she moved quickly forward, more confident in her route with the light on. Dilan struggled to keep up; the light behind Sena was much dimmer.

Finally, Sena slowed and turned toward the hover next to her. They had passed by at least twelve or thirteen of them. She had been correct. The ones here in the front were the only options.

The girls spent just a few moments looking over the nearest car. It shone, just like the first one, as the light reflected back into their eyes. Sena opened the door on the driver's side. As she expected, the interior light came on. Both girls looked inside. The interior was clean and smelled new.

"We might be in luck," Sena said. "I think it's new."

"Can you fly it?" Dilan asked.

"If I can start it, I can fly it," Sena replied as she climbed into the driver's seat. A few seconds later the hover was floating fourteen inches off the ground and emitting a quiet hum.

"I've never heard a hover so quiet," Sena said. "This is the one. Let's figure out how to open the hangar door."

"What about da?" Dilan asked. Sena loved the way her little sister still called their father "da". That's what they called him when they were small. It reminded Sena how young her sister really was, despite the maturity she often displayed.

"I'm sorry Dilan," Sena began, "We saw him get attacked. Remember a few minutes before he was bitten, when that doctor from Poland was bitten? She stood back up and attacked someone else right away. I don't think dad is himself anymore." Sena's words trailed off as she fought back tears.

Dilan apparently had no such reservations. She wept openly. Sena reached over and laid a hand on the side of her little sister's head, like their mother used to do when they were sad. Dilan turned to look at Sena, and Sena could see the resolve growing inside her sister.

"Let's get out of here," Dilan said, "for da."

Without any further words, the two girls exited the hover, each moving in opposite directions along the large bay doors at the front of the hanger.

Outside the hanger, Hasan Tabak sniffed the air. He had not seen his daughters flee the bunker, but he knew they were gone. That's what he told them to do. He had taught them well, he knew. And now, he wanted them to join him and his colleagues in their hunt. Hasan didn't feel any particular emotion as he searched for his daughters. They were perversions, just like he had been only minutes earlier. But now he was Chosen. He was special. Hasan only wanted the girls to be saved, as he now was. It mattered very little that they were his daughters.

A group of the Chosen followed Hasan as he moved toward the large hanger on the property, branching out slowly as they neared. They could smell the young girls. As they approached the hanger, a quiet hum sounded from inside. Hasan was surprised how well he could hear it. His only experience with the hanger was the day they arrived, when he flew his hover in and parked it. But he knew from conversations with their mechanic, that the hangar was well-insulated. He also knew what the sound was. His daughters had activated a hover. They were going to try to escape. He could not let that happen.

"Over here," Dilan called out quietly. Sena rushed over and, together, they looked carefully at the controls affixed to the wall on the right side of the large moving doors.

"There's a green button," Sena said. "Green means go. That's got to be it."

"How are we going to push it and still get in the hover and take off before the monsters find us?" Dilan asked. "I mean, they're probably outside right now."

"You're going to have to push it Dilan," Sena replied. "You can't fly, right? Hopefully the door will open slowly, or maybe it won't open for a few seconds. We'll leave your door open. You push the button and then run as fast as you can. You can do it."

"Yeah, I know I can do it, but I still don't want to."

"We don't have any other choice."

"Okay, open my door on your way back, then keep it running. As soon as I get in, you better be ready to take off."

"I will little sister. We're going to make it. Give me thirty seconds before you push it."

Thirty seconds later, Dilan hesitated. Her pulse was racing and she felt out of breath, even though she hadn't moved yet. She reached toward the green button on the wall, but stopped half way.

"Push it."

Dilan barely heard Sena's whisper. She had to be strong. She moved her hand the rest of the way toward the button. She pressed it, then ran. Nothing happened. Dilan stopped moving and turned back around toward the wall. She had just taken a step back toward the control panel when an alarm sounded. In the silence of the vast hanger, it was deafening.

She turned and ran.

The alarm had been activated. The Chosen were running around, looking for the source of the noise. One of them walked up to Hasan.

"They cannot open the door unless the remote locks are disengaged. We can go in after them the back way."

"Do that," Hasan said. "I will wait here."

"What happened?" Sena asked loudly as Dilan climbed inside the hover and closed the door, locking it as soon as she sat down.

"I don't know. I just pushed the button."

"It must be alarmed. What are we going to do?"

Dilan stared at her sister, a perplexed look crossing her eyes. "What do you mean?"

"The door isn't opening, so we can't get out. That's what I mean?" Sena replied.

"Sena, crash through the door."

"You think that will work?"

"I don't know. You're the old lady around here. You've flown these before. Aren't they supposed to be strong enough to avoid being crushed if they run into things?"

"Yeah, I think so," Sena replied.

"Then crash through the door," Dilan said.

Dilan made it sound so simple. Sena wasn't sure it would work. But it didn't matter now, as a small crack of light reflected in her mirrors. Sena turned around. "They're inside. They came through the back door."

"Go!" Dilan said under her breath.

Sena grabbed the stick and hit the thrusters. The hover shot forward, crashing through the large hanger doors. The impact caused a sharp pain to flow through Sena's hand and into her arms and shoulders as she held tightly to the stick. She couldn't see. They faced the sun as they exited the hangar. The bright sunlight outside blinded her. The hover bumped over something in its path.

"What was that?" Dilan asked quietly. "Are we free?"

"I can't see yet. I need to slow down. If we hit something, we might not get away."

"I don't like that," Dilan replied. She turned around to look out the back of the hover, her eyes adjusting to the bright light as she faced away from the sun. "They're coming. Go!"

Behind them, Hasan Tabak lifted himself off the ground and stumbled toward the retreating hover. His comrades raced past him, chasing his daughters as they fled. But then the hover began to slow.

"I can't see," Sena yelled. "Wait, it's getting better. The windshield is darkening, or something."

"Then go!"

Before Sena hit the thrusters again, the hover rocked to the left. Then violently to the right.

"They're here!" Dilan screamed. "They have us. Go. GO!"

Sena recovered and slammed her foot to the floor.

Outside the hover, the Skins held tight to the panels. One had climbed on top, his perch tentative. As the hover flew forward, the Skin on top of the hover flew off the back, crashing into the pavement. He didn't move. Another Skin grasped tightly to the bottom of the hover, wedging his hand into a small gap between the rear thrusters and the rear fender. As the hover shot away, his hand ripped from his body at the wrist, blood spurting from the open wound as he too smashed into the ground and lay still. Others had fallen away but recovered from their impact.

Eventually, they stopped their pursuit. The hover was gone. The Tabak girls were gone. Hasan, now recovering from being hit by the hovercraft on its initial departure, stood and faced the direction to which the small vehicle had fled. The girls got away, but he would find them—soon.

18

"You've got to watch this, sir," the man said as Director Adal Jass walked up to the group surrounding the monitors. They had set several screens up side by side in the lounge area to watch the near-naked men and women as they attacked other humans, first in North AM, and then across the globe.

Adal had told the group, several weeks earlier, that they had lost communications with the outside world. In reality, he had just shut everyone else out. The only communication with the outside, and the information they might learn from others, was his to control. The small group in Rio believed the only way they would ever know what was going on, or whether someone with a vaccine was close, would be by watching USCAN. Jass let them believe it.

Director Jass still had access to the various boards of the IIA database, but there weren't many posts. He knew little more than his comrades about the Skins; but at least he knew what the monsters were being called by others, and from where they had come.

Every couple of weeks, Adal sent a team outside to gather provisions. They had several protective suits with canned air, and were able to travel freely in hovers without risk of contamination. But they had no real need to go out. They didn't have enough air canisters to get them all the way to North AM where the teams from Toronto and Boston were vaccinating people. So, they waited, and watched.

Over the past couple of weeks, they had watched the hairless, and often unclothed men and women attack others. They had no idea why this was happening, but it was frightening. They followed the rescue groups, praying that they would escape the monsters. They all knew that their only hope for survival was to get the vaccinations from one of those teams.

"What are they doing now?" Adal asked.

"They seem to be gathering in central locations, rather than just wandering around like before," the man replied.

"It's like . . ." a woman began, "it's like they're all moving together, communicating with each other somehow. But none of them use any tech."

"Yeah," the first man continued, "they have to be communicating somehow. I mean, look over here." The man pointed to a screen on the left. "They're all gathering around that little home there."

"Where is that," another man asked.

"Somewhere in France, I think."

"You mean," Adal began, "that these . . . things . . . are all over the world?"

"Yes sir, we don't know when they arrived in Asia, but we first saw them in western Russia about a week ago. Since then, they've shown up all over the place."

"And I suppose they're still outside here, in Rio?" Adal asked.

"Yes sir."

"And is anybody stopping them?"

"Well, those people we saw first, from North AM, have been fighting them. Other groups are trying to fight too. But the monsters are increasing in numbers much faster than those small groups are killing them. Not enough people have firearms. And, as of two days ago, we can't find the group in North AM anymore."

"So, how many people are alive out there, apart from the monsters?" Adal asked.

"There's no way to know. We can't see very many. It looks like the monsters are winning. They're killing everybody who survived Anthrax E."

The room grew quiet as each person assimilated the news. Adal knew they were all thinking the same thing, but nobody had said it out loud until now. Each of them believed that Adal had lost contact with survivors in other bunkers. He knew they were thinking that the other bunkers had probably succumbed. Again, he would not disabuse them of that belief. His control, what little he had left, would only remain so long as he controlled communications and information.

Finally, a petite woman with red hair and thin, wiry glasses spoke up. "So, are we alone?"

Nobody answered. Eventually, every person in the room wandered off to his or her private quarters.

From his little sanctuary, South AM Director Adal Jass looked at his watch. The screen displayed the words "new message". Adal touched the screen and read the small message displayed there. He stared at the words, not fully comprehending their meaning, or why he had received the message in the first place.

"They're here! They're flushing us out!"

The message came from Latisha Bodily in Boston. It was her first contact with Adal in over two months.

JULY 19
PANAMA CANAL, PANAMA

Hubert struck a lighter and lit the pile of dead leaves and grass. The flame grew quickly as the others added to the pile. Soon, the fire spread to nearby plants and weeds in the small clearing. The latest drought was a blessing in disguise as the brittle plants caught fire.

"Hurry," Hubert said quietly, "they could be anywhere."

Hubert, formerly a military special agent for the Argentinean government, had secured a room for his family in a military bunker near Buenos Aires when the plague had found its way to his country. Now, months later, he, his wife and daughter, and two others ran for their lives, hoping to get across the old Panama Canal before the monsters finished devouring the remainder of their friends from the bunker—or whatever it was the monsters were doing back there. Of the 67 people who had inhabited their bunker, only five were left.

The Skins had flushed the Argentinians out of their temporary hiding place just south of the dilapidated Canal. Hubert and his group were supposed to be meeting up with a group of survivors from Brazil. Together, they had planned to head toward a bunker in Mexico, somewhere along the Gulf. Someone named Shift Bader had contacted them and given them coordinates. It was supposed to be safe. But the Brazilians had never made it to the rendezvous point. Hubert wasn't going to worry about them though. Almost everyone in his group had died, and now, the only four survivors beside himself needed his leadership and guidance.

As the flames grew, they spread rapidly through the underbrush. The smoke swept up and over the tall trees of the jungle canopy on a breeze blowing from the west. Through the smoke, Hubert could see the shape of a man appear. He was standing on the other side of the clearing, perhaps as much as 100 meters away. Soon, other human figures appeared next to him. But they had stopped advancing, the fire presumably making their path more difficult.

"Is that the Brazilians?" Hubert's daughter Gemma asked, squinting to try to see through the dense cloud of smoke that was billowing up from the fire they had started.

"I don't think so," Hubert replied, "it looks like there are too many of them."

"Then why aren't they moving?"

"The fire did what I hoped it would do. They feel pain too. They don't want to get burned."

"Then let's get out of here while we have a chance," Hubert's wife, Ange said.

A loud cracking sound echoed through the jungle as the fire spread, followed by the thud of a branch crashing to the ground. The fire had engulfed nearby trees and was now on the verge of raging out of control. Several other branches splintered and fell from trees all around them. The roar from the fire and the groaning and creaking from the trees made it difficult to hear each other speaking. Hubert's small group of survivors backed away from the powerful fire quickly, hoping the Skins on the other side of the conflagration were doing likewise.

"Okay, let's go," Hubert replied, keeping an eye on the horde of Skins gathering on the other side of the inferno. He placed his hand on his daughter's back and guided her away from the fire. He waited until the others followed, then began to turn to follow them. Hubert took one last look before he turned. What he saw was not a comforting sight. The Skins were moving left and right away from the central fire. *They're trying to go around*, Hubert thought. He was grateful the fire caught so easily and had spread so quickly, but he was worried it wouldn't be enough.

"Okay, run now," Hubert said as he caught up to his family moments later.

The group began to run again. Hubert knew that everyone was tired from their prior escape just minutes earlier; but they had new life. He hoped the fire would buy them the time they needed to cross the Canal.

They reached the edge of the deserted, concrete Canal within minutes, and the horde of Skins had not caught up. But Hubert knew they would. He needed to get everyone across without starting a panic; he thought that their only hope was to get across the gap and hide in the warehouses on the other side. But even if they made it across, he was terrified to think that even the huge, empty canal might not stop the monsters. He had seen them jump.

Hubert had led them toward the Miraflores Locks, just north of Panama City. He knew there were bridges across the canal, both to the north and to the south. But he had intentionally avoided the bridges because there was nowhere to hide from the monsters on the open highways leading to the bridges. Hubert had been told there was a small service bridge built in the lock structure at Miraflores and that it was passable when the lock gates were closed. The canal was thirty-four meters across and as much as twenty-five meters deep and there were a limited number of places to cross safely—only the bridges and these canal lock gates. He was hoping the locks were closed. If there was no way to cross at the locks, he would have to hope they had time to go to one of the bridges.

Arriving at Miraflores, Hubert could tell the locks were partially open, which had allowed the canal to drain. There was a five-meter gap between the two gates of the lock that they would have to jump across.

"It's so far," Gemma said. "I don't think I can make it."

"I'll go first," her father replied. "Watch how I do it. You follow my lead and you'll be fine."

Hubert backed up several paces then ran forward as fast as he could. He pushed off from the end of the gate, flying over the open space. He landed safely on the other side, bending his knees as he touched down. Then he rolled to stop his momentum, and stood back up.

He was encouraged and grateful they had come out of the jungle at this location.

"Did you see that baby?" Hubert said enthusiastically as he turned to face his friends and family on the other side of the chasm. "Now it's your . . ." He stopped talking as he viewed the scene unfolding behind them. The Skins had come around the great fire that was roaring behind them in the jungle. And they were moving fast.

"Jump!" Hubert yelled from across the gaping hole.

"I can't!" Gemma yelled back. "It's too far." She began to cry, and Hubert knew she felt stupid for it. *Sixteen-year-olds shouldn't be afraid of heights,* she had told him last summer standing on a high platform above a swimming pool. Then, Hubert had told her she didn't need to jump. This time, she didn't have a choice.

"You can do it, baby," Gemma's mother whispered, standing next to her.

"I'm going," Benoit said. "They're too close. We can't wait for Gemma." Benoit, a 64-year-old politician, jogged back several paces. A couple days earlier, he had been hit by a stray bullet as the group fled their bunker during the Skins' initial attack. It only grazed his shin, but it was enough to cause him to limp. He began to race forward toward the gulf that separated Hubert from the others.

Benoit's speed wasn't enough. Hubert could see the man wasn't going to make it, but couldn't form the words in time to stop Benoit's rush forward. Benoit leapt. The gap wasn't that far, but the distance to the bottom of the chasm below was as much as twenty-five meters, or more. Hubert watched in horror as, in mid-air, Benoit looked down and began flailing his arms and legs. Benoit wasn't going to make it, but he reached his hands out for the ledge at Hubert's feet. Hubert dropped to his stomach, reaching toward Benoit; but he wasn't able to react fast enough. Benoit fell. A few short seconds later, his body crumpled against the cracked and dirty concrete far below.

The Skins were coming. Rogelio, the last survivor of the small group, ran forward. He made it, easily. As Gemma watched the ease at which the young, handsome mechanic made the leap, her eyes lit up. Squeezing her mother's hand, she ran forward. As she took the last step toward the gulf that separated her from her father, her mother screamed. The effect of that scream, and the gurgling noise of the monsters as they tore into Ange's flesh caused Gemma to lose balance. She stumbled and fell over the edge.

Rogelio ran.

Three seconds later, Hubert stepped off the ledge to join his daughter far below.

Within seconds, more than 200 nearly-naked figures easily leapt over the old canal to give chase to the man running down a lonely highway. Easily clearing the chasm, the Skins began to leap skyward, traveling as far as thirty or thirty-five meters through the air. They landed all around Rogelio and brought him down swiftly. Within moments, the group fell back as Rogelio rose from the ground, ripping and tearing at his clothing. He was one of them.

19

"You think that man, Shift, is really from the United States?" Dilan asked after Sena hung up the com.

"I guess. Why would he lie to us?" Sena asked. "And he had the right accent."

"I don't know. But I don't trust anyone anymore. I didn't even think anyone would be alive anywhere, now that the monsters are out."

"Yeah, I was worried about that too."

"I guess we should try to do what he says though, don't you think?" Dilan asked.

"You mean cross all of Russia and then Canada. Then go all the way down through the U.S. and into Mexico? How would we even do that? The monsters, or, what did he call them?"

"Skins."

"Oh yeah, the Skins. That's what dad said the Americans were calling them. The Skins won't leave us alone. They would chase us all the way."

"Well, we should try," Dilan said, pouting. "We're going to die if we don't."

"We might die if we do," Sena replied. "You heard him. He said there are so many Skins around them that we'd have a difficult time getting past them."

"It can't be worse than it is now. I mean, we only get a couple hours break before they catch up to us."

"You're right Dilan. In fact, we need to get moving."

The two girls got back into the hover. They had been lucky too many times, but they had to stretch their legs. Sena knew that their luck wouldn't hold. She wanted to get to Mexico, but she didn't want Dilan to get too excited about it. Ever since the day they had been chased by their former friends from the compound in Turkey, they had been hunted, like animals. That would only get worse, according to the man named Shift.

Sena started the hover. She had just pulled onto the road when they heard the unmistakable sound of thunder. But this thunder was made by the feet of hundreds of Skins. They had caught up again. It was time to move. Sena decided right then that they would take the chance. She would head east. The next time they stopped, she would enter the codes to track their course toward Mexico, many thousands of miles away.

JULY 29, 2093, LATER
URAL MOUNTAINS, RUSSIA

"They're still right behind us! Go faster!" Dilan said, loudly. She stifled a scream. She had done it plenty of times. Sena had insisted that screaming made it hard to concentrate, so she was grateful Dilan was trying to stay calm.

"I can't go any faster," Sena replied, quietly. She was focused. The mountain passes and curves were slowing her down. But it didn't slow the Skins down. Every other time they had fled, they lost the Skins—at least temporarily. But this time was different. She didn't know if they would make it. They had no weapons with which to fight, and now, things had just taken a turn for the worse.

"Dilan, the energy cores are getting low."

"What? How?"

"I guess these old roads can't charge the batteries."

"What are we going to do?" Dilan began to cry.

"I don't . . ." Sena's reply was cut short as the hover was pushed to the side by something unseen, as though a gust of wind had blown by.

"What was that?" Dilan asked, very quietly.

Sena looked out the windows around her, trying to maintain her precarious control of the hover on the sharp curves of the road. She could see the Skins behind them on the dashboard screen. They were still a bit behind them, but seemed to be gaining ground. She couldn't see anything else. "There's nothing out there."

Suddenly, a large shape dropped down out of the sky in front of them. It was some kind of flying craft, unlike anything Sena had ever seen. It kept its speed even with the hover as they continued up the winding canyon.

"What is that?" Sena asked.

"Are we going to run into it? Do we have to slow down?" Dilan asked in response. "We can't slow down."

"I don't think so. It's keeping the same speed."

Before either girl could say another word, a beam of light shot from the craft in front of them and over the top of their hover. Dilan looked back to see where it was directed. Sena watched the dashboard screen which had been displaying the Skins behind them for the past ten minutes. Behind them, the horde of Skins broke apart as the beam of light sunk into the roadway between the leading Skins and the hover. Two seconds later, the roadway blew apart, sending chunks of rock and fragments of road in all directions. The Skins, at least those at the front of the horde, were scattered as well, body parts flying through the air along with asphalt and dirt. Whether they were dead, Sena couldn't tell, but they had certainly stopped their pursuit.

"What was that?" Sena asked slowly, emphasizing each word.

"Some kind of gun, I think. Maybe someone up there is trying to help us."

"It would appear that way. How can we communicate with them?"

The girls drove on in silence for only a moment before the rear hatch door of the flying ship began to lower. Fifteen seconds later, the door had lowered to a point just below horizontal, creating a ramp up into the ship.

"You think we should fly into that thing?" Dilan asked.

"No, I don't."

"Then think again sister, because the Skins are back."

Sena looked down at the monitor again. The Skins had regrouped. Certainly some of them were dead, or too wounded to proceed, but not all. They were again in hot pursuit. And they were closer than they had been in many days. The charge indicator on the hover was not in the red, but engine shut-down was near; perhaps in minutes. With the Skins so close, they had only one option.

"Okay Dilan, let's go in there. Whoever is in there may not be friendly, but I'm willing to bet that they're human at least."

The rear hatch closed as the hover slowed to a stop inside the landing bay of whatever it was they were now inside. A loud clank signaled that it had shut and locked, and the girls could feel the ship move upward, likely off the road. The darkness surrounding the hover was absolute, save one small, blinking, red light at the far end of the cargo bay in front of the girls. Sena opened her mouth to speak, but stopped abruptly as lights came to life all around them outside their hover. They had flown into a small hanger. It was gray and industrial, but clearly new. It was clean and neat, with everything in its place—at least as far as Sena could tell.

A moment later a voice penetrated the strong hull of the hover.

"Welcome to my ship," a gentle male voice said. "My name is Thomas. You are safe now."

"Myślisz, że nas słyszy?" Dilan asked.

"Please speak in English if you wish me to respond," Thomas said.

"I said, 'Do you think he can hear us?'" Dilan replied.

"Yes, I can, obviously," the male voice replied.

"Well, I guess the only way to keep our secrets is to speak Polish," Sena said in her native tongue, in a whisper barely audible even to her sister." Then, addressing the man whose face they had not seen, Sena asked, "Where are you?"

"I'm in the front of the ship. I'm going to turn on the scrubbers and decontaminate your ship from the outside. Do not be alarmed. It will only take a few seconds."

A loud hiss came at the girls from all angles and a fine mist shrouded the hover, causing Dilan to gasp.

"I don't think it will hurt us," Sena said over the noise. "He said it was a scrubber. I think that means he's killing the Anthrax E on the hover, like when we left the bunker after dad . . . "

"Does that mean he hasn't been vaccinated yet?" Dilan asked, trying to keep her mind off the death, or whatever it was that had happened to Da.

"I don't know. Let's see what he says next."

The girls waited in silence as the scrubbers finished cycling around them. Then the voice spoke again.

"Now, I need to know something important. Have you been vaccinated?"

"Yes," Sena replied. "We were vaccinated in a bunker a few weeks ago. Have you been vaccinated?"

"No, I have not. That is why I have to decontaminate your hover. I need you to open all the doors and the rear hatch of your craft and then stand next to it."

"Why?" Dilan asked.

"I need to decontaminate the interior of your craft, along with you and your other belongings. The technology I'm using here is state of the art. You've seen how it works from the inside of your hover, but now you'll get to feel it in action."

"Will it hurt?" Sena asked, clearly giving in to her fears despite a promise she made to herself to be brave.

"No, it won't. At least I don't think it will. But it is loud, as you've already witnessed. It won't damage your hearing though, so no need to worry about that. Mostly, if I understand the tech properly, it will feel ticklish at first, but then feel like a mild sandpaper scraping over your skin. If the literature is correct, however, it will not leave any marks and the scratchy sensation will last only a few seconds after the process is complete."

"I don't like the sound of that," Dilan said, looking at Sena.

"I don't think we have any choice."

"You don't have any choice," the man said. "But I assure you that this is for your own good too, not just mine. I have saved you from the monsters. But now you are confined to the rear of this beautiful ship. You won't be able to access the rest of the A-400, because I can't decontaminate your bodies from the inside. But every spore we can kill is better, don't you think?"

"What is an A-400?" Sena asked.

"That's the ship you're in. State of the art. Straight out of the factory. The only ship of its kind, I think."

"Well, let's get this over with," Dilan said.

"Okay, here we go," Thomas said, a little too excitedly.

The loud hissing started again, but this time significantly louder than before, without the walls of the hover to dampen the sound. And Thomas was right, it did tickle. Before long, however, Sena began to feel the effects of the scrub. It began to burn, but not intolerably so. Approximately twenty-two seconds after it began, the hissing sound died out and the air cleared.

"Tell me ladies, what is the color of the light you see at the front of the bay?"

"Green," Dilan replied.

"Good, that is the color I register up here as well. Green means we're all clear. The entire bay in which you stand, and all items within the bay are now Anthrax E free, at least for as long as you don't breathe." Then Thomas laughed. "While that doesn't mean much to you. Someone like me, who hasn't been vaccinated, really appreciates that knowledge. Of course, you might still carry the disease inside of you, so I won't be able to meet you in person, unfortunately. We'll check that light every once in a while. Look around. Give me a few moments to program the ship for our next destination. Then I'll see you at the front of the bay, next to the glass windows."

Several minutes later, Thomas rapped on the big glass window separating the front and back of the ship. Sena and Dilan turned and walked toward him. Sena felt safe, for now, and Dilan's face showed that she was comfortable, at least for now. The man had apparently not been vaccinated. That meant he couldn't get near them.

"I'm very happy to have you on my little ship," Thomas said, his voice coming through a small panel to the left of the windows. "What are your names?"

"I'm Sena," Sena replied. "And this is my sister, Dilan. Thank you for saving us."

"Well, that was no problem at all. I only did what any other person would have done."

"Sure, but there aren't many other people out there, so we really appreciate it."

"Are you alone here?" Dilan asked.

"Yes I am, and I've been alone for a long time. I had some friends out there, in New Zealand," he said, pointing a thumb over his shoulder toward the front of the ship. "They're all dead." Thomas paused a moment before continuing. "And I've been watching those creatures kill people all over the world. And you know, when I saw you two down there, I wanted . . . no, I needed, to do something. I lost some good friends out there; friends I promised to protect. But I couldn't. So, maybe they'll see me from Heaven, or wherever, and this will help them feel better about me."

"What happened?" Sena asked. "Was it Anthrax E?"

"Yes. I was living with them in New Zealand. They rescued me from . . . We'll, never mind that. But I couldn't save them. My conscience . . . " Thomas wiped a tear from the corner of his eye, choked back a sob, and continued, more slowly. "I've been beating myself up over it. I flew back over their little village. They were all dead, lying all over the hills and in the streets. I couldn't save them."

Dilan and Sena both wiped tears from their eyes. Thomas' tale was no different than so many others around the world. But Sena could see the man's pain and she had a hard time controlling her own emotions.

"I don't know why I even told you that," Thomas continued a few moments later. "I've just been so . . . lonely."

"If you're alone, then who's flying the ship?" Dilan finally asked.

"It's flying itself. But we're not moving very quickly. There's no need to go fast. We have nowhere to go, that I know of."

"I don't understand," Sena said. "If nobody is flying, and we're not moving very fast, how are we staying in the air? This isn't a helicopter."

"No, it's not a helicopter. As I said before, this is called an A-400. That's just a model number. If I could name it, it would be the 'Franconi.'"

"What's a 'Franconi'?" Dilan asked.

"Ha ha. I'm a Franconi. That's my last name."

"Well, Thomas Franconi, what do we do now? Are we your prisoners or something?" Sena asked.

"Heavens no Sena. You're my guests. The ship is magnificent and comfortable, back there and up here. But unfortunately, I have nowhere to take it. I just fly around, watching for . . . I don't know . . . people in trouble, that need rescuing, I guess." Thomas smiled sadly. "I land when I need to, to recharge. But I never get off. I can't, as you can imagine. I'll get sick. And now, with you back there, I can't even visit the rear of the ship. Of course, all of the services any of us need to survive are available in front and back. So, consider the back of the ship your home. The doors separating us will be locked so that neither you, nor I will accidentally get me sick."

"Okay," Dilan replied.

"So, what do you think?" Thomas asked, smiling. "I know it isn't very big."

"I think this is way better than that hover we've been flying around in for the past two weeks," Dilan said.

"I imagine that was tough. You're probably starving. Why don't you get something to eat from the wall unit? We can talk any time; and I'd love to hear about everything you've gone through."

20

Shift Bader and his small band of survivors had stayed ahead of the Skins, crisscrossing the continent and hiding in the best shelter they had found to date in Cabo Rojo, Mexico. The Skins had finally flushed them out of their Mexican hideout. As Shift's group fled, they intentionally destroyed an underwater tunnel from the mainland to a small island retreat. The bodies of dozens of Skins had been ripped apart by the explosion. As the saltwater from the Gulf of Mexico poured into the wrecked tunnel, it engulfed and consumed the bodies of hundreds more, drowning many and causing their flesh to burn and boil. Shift's small group had correctly predicted that the Skins' bodies could not survive the salt of the sea.

While hundreds more Skins watched from the shoreline, Shift's small group escaped into the Gulf of Mexico by boat. They had headed for a rendezvous with the only other group of survivors they knew of—five people returning from the moon to the space port at Cape Canaveral, Florida. The group planned to flee to the moon; but the ship coming to rescue Shift and his friends had not arrived yet. If Hasani, Jonas and the other survivors from the moon didn't arrive soon, the Skins would find the small group, and it would be too late.

The Skins were unable to follow Shift's group across the sea; yet incredibly, although not unexpectedly, the Skins had tracked the small group of survivors to Florida. They were already approaching the shuttle base.

"*Canaveral, do you copy?*" The clear message signaled the shuttle's arrival.

"Yes, we copy. Is that you Jonas?" Shift Bader asked.

"*Yup, we're inside. Approaching now. We expect to land in about five minutes. Is everything ready?*"

"Yes, but we have a little problem. The Skins are outside, snooping around. They'll hear you any second now. Then they'll know we're here. Once you land, *do not* open the doors until I tell you to. We're working out a plan."

"*Okay, you'll see us land, obviously. We'll wait for your signal before we do anything.*"

Cain looked up, and his gaze was followed by more than 1,200 Skins, each one eager to move toward some clearer goal. The sound was growing louder, but Cain couldn't place it. Then he saw it. A ship speeding toward them through the air. It was headed straight for them, as if it meant to crash into them.

No, that isn't right, he thought. *Where are we? Florida? Yes, a shuttle base must be nearby*. Searching the land around him, using the eyes and ears of his followers, he saw the enormous base. Some of his troops were only a few miles from the gates. They now sensed his command. They moved eastward.

A few minutes later, they easily tore down a chain-link fence on the outer perimeter of a massive compound and began a frantic search for the perversions.

Shift and his friends watched out the large windows of the space port at Cape Canaveral as the shuttle began its descent to the runway below them on the tarmac. Shift's eyes followed the ship. It was huge—and loud. There was no way it would avoid the Skins' observation.

"*. . . We're down. Piloting to the terminal now.*"

"Good," Nelise Fabrisio replied, peering out into the early morning light. "Bring her around to bay door 152. I'm sending the ship directions now. We'll be making our way to the shuttle from there."

"*What are the Skins up to?*" Hasani Chalthoum asked through the com.

"The Skins are on the ground, just inside the perimeter," Mike Petrovsky called out. "But they look like they're still searching for us. Time is running out though. They know we're here. We've got to get out of here."

"*Okay,*" Dr. Jerad Beaudoin said, "*we're at 152. Ready for charging.*"

"We're sending the jet way out to meet you," Nelise said. "Once it's connected, we'll head your way."

"Guys," Mike called. "The Skins are inside the base."

Shift turned to the monitors Mike was watching. The Skins were inside. This was it. For all he knew, the survival of the human race depended on this moment. He looked upward and said a silent prayer.

Cain knew the perversions were on the base somewhere. They were evading him, but he would find them. Their stench would uncover their hiding place. But he had to hurry. The shuttle made him nervous.

Cain's troops rushed from building to building, searching for the perversions inside the massive air base. They scrambled over rooftops and under vehicles and machines. They were like a swarm of ants, hell-bent on devouring everything in their path. Only they weren't devouring anything. They were saving their anger and ferocity for the perversions. Cain had given them free reign.

Cain watched as his troops searched the base. *Why haven't they uncovered the perversions yet? What is going on?* His grip on them was weakening, and clearly, their aptitude for the hunt was flagging as well. But he had a backup plan. He would stop the perversions one way or another. Using his unnamed power, some form of mutated telepathy or telekinesis that he'd not quite figured out, Cain directed troops stationed at hundreds of communications centers around the world. His power was not entirely gone. On his signal, his army began destroying equipment and buildings and pulling down cellular towers, effectively shutting down communication ports the world over. What little communications remained would scarcely benefit any people still evading his troops.

AUGUST 11, 2093
ABOARD THE A-400

"Sena," Dilan said as she set a mug of hot chocolate down on the table that separated the girls from one another in the back of the A-400, "I was thinking again about that man, Shift. He told us to go to someplace in Mexico. Couldn't we go there? Thomas could get a vaccination and we wouldn't be stuck in this ship. We've only been in here a few days and I'm already going crazy."

"Thank you for reminding me," Sena replied. "Let's talk to Thomas. I would love to walk on solid ground."

The sisters stood and walked to the front of the compartment. Sena pressed the com button to hail Thomas.

Thomas' face appeared on the screen after a few moments. "Hello Sena, Dilan. How are you holding up back there?"

"We're doing fine, Thomas," Sena said. She hesitated before going on. "Do you know someone named Shift?"

Thomas looked thoughtful for a moment, then replied, "I believe I have heard that name somewhere. Why?"

"He told us to go to Mexico, back before you rescued us. That's where he com'd us from. Some underground bunker, I think." Sena felt self-conscious, not sure how to continue.

"And . . ."

"Well, you said you didn't have anywhere else to go . . . we wondered if you would take us to Mexico."

Thomas sat quietly, his face contorting as he stared at the girls. "I think," he began slowly, "that that would be a good idea. Do you have coordinates?"

"Well, no." Sena looked at Dilan for help.

"I think it's in a place called Cabo Rojo," Dilan said. "Shift said it was on the coast of the Gulf of Mexico."

"That may be good enough," Thomas said with a smile. "If we get close enough, we'll call this Shift character and he should answer. It won't take more than a few hours to get there. I know you haven't seen it in action yet, but the A-400 is a very fast ship."

"Shift, Shift, this is Thomas Franconi. Can you hear me?" No answer. Thomas had located Cabo Rojo on the Gulf coast of Mexico and had been flying slowly around the area for the better part of two hours. Shift did not respond.

Thomas didn't know Shift, and couldn't remember his last name, but he had certainly heard of the man. Through connections he didn't divulge to the girls, he had come to know of the man's exploits.

"Sorry ladies," Thomas said to Sena and Dilan. "Either they've left or . . ." he didn't finish what he was thinking, *that they had been found by the Skins*. Through onboard scopes of some kind, they could see a few Skins on the ground, as they made several passes high above the shoreline. But they were leaving, headed north away from the area around Cabo Rojo. Thomas was afraid it meant they had found Shift and were now looking for other humans. He didn't want to say anything to the girls about that.

Thomas moved slowly northward, up the coast, having nowhere else to go.

Less than two hours later, Thomas noticed a large number of Skins headed northeast along the coast, in a hurry; they were jumping thirty or more meters at a time. Maybe they had located Shift, or other survivors. He had only seen this type of movement when the Skins were on the hunt, like they had been the day he rescued Sena and Dilan in the mountains of Russia. He turned the ship slightly to the east and began to follow them. As he turned, he com'd the girls in the back.

"Did you find them?" Dilan asked, excitedly.

"No. I'm sorry," Thomas replied. "But I've just seen a large group of Skins headed northeast from Cabo Rojo. I've turned the ship and we are now moving with them. It looks to me like they're following someone. They're acting the way I saw them act when I picked you two up."

"You think they've found Shift," Sena said. It was a statement.

"Yes, I do."

"Hurry then."

"I am. Unfortunately, this group is headed the same direction as a smaller group we saw a couple of hours ago. If this large group is headed toward Shift, the others ahead of them may have already caught up. We may be too late. I just don't want you to get your hopes up."

Thomas left the com screen on, but went back to his controls. He accelerated past the group of Skins and began looking for the first group. If they were headed northeast, and they were chasing Shift, it meant Shift had escaped into the Gulf and was probably headed toward the southeastern United States or into the Caribbean.

There were hundreds of them, and they appeared to be coming from all points on the compass, from the north to the west, converging on the space station at Cape Canaveral, Florida. Thomas was minutes away from arriving there himself, when he saw a shuttle take off from the landing strip at high speed and disappear into space. He quickly picked up his com unit and started calling, through every available frequency, hoping someone on the shuttle would hear. He was surprised to see that most frequencies were silent, as though communication ports had been shut down.

"Shift, Shift, do you copy?" He paused for a response. "This is Thomas Franconi. We're at the base." Another pause. "Shift, this is Thomas Franconi." There was no response. Thomas continued forward, passing over the facility as the girls watched from their vantage point in the back of the A-400. Skins were roaming all over the base, converging on the site from which the shuttle had just launched.

On the shuttle, the new arrivals caught their breath and wept over the loss of their colleague, Dr. Andrew Jones, who had been trapped by a wave of Skins as the group fled toward the safety of the shuttle.

Dr. Jonas Sampson sat with Jerad Beaudoin on the bridge, discussing their luck at having no problems during take-off, apart from losing Andrew. Amongst the noise and commotion reaching the bridge from the lounge behind him, Jonas heard some garbled words. He was distracted by the sobbing of someone nearby and only heard part of the message.

". . . this is Tho . . . coni."

The words made no sense. Jonas couldn't tell if the voice had come from someone on the ship or from the ground through the ship's com board. Then the voice was gone. He tried for several minutes to find the source of the voice, even checking the shuttle's com registry, but he failed to find the source. No coms from the ground registered on the ship's computers. He didn't think to check air coms.

"Did they even hear you?" Dilan asked, pouting.

"I don't think they did. I'm sorry," Thomas replied.

"Maybe you could try it again later?"

"I don't think it will work. It looks like nearly all communication ports in this area are out. It just happened. When I was trying to hail the shuttle, I opened every frequency available, then watched them shut down, one after another. It was like some kind of chain reaction. I can't be sure whether my message got through to the shuttle or not. But they didn't stop and turn around—not that a ship that big could anyway."

"So now what do we do?" Sena asked. She wasn't quite as disappointed as her little sister appeared to be. But the thought of having to live on the A-400 for the rest of her life was beginning to look more likely. In the moments after Thomas' explanation about coms going out, she began to worry. "I mean, we can't live on here forever. I've got to have my feet on the ground."

"I understand, Sena," Thomas said quietly. "Perhaps we can find some place for the two of you to live, and I'll let you out there."

"I don't want you to leave us, if that's what you're thinking," Sena said quickly. "I just want to be able to stretch my legs. There has to be someplace we can go that has real food—fruits, meat, something—and no Skins. We could leave the ship sometimes, but always come back to you."

"We could go to New Zealand, I guess," Thomas replied, a smile lifting the corners of his mouth. "I don't think the Skins are there; and there's tons of orchards and farms. Shall we check it out?"

"Yes!" Sena and Dilan both cried out at once.

Thomas checked his gauges to make sure the ship was adequately powered, then turned the ship toward the southwest.

SEPTEMBER 22, 2093—PRIVATE COM

"Adal, good to hear from you," Thomas said when he answered the com. He was surprised to receive the communication at all. While he had only tried a few times since losing sight of the shuttle leaving Cape

Canaveral, he had never been able to establish communications with anybody. Not the shuttle. Not Adal Jass. Not SEC-GEN Davis. As far as could tell, coms around the world had shut down at about the same time the shuttle left Earth. Not that it really mattered. He didn't have anyone he needed to talk to.

Now, he really didn't want to talk to Adal Jass again and considered not answering. But if Jass had located him somehow, he would be suspicious, and angry if Thomas didn't answer.

"*Hello Thomas. Where are you?*" Adal said.

"I'm in New Zealand, as we agreed."

"*That was months ago, Thomas. What happened in Antarctica?*"

Thomas frantically reviewed his encounter with the González brothers to make sure that what he said made sense and would not give away his betrayal. "I don't know. I never made the trip. Your people never showed up."

"*That's not what I heard. I heard they landed and were met by a hover. The pilot of their ship said a man exited the hover and spoke to them before he left.*"

"Sorry Adal. It wasn't me."

"*The pilot wasn't able to give me a description of the hover driver. Are you sure it wasn't you?*"

Thomas could hear the suspicion in Adal Jass' voice, but he tried to remain calm. "Sorry Adal. I don't know anything about it and they didn't reach me."

"*And you didn't transport Davis' people to Antarctica either?*"

"No, I never saw them either," Thomas answered with more confidence, since he truly hadn't seen them.

"*Fine, Thomas. Why don't you come to Brazil and join us?*"

"You want me to join you in your bunker?"

"*Well, not exactly Thomas. I want you to remain in your ship, but nearby, so that we can leave if, or when the need arises. It seems we have better communications with locations close by. It has taken me months to locate you, you know. You are much more valuable to our cause out there in your ship, but perhaps not so far away.*"

Thomas hesitated. He didn't want to go to Brazil, but he couldn't think of a good reason not to. And Jass would become suspicious if he said no. *What could Jass really do to me if I don't go?* He wondered.

"*Thomas, are you still there?*"

"Sorry, Adal. I was just thinking about the things I would need to do here before I could come to you." Thomas cringed at his flimsy excuse.

"*Like what? You're totally self-contained.*"

"Yeah. I guess I just need to make sure I have full power, then I could leave."

"*You haven't found a lady friend there to keep you company and distract you from coming to help me, have you?*" Adal asked conspiratorially.

The question made Thomas think about Sena and Dilan. The best way to protect them was to keep them in the dark about Adal Jass; and to keep them a secret from Jass. "No Adal, I'll be there in a few days."

21

"I think it's about time," Dr. Angel Robertson said, squeezing her husband's hand to get his attention.

"Time for what?" Street Kimball asked. He rolled over and laid his hand on Angel's side. They had just gone to bed. It was still early, but Angel had a hard time sleeping at night due to the massive bulge where her flat, toned stomach used to be; and Street had put in a long day in the fields.

"Time to call Marilyn. I think the baby's coming."

Street sat bolt upright and flung his legs over the side of the couple's king-size bed.

"Let's go pretty lady!" Street said. He walked over to the wall and flipped the light switch. The bulbs in the ceiling illuminated the room giving Street a perfect view of his wife, lying in bed, curled in the fetal position.

"What's wrong babe?" he asked.

"I don't know," Angel replied. "But something seems to be a bit off. It hurts."

Street rushed over to his dresser and picked up his MEHD. He touched Marilyn's face on the home screen and it immediately dialed.

"Hi Street, how are you?" Marilyn asked through the MEHD, only moments later.

Street put the MEHD on speaker so Angel could hear. "Marilyn, Angel says she thinks the baby is coming, but it hurts."

"What do you mean? Like contractions?"

Street looked over at Angel. She was shaking her head.

"No, she thinks it's something else," Street replied.

"Okay, I'll be there in ten minutes."

As the MEHD disconnected, Street walked over to the side of the bed where Angel lay and knelt down. They had only been married for a few months, but they'd been together for many more. Once Shift Bader was elected Mayor of their small community, they had all had to learn what powers that gave him. Eventually, the group determined that Shift had the power to legally marry people. His first order of business was to marry Street and Angel. Neirioui Safar and Hasani Chalthoum were married immediately thereafter. They held a big wedding party for both couples. Well, as big as it could be with only sixteen people. The day following the festivities, Mayor Bader appointed Jonas Sampson as his Deputy Mayor. Jonas married Shift and Anta in a quieter ceremony.

Now, a few months after Street and Angel had officially tied the knot, their baby was on the way. It was early, but only by a few days. Nobody was too worried about the health of the baby.

Neirioui had delivered a healthy baby girl, already immune to AE, a couple of weeks earlier. The difficulty was that nobody knew for certain whether Sami Chalthoum was immune as a result of the vaccine or because she inherited her mother's natural immunity. Shift and Anta's baby boy, Yurgi, had received an immunization early in the pregnancy following some difficulties Anta had on the moon. Nobody knew whether Yurgi was born immune as a result of Shift and Anta's immunizations, or due to the one he received directly while in the womb.

But neither Street nor Angel was naturally immune, at least not that they were aware of, and the baby had not yet been immunized due to potential complications with dosages. So there could be difficulties with this baby.

"Can you tell what's wrong?" Street asked Angel as she crunched herself up tighter into a ball on the bed.

"No, it just hurts," Angel replied. Tears began to form in her eyes. "But I don't think the pain is as bad as Anta had with little Yurgi on the moon."

"That's good." Street had never seen Angel cry. She was tough—a little too tough sometimes.

They sat together in silence for several minutes, Street holding Angel's hand and rubbing her back, until they heard a knock at the door. Street stood and jogged to the front door of their modest home, which sat on the hill over-looking the Snake River. He didn't want to tell Angel, but he was very worried.

"She's in the bedroom," Street said as soon as he saw Marilyn's face.

"Thanks Street. Shall I just go in?"

"Yes."

"Why don't you give me a few minutes with her, alone? Perhaps you should call Anta. Angel would probably like to have her best friend here."

"Okay," Street said, closing the bedroom door behind Marilyn.

"What's going on?" Marilyn asked as the door closed behind her.

"I don't know, but it hurts real bad. I didn't want to tell Street, but I'm bleeding."

"Maybe your water broke," Marilyn replied.

"No, it's just blood—I'm sure." Angel pulled back the cover. Dark red blood stained the sheets under Angel's pelvis.

"Okay, you're right," Marilyn said. Her voice was calm. Her medical training and experience delivering children before AE had taught her how important it was to remain calm, even when something bad happened. "I need some help. Street is calling Anta. When she gets here, we're going to take care of this. I'm going to call John over as well, if you don't mind. I may need his assistance."

"Call whoever you need. I'm not bashful." Angel smiled a bit, but it faded quickly as the pain strengthened.

A few minutes later, Street peeked his head in and announced, "Anta's here."

"Street," Marilyn began, "will you please call John as well? I am going to need his help too. Thanks."

Within minutes, John arrived and knocked quietly on the door.

"Come in," Street said as he opened the front door. Street's face betrayed some emotion which John couldn't quite place, and he folded his arms as John crossed the threshold and entered the living room.

"I'm not sure exactly why I'm here," John said, a bit worried by Street's body language.

"Marilyn needs your help," Street replied. "I don't know why, but she asked for you."

"Come in John," Marilyn called from the bedroom.

John looked at Street, shrugged, and walked toward the bedroom.

"Close the door," Marilyn said as John walked into the room.

John looked back at Street. Street sat, hard, on the living room couch and grunted. He was frowning. John tried his best to give Street a look that said "I'm sorry," but he wasn't sure he pulled it off. For some reason, Street seemed upset.

Inside the bedroom, Marilyn directed John to wash up as she continued to prep Angel for delivery.

"What's going on?" John asked. "Why do you need me?"

Just then, Angel cried out in pain. It was a frightening sound and John took two steps back, almost involuntarily.

"Angel, I'm going to give you a mild sedative which should help with the pain. Is that okay?"

Angel nodded her head.

John looked back and forth between the three women. He could sense that Angel was in trouble. He knew that Marilyn's sedative could knock Angel out. Angel must have known it too. But Angel clearly trusted Marilyn as she turned slightly in the bed to receive the medication. John watched as Marilyn lifted a small device and placed it against the skin on Angel's back.

"You're going to feel a little pinch," Marilyn said as she held a small electronic device against Angel's skin just below her right shoulder blade. Within seconds, Angel's breathing became shallow and her body relaxed. Marilyn stood up and stretched. Then she looked at Anta and John.

"Angel is having the baby. It's breach and there's lots of blood. We need to do an emergency C-section, and it needs to be right now. Anta, you will be my nurse. John, you will be my gopher and help with anything else I ask."

"I don't know anything about delivering a baby," John said. "I'm very uncomfortable here. Shouldn't Street be helping, or *anybody* else?"

"No John. I need you," Marilyn replied. "We need to know that this baby isn't contaminated with AE. And you're the only person who can help figure that out, seeing as Angel is indisposed at the moment."

"So I just need to run tests on the blood then?" John asked, hopeful.

"That will be your job as soon as we deliver this baby and take care of her mother."

"*Her* mother?" Anta asked.

"Yes. It's a girl."

APRIL 25, 2095, LATER
SUNNY SLOPE, IDAHO

"Street," Marilyn said, trying to get his attention. "Street!" she said louder.

"Oh sorry, what?"

"Street, look at me."

Street was peering at Angel, lying in their bed under the covers. She appeared to be sleeping. Marilyn knew that Street must have heard the noises and cursing from John while they tried to deliver the baby. *That's probably why he looks so upset*, she thought.

Anta was in the room too, and Street's eyes kept drifting over to her, then back to his wife. Anta was holding the baby, and the baby was crying. Street may not have understood, but there was nothing abnormal about that.

Finally, Street looked over at Marilyn, who was standing beside him just outside the bedroom door.

"Street, your little girl would like to meet her father. Would you like to hold her?"

Street turned back toward the bedroom. "Uh, yeah. But what about Angel? Why isn't she holding the baby?"

"Can I have your undivided attention for a minute?" Marilyn asked, pulling gently on Street's arm. "Come sit down for a moment, please."

Marilyn pulled Street across the living room away from the bedroom. She had to push him onto the sofa and stand in front of him to get his attention. When Street finally looked at Marilyn again, she began speaking to him in the way only a practiced medical practitioner could do.

"Street, your baby is beautiful. She is healthy and immune. She is going to be fine and strong, just like her father."

"Oh, that's good," Street replied, his voice sluggish and full of worry. "But how is Angel?"

"Angel had a very rough delivery. We had to perform an emergency C-section. Do you know what that is?"

"No."

"Without going into great detail, it's basically a medical procedure where we cut open Angel's stomach area and pull the baby out that way, rather than the baby being born in a traditional way." Marilyn was extremely uncomfortable having this conversation with Street. In fact, she couldn't remember ever being so uncomfortable speaking about the birth of a new child. Most fathers had some idea what was going on. But Street was a tough football player—at least he was—and he was new at this. It was clear that he was having a difficult time with the conversation as well.

"Uh, okay. But . . . well . . . the baby came out okay, right?"

"Yes, the delivery was fine. But Angel had a very tough time. She lost a lot of blood."

Street's face drained of color at the mention of the loss of blood.

"You remember that I had John come in to help me, right?" Marilyn continued. Street nodded his head, his eyes narrowing.

"I probably should have explained to you why that was, but we were in a hurry. I know it must have been hard for you to have another man present at the delivery of your child, and not you. But I didn't want you to see Angel that way. And, here's the important part: I knew that Angel was losing blood and I thought we might have to give her a blood transfusion. John is the only person in our community with the same blood type as Angel. If John hadn't been here, there is a very good chance your sweet wife wouldn't have made it."

Street's countenance changed immediately, and tears formed in his eyes. Moments later, he said, "So, John saved Angel's life?"

"Yes Street, and Anta too," Marilyn replied. Without John and Anta at my side, I could not have performed that surgery. I needed John's blood and I needed Anta's confidence. Anta gave me the strength I needed to work with your wife for all of those hours. I think you may wish to thank each of them for their contribution."

Marilyn smiled at Street. Street smiled back, tentatively, then lowered his head. A tear dropped onto his lap, and he tried to wipe it away as it soaked into his flannel pajama pants.

"Where's John?" Street asked.

"He's gone home to rest."

"I need to talk to him."

"Yes, Street, that would be nice. But maybe you should go meet your daughter first."

Street lifted his head and a smile lit his face. "I *do* need to meet her." He stood and walked into his bedroom, Marilyn trailing close behind.

Anta lifted her head at the sound of Street's footsteps.

"Hi Street," Anta said. "Your little girl is beautiful. You should be very proud. And her mother is stronger than any of us ever knew."

"I think I need to thank you Anta, for helping Marilyn. I'm not really very good at this. But, thank you."

"That's just fine, Street," Anta replied. "It was my pleasure. I love you and Angel very much. And this little girl is melting my heart right now. She looks just like her mother. Like a little echo of her mom."

"Can I hold her?" Street asked, quietly.

"Of course. Come over here and sit down. I know you never held little Yurgi. Have you ever held a baby before?"

"No. Will you show me?"

Street sat down in the chair Anta had just vacated. He held out his arms as Anta stretched hers forward.

"It's very easy Street. You'll get the hang of it in no time." Anta placed the baby into Street's arms. "Hold her head so it doesn't fall backward. Yes, like that. Babies like to be bounced a bit, but not too much. There, just like that."

The baby had been whimpering a little as Anta laid her in Street's arms, but with a gentle bounce, she stopped. She stared at her daddy's face and Street's face crumpled.

"Street, what's wrong?" Anta asked.

"Nothing. She is beautiful. I can't believe I helped make this. I can't believe she's mine. I feel . . . I don't know really what it is. I've never felt like this before."

"Street, that's love," Anta said. "And not the kind of love you feel for Angel or your friends. That's the kind of love that only a parent can feel. It's wonderful, isn't it?"

"Yeah, it is. Nothing bad is ever going to happen to this little girl. I'll make sure of it."

"I know you will. You're going to be a great father."

"Street, is that you?" Angel's voice was quiet—just loud enough for them to hear.

"Yeah baby, I'm here. Are you okay?"

"I'm feeling very tired, but I'm going to be fine," Angel replied, lifting her head slightly and turning to face Street and Anta. "How is our baby? Is it a boy, like you wanted?"

Hearing Angel's voice, Marilyn walked over to the bed and began checking computers. She lifted the sheet draped over the lower half of Angel's body and looked around for a moment. Then she laid the sheet back down and smiled. She gave Street and Anta a 'thumbs up' sign and walked back over to the doorway to watch from a distance.

"No babe, it's a girl, like *you* wanted."

"I'm sorry Street," Angel said.

"Don't you ever be sorry," Street replied. "This little girl is ours forever and I love her more than I can possibly tell you!"

"I'm very glad to hear it."

"What are you going to call her?" Anta asked.

"What about 'Echo'?" Street asked.

"Echo? Why?" Angel asked.

"Anta told me our girl looks just like a miniature you, like a little echo of you. And she's right. She's just as beautiful and strong as you babe."

"I like it," Angel replied. "Echo."

"It's a beautiful name," Anta said. "Echo Robertson. Can I tell the others? Everyone is waiting outside in the yard. They are so excited to see your little girl and to congratulate you both. And Angel, even though you scared us for a while there, it looks like you're going to be fine."

"I don't want to know about it," Angel said. "Just let me believe it was easy, okay?"

"Okay. That was the easiest delivery I've ever been a part of, except my own." Anta smiled. "Of course, it's also the only other one I've been a part of besides my own."

Angel smiled. "Thank you Anta."

"Marilyn and John deserve all the credit."

"John?" Angel asked.

"I'll tell you all about it, after I've spoken with him," Street replied. "I think we owe him some home-made cookies, or something."

22

"The only word I heard was 'Idaho,'" Mike Petrovsky said. "The rest was all static. Sorry."

"Where did it come from?" Street asked.

"Rio de Janeiro, Brazil. I've spent hours slowing it down and speeding it up. I can't hear anything else beyond the static."

"I feel kind of stupid for asking," Shift began, "but you *have* tried to contact whoever it is down there, right?"

"Uh, yeah boss. That was a stupid question."

"Hey, one of my teachers told me that there are no stupid questions," Shift replied, smiling.

"Well, there are; and that was one of them. Of course I've tried to contact them. But no, I haven't reached anyone. I've also logged into USCAN and reviewed some scratchy and unreliable feeds from the area around where I think the sounds are coming from. Nothing there either."

"So, I guess we need to go investigate, right?" Shift asked.

"Hey, I'm down," Street replied.

"I can't pinpoint the exact location, but it came from somewhere near the center of the city."

"I've never been to Rio," Street said, "But I'm thinkin' that city is pretty big, right? So, 'somewhere near the center of the city' isn't that helpful bro." Street's sarcasm was obvious.

"It's not a large area, but it used to have a huge population," Shift said, "mostly in high-rise apartment buildings and condos. I've got a truckload of the vaccine sitting in the safe room. I guess we should take it out and dust it off. There might just be someone down there who could use a dose or two."

JUNE 21, 2095
SUNNY SLOPE, IDAHO

"Happy Birthday dear Yurgi. Happy Birthday to you!"

Sitting on his mother's lap at a picnic table on the deck in the backyard of the Bader's small home, little Yurgi Bader bent over his chocolate cake and blew hard, just like his mom had shown him earlier that morning. The lone candle shifted in the soft breeze and went out.

"You did it!" Anta said, squeezing her son tenderly. A happy smile lit his small, one-year-old face as everyone around the table clapped and cheered. For a one-year-old, he was a pretty smart kid. He had been named in honor of Dr. Yurgi Shevchuk who had been their mentor and friend in the bunker and directed the effort to develop the E-rase vaccine. They considered Dr. Shevchuk to be the foremost reason they were alive. When the bunker near Boston had been overrun by the Skins, Yurgi had been attacked and bitten. He turned into a Skin, causing significant grief for Shift and Anta. They had cried for the loss of their dear friend. Whether to name their son "Yurgi", after the great man, was never a question.

"Happy Birthday kid," Shift said, bending down to kiss his son on the forehead.

While birthday cake was cut and passed around, Yurgi hopped off his mother's lap and wandered over to a shady spot on the deck where his future playmates, Sami Chalthoum and Echo Robertson, lay side-by-side in a small portable crib. They were no fun. Moments later, Yurgi wobbled away on unsteady legs to chase the chickens who had carelessly sauntered into the yard again. Pigs lazed about in a trough on the side of the yard, enjoying the warmth of the sun on their pink skin after the previous night's thunderstorm.

The day was beautiful. In fact, life was beautiful. Though the devastating effects of AE were still felt and seen everywhere they went, new life had revealed itself again during the group's second spring in Sunny Slope. The cattle and other animals, shipped by train across the country over a year earlier, had thrived on the grassy hillsides.

A few baby animals had been born again this spring, immune, just like Echo and Sami. There had been no need to inoculate the new arrivals. Chickens produced eggs in abundance, and the copious fruit trees of Sunny Slope continued to produce more than enough for the small group's needs.

"Yurgi! Do you want some cake?" Anta called from the small porch.

"Yay!" he squealed. He stood slowly and tottered back from where he had sat down to play with a dandelion. The white seeds from the dandelion spread out behind him on the breeze as he walked.

"Shift," Street began as he pulled his friend away from the group, "it's time we went down to Brazil." Despite some early trepidation about leaving the group, Street was getting restless.

"Yeah, it probably is," Shift replied. "Anta has dreaded this, but I don't see how we can keep putting it off."

"If you go, who do you want to go with you?" Shift asked.

"That's easy," Street replied. "You and Jon."

"Jon? You think Steve, or Suvan, would actually sanction that?"

"Hey, he's his own man, right? He's not a kid anymore, and I trust him with my life. So, yeah, that's who I want to go."

Jon was definitely not a kid anymore. At seventeen years old, Jon Porter stood an imposing six foot three inches in height and weighed nearly 210 pounds. His strength had grown tremendously as he farmed the land around Sunny Slope. And he was not afraid of anything.

"If you can convince Steve, and Suvan, to let Jon go, then I can probably convince Anta to let me go. But you, my friend, may have the most difficult time. Angel is one tough mother. So, good luck with that."

Street laughed. He loved his wife. And she was one tough mother, as of two months earlier. But Street knew he would have no difficulty convincing Angel that it was time to go. He and Angel had spent the last three nights discussing this very topic. Her fascination with the effects of AE so many months ago had worn off. She wanted Street to go. She would miss him, but she was smart enough to know that they had a responsibility to find anyone still living in order to help the human race survive. But Shift didn't know that.

"Okay boss, I'll work on Angel, and I'll talk to Jon. You go do your job and get Anta to agree. It's time to go."

"Alright, but I'll wait until the party's over to talk to her, if that's okay with you. I'd like a piece of cake."

JUNE 23, 2095, 8:15AM
SUNNY SLOPE, IDAHO

"You ready boss?" Street asked.

"Yup," Shift replied. "Where's Jon?"

"He's on his way."

"How did he convince Suvan to let him go; or is she mad at him?"

"Naw, I guess it was pretty easy," Street said. "He just had to promise her that if he found a hot Brazilian chick, he'd leave her there."

"Yeah, I bet."

The small group had all turned out for the send-off. Jon and Suvan were the last to arrive, as usual. When they finally arrived, the hugs started, and the promises were made.

"I'll be back Yurgi," Shift said, kneeling on the cool grass in front of his son. The morning dew wet his jeans as he wrapped Yurgi in his arms and kissed him on the forehead.

"Mon-tey?" Yurgi said, looking into his father's eyes. The people around them laughed quietly. When the men had decided they were leaving for Brazil, Suvan had shown Yurgi pictures of the jungle, and the monkeys.

"Sorry kid," Shift replied. "I don't know if we'll be able to find a monkey. But if we do, I'll try to catch him." He knew that Yurgi probably didn't understand.

"If you find a monkey, alive" Anta whispered under her breath, "I'd like to see it too."

"I'm sure we all would."

Shift patted Yurgi's head as he stood up. He reached out to Anta, who moved toward him and placed her head on his shoulder as they embraced.

"I love you Anta," Shift said quietly.

"I love you too. Take care of Jon, and Street. Bring them both home safely."

"I will."

As Anta and Shift ended their embrace, Shift turned to Street. He was just walking away from Angel and Echo, his cheeks wet with tears. Jon walked over too, with Suvan holding tightly to her mother behind him.

The three of them walked to the waiting hover. It was the same Fluxor that had saved them in battle so many times in the past. It was their friend. Shift and Street had thought of no other vehicle when planning the trip.

The three men climbed in and, waving their goodbyes out the windows, sped off.

JUNE 23, 11:30AM BRT (BRASILIA TIME)
RIO DE JANEIRO, BRAZIL

"They're on the move," Director Adal Jass read on his watch. "Our contact says they carry over 300 doses of AE with them."

"How are they kept?" Director Adal Jass typed in reply.

"They're in a safe box on the hover."

"Watch them carefully," Jass replied. "The plan remains in place. Those against us will be taken out."

On the other end of the communication, Thomas Franconi shuddered.

23

"What are you doing Adal?" Dr. Nic Heiberg asked as his friend and boss quickly slipped his hand into the old locker.

"Just checking the time," Director Adal Jass replied.

"Then why do you look like you just got caught with your hand in the cookie jar?" Nic probed, smiling.

"That's not your concern," Director Jass replied curtly as he walked quickly away from his friend and out of the room.

Nic was surprised at Adal's tone and behavior. They had been acquaintances for nearly a decade and had, over the past two years, become friends. Not once, in the more than two years they had been stuck in the Rio bunker, had Adal ever spoken to Nic this way. This sudden attitude change was disconcerting.

"I'm sorry for asking Director," Nic said to Adal's back as the Director turned a corner out of Nic's sight. "But I'm not satisfied with your answer," he continued under his breath, turning toward Director Jass' locker.

Nic walked quietly to the locker and slowly lifted his hand to the handle. He pulled gently. It was locked, of course. But Nic knew that this old furniture was falling apart, just like everything else in the bunker.

Nic removed a pocket knife from his pocket and carefully inserted the long blade between the two doors of the locker. Pushing gently on the knife's handle, he wedged the blade further into the gap. A slight push downward on the knife's handle caused the left-side door to pop open. Nic glanced over his shoulder at the doorway to the room, then opened the door and peered inside.

There, lying on a shelf at eye level was a "smart watch", with vast communication capabilities. Maybe Adal had been telling the truth. Maybe he *had* just been checking the time. *But then why was he so brash and guilty-looking?* Nic wondered.

Nic removed the watch and turned it over. On the screen was a short sentence. "Watch them carefully," it said. Nic knew there must be more, but he was nervous. He was prying into the private affairs of the Director, the man responsible, or so they all believed, for their safety from Anthrax E. But stronger than his nervousness was the pull to find out who was watching whom. What did the message mean?

Nic scrolled through the messages. He was confused. But more than that, he was scared.

One old message talked about killing other survivors. Other messages, older still, talked about an ancient plan to wipe out the human population and start fresh with people from a pure Germanic race. These messages referenced the Nazis and plans of biological warfare more than 150 years earlier. There was a conversation, much more recent, about a search for something in the Sahara Desert.

Within thirty minutes of first picking up the watch, Nic began to fear that the release of Anthrax E may not have been an accident. He had questions about whether its discovery in Egypt had been accidental, but there was no mistaking the fact that, once it was unleashed in December 2092, certain members of his group, and others throughout the world, had conspired to keep any successful vaccination or cure away from the public. They had intended to reserve life for themselves and re-populate the world after the "weak" and "filthy" members of the population had died. And it seemed that Adal Jass considered the entirety of humanity to be "weak" and "filthy".

Moments later, as Nic contemplated what to do with this new information, he remembered an exchange he had with Adal more than two years earlier, when they had been in the bunker for only a few weeks. He vaguely recalled some news article alleging that the government was behind the Anthrax E madness. Adal had denied it then. Adal had lied.

Nic's fear and sorrow threatened to overwhelm him. Was he unwittingly part of some horrible design to destroy mankind? Was he responsible for it? It was obvious that Director Jass knew what was going on—it was *his* watch. Many of the messages had been his. In fact, Adal appeared to be a central figure, or perhaps *the* central figure in that plan. And, amazingly, Adal was in communication with someone alive outside the bunker. Apparently, he had lied about that too. Not only had Jass told them, more than two years earlier, that communications were out, but they had also lost their link with USCAN. *Was it all part of Adal's plan? Was it all a hoax?* He wondered.

Nic knew he had to do something. *But what?*

JUNE 23, 12:14PM BRT (BRASILIA TIME)
RIO DE JANEIRO, BRAZIL

"Frans, may I speak with you for a moment?" Dr. Nic Heiberg asked his associate.

"Sure Nic, what's going on?" Dr. Frans Sillman replied.

"Frans, what I'm about to say to you is secret. Can I trust you to keep it that way?"

"Of course Nic. You know I've always got your back."

Dr. Heiberg and Dr. Sillman had each been invited to the bunker in Rio more than two years earlier when it appeared that Anthrax E could, or would spread through South AM. They had been tasked, like so many others around the world, with trying to find a cure, or creating a vaccine. They had not been successful, and even after the vaccine was created by others in North AM, they had lost communication, according to Director Jass, with the outside world. The whole group in the Rio bunker had lost faith that they would ever be rescued.

"What I'm about to say will shock you, but you must believe me," Nic said quietly, looking over his shoulder.

"What is it Nic?" Frans was beginning to get nervous. Nic was acting strangely and it was disturbing.

"I believe that Adal, and probably others, intended for Anthrax E to wipe out the world. I think he intends to kill us too."

"What are you talking about?" Frans asked, so quietly that it was likely Nic would barely hear him.

"I'm talking about a conspiracy to destroy the world. Adal has been communicating with the outside this whole time, when we thought we were alone. I read it on his watch. And the last message, from someone in the United States, talks about someone traveling, carrying 300 doses of a vaccine. It said, 'they're on their way.' And Adal's response was that anyone against him will be killed."

"Adal has contacts on the outside? People are alive out there?" Frans whispered. "You better start from the beginning."

After Nic had relayed the information he had learned, Frans asked, "So, why do you think *we're* in danger? What makes you think that you and I, or anyone in here, is 'against' Director Jass?"

"I don't know really, but I have a bad feeling. I mean, isn't it strange that we didn't know about any of this? I feel like I've been kept in the dark. He told us he had no contacts outside the bunker. USCAN went down as we watched the monsters kill any remaining humans we saw. He led us to believe, and *let* us believe that there were no other survivors out there. He clearly intentionally kept us out of the loop. And, here's something else you never knew. A few weeks after we sealed the doors here, I came across a news article from Germany. It alleged that the government was behind the release of Anthrax E, and that it was an intentional attempt to wipe out the human race. I showed it to Adal. He denied it and assured me that the government had nothing to do with it. He was quite defensive, but I thought nothing of it then and dismissed it as a conspiracy theory. He asked me to make sure nobody else saw the article."

"So you think that article you read might have actually been true?" Frans asked.

"No, not necessarily. I think the release of Anthrax E was likely an accident. But, to answer your question about why I think we may be in danger: I think that, because of the way Adal acted then, and the fact that he kept so much information from us, we have never been part of his inside group. If we just go along with whatever he has planned for these people coming from the States with the vaccine, we will be no better than he is. But if we don't go along with it, we will clearly be acting against Adal. Then, according to his last message on his watch, we will be 'taken out.'"

"That makes sense. I think I agree. But what are we going to do about it?"

"Well," Nic said, "if there are people coming this way, or that exist anywhere, that have a vaccine, we need it. We can't survive much longer without it, right? So, we need to find them before Adal does. We may even need to remove the threat ourselves."

"You mean . . . kill Adal?" Frans asked, his eyes growing wide.

"Yes, or at least remove him from power . . . somehow."

"How? And how do we know who's with him and who is in the dark like us?"

"I don't know," Nic replied. "But since Adal put himself here, and selected the majority of the others to be here with him, I think we can assume that all of those he personally selected to be here are in this with him."

"Yeah, that's probably a safe assumption."

"Then we need to figure out who was not selected by Adal. Neither of us was selected by him, and I know a couple others."

"I think I can find it all out if I have a little time on the computers," Frans said.

"Go for it. And let's hope we can trust them."

JUNE 23, 3:36PM BRT (BRASILIA TIME)
RIO DE JANEIRO, BRAZIL

"Do you have a list," Nic asked.

"Yes," Frans replied, handing the list over to Nic.

"Only fourteen of us?" Nic asked, the corners of his mouth twisting as he scanned the page.

"Yes, only fourteen."

"But we have the element of surprise," Nic said. "We'll need to talk to each of them separately, so as not to arouse suspicion. With a few select questions that I've been working on, we can probably figure out if they know anything. If we believe they are in the dark, we'll bring them up to speed and see if they'll join us."

"But what if they don't believe us, or won't join us?" Frans asked.

"We have to make them believe. We have to convince them that they are in danger—that there is a plot against their lives."

"And that it's imminent," Frans added. "Plus, if they know there are people out there, alive, and that a vaccine is on the way, but that they have to fight in order to live long enough to receive it, I think we can persuade them."

"Is there anyone on that list that you don't trust?" Nic asked.

"I think I trust all of them except Marina. She's been pretty chummy with Adal and rather cold with me ever since she got here."

"Okay, then we leave her out," Nic said. "We don't want her to go running to Adal or anyone else before we have the chance to carry out our plan."

"And what's the rest of the plan?" Frans asked.

"This is what we'll do . . ."

24

Under ordinary circumstances, a trip from Idaho to Brazil, by hover, would never have been undertaken. Not because it was impossible, but because it would take too long. A flight would take mere hours, but by hover, the winding and sometimes dilapidated roads of Central AM increased the travel time significantly.

Their trip had started out uneventfully. Shift, Street and Jon had taken turns driving and sleeping so they could put more hours in, sleeping at night in whatever hotel or motel they came across when they felt it was time to stop. They picked up the Pan-American Highway in Albuquerque, New Mexico and followed it through Texas and most of the way through Mexico. They didn't see a living soul and encountered no significant delays apart from a few traffic jams—places where abandoned and rusting vehicles blocked the highways in the larger cities—until they reached the jungles of central Mexico. It had been nearly two and a half years since anyone had performed any maintenance on the infrastructure. Nobody had kept the heat- and humidity-fed jungle growth from encroaching into and over the cities and highways—there was no one alive to do so.

"I can't believe this," Jon complained as he steered the hover over and around gnarled roots tearing up the road and thick vines hanging overhead.

Street, sitting next to Jon in the front, opened up the map on his MEHD. "Looks like the jungle should clear out in a bit, when we get closer to the coast."

Shift, lying down in the back seat, spoke without opening his eyes. "Sounds right to me. I think we're supposed to go in and out of jungle patches from here to Panama, but then it'll get bad again until we get to the Pacific coast in Peru. So, we've just gotta suck it up. It's not going to end any time soon."

"Do we really have to go all the way to Argentina along the Pacific coast," Jon asked, "before doubling back to Rio? That's going to take forever."

"That's where the highway goes," Shift replied. "The alternative is to cross through the Amazon jungle. There's a bridge at Manaus on the Amazon River . . ."

"Never mind," Jon complained. "The less jungle, the better. I think the tree roots are interfering with the pulsar energy modules in the highway. The power gauge keeps rising and falling every few minutes. I hate to think what the Amazon jungle has done to them."

Street chuckled. "Argentina, here we come," he said and sighed.

JULY 7, 2095
RIO DE JANEIRO, BRAZIL

"I think we're here," Jon said, pulling over to the shoulder of a raised portion of highway.

It had been fourteen days since they left Sunny Slope, Idaho, but Street, Shift and Jon had finally arrived on the outskirts of the once-great metropolis of Rio de Janeiro.

"So, this is it, huh?" Street asked, sticking his head up between the front seats. "Looks dead, just like every other place."

The men hadn't seen a human, alive, anywhere along the way, but they'd seen thousands of human and animal remains. In each of the cities and towns they'd passed through, the dead still lay where they had fallen, more than two years earlier. There was no longer the horrible smell of decay and death. The bodies of the dead had dissolved over time, from the inside out, and had certainly stunk terribly for months. Now, all that remained of them were the bones. Even the clothing they had worn was gone in most instances; decayed by the heat and humidity, and swallowed up by the land.

"How long 'til we get where we're going?" Street asked.

"Did you remember how big Sao Paulo was?" Shift asked in reply.

"I was trying to sleep when we went through Sao Paulo," Street replied. "Why?"

"Well, I read there were more than twenty million people living there—before this all started. Sau Palo stretched out forever. Not like New York City, where you could cross the island on foot in a couple of hours. It was *big*, as in, we drove for a couple hours. And the plants had overgrown all the infrastructure. It was amazing. Unfortunately, I think Rio is about the same size."

"So, that's what we have to look forward to, huh?" Jon asked. "Even though we made it to Rio, it could be hours before we get where we're going?"

"Yup," Shift replied casually.

"It's so different from Sunny Slope," Jon said. "I'm not loving it."

"Yeah, but we live in the desert. Central and South AM are tropical, obviously. Someone told me once that the native vegetation has to be cut back on almost a daily basis. There are, or there *were*, people whose only job was to cut out vines and roots to keep the highways clear. There's so much more rainfall here."

That was certainly true. Throughout the region, the travelers had seen evidence of catastrophic mudslides and floods, likely from torrential downpours or hurricanes over the years. The damage left in the wake of these storms had never been repaired. And it had rained off and on for the last six or seven days.

In Costa Rica, Street had barely missed flying the hover into a massive sink hole that had formed in the middle of an urban highway. After that, they had traveled more slowly, and more carefully. They weren't used to those kinds of obstacles.

In Sunny Slope and the surrounding towns in Idaho, the group maintained the roads, bridges and buildings they needed. Nobody had traveled farther than twenty-five miles to Boise in many months. They had not considered that the world might begin to fall apart so quickly after the humans were gone.

Now, as they drove into tropical Rio de Janeiro, where rainfall approached 45 inches per year, the native vegetation was slowly creeping up the sides, and through the windows of the wood and brick homes on the outskirts of town. In the urban centers, the concrete and steel structures still held fast, but the plant life was certainly gaining traction.

The elevated highways were in fairly good condition still, but the plants that once grew on the fringes of surface streets had grown through and over many paved surfaces. And likely under them too. It was a wonder that the Fluxor was still able to operate despite the probability that the pulsar energy modules embedded into the tarmac were, or would soon be choked with the roots of the jungle plants.

It was with great satisfaction and relief that they finally entered the city proper. They could see Corcovado Mountain to the north. On the top of that massive granite dome, far in the distance, stood the statue of Christ the Redeemer, shimmering in the sunlight as if it had just been polished.

"Look at that," Street said. "I've wanted to see that all my life!"

"Is that Jesus?" Jon asked.

"Yes sir," Street replied. "That's my Lord and Savior. Well, a statue of him anyway."

"You still believe in that, Street, after everything we've been through?" Jon asked, stretching.

"Yes, I do. I'll never lose my faith."

"I hope you don't, Street," Shift said. "It makes you human."

Street smiled. "Shift, it would do you some good to have a bit of faith too."

"I try dude."

"So, where to gentlemen?" Jon asked, steering the conversation away from religion as he steered around a large hole in the road with vines creeping out and across the tarmac.

"Just stay on this road," Shift replied. "We'll head toward the city center and find some place to stop for the night. Then we can give Mike a call. They're probably waiting for us already."

JULY 7, 7:50PM
RIO DE JANEIRO, BRAZIL

"We're here!" Street typed into the web chat.

"Awesome!" Mike replied. "Let me get everyone over here. They've been harassing me for three days. Have you tried a holo?"

"No, but Jon is bringing one up to the room from the hotel lobby right now."

"Check it out. I'll wait."

Communication systems all around the United States and many places throughout the world had gone down twenty-three months earlier as the small group of survivors fled Earth on a shuttle headed for the moon. They didn't know how it had occurred, but had assumed the Skins were behind it. Since their arrival in Sunny Slope, Idaho, Mike had been able to reestablish functioning landlines in town, the only place they had really needed to communicate. And, periodically, electronic and digital communication systems in different places around the world would go in and out, probably as satellites moved into and out of range as they orbited the Earth. That's how they had heard the noises coming from Brazil in the first place.

Maintaining electric power had initially been a harder matter. Using guidebooks and information downloaded from the Net many months earlier, they had figured out how to maintain the small substation in Marsing, Idaho. The hydroelectric dam upstream on the Snake River was still functioning with minor, periodic maintenance. If that ever broke down, the group could be in trouble. Recently, they had been working on maintaining some small wind turbines around Sunny Slope and Marsing that were capable, they hoped, of generating enough power for at least their basic needs. But they didn't know how to remedy the intermittent communication problem.

"It works!" Street typed moments later. "I'm calling you now."

"Well, hello there my friends," Mike said, smiling, as he looked at Street, Shift and Jon in the holo seconds later.

Within minutes, the fifteen people of Sunny Slope had gathered in Mike's tech lab inside his small home. The lab was furnished with all of the latest and greatest gadgets and computer systems Mike had been able to find. He had traveled to several different stores in nearby Boise and taken anything he thought would be useful. At the time, he felt guilty for taking things that he hadn't paid for. Now, of course, every one of the survivors had grown accustomed to filling their homes and closets with whatever they needed and desired. There was no one else with which to share, and nobody to accept payment for the goods.

"We're all here guys," Mike said after everyone had gathered around.

As the people closed in around the small holo in Mike's lab, the group in Sunny Slope saw the three travelers sitting in a large, comfortable hotel suite. It had been four days since they'd last talked. Their only communication in that time had been through text-only transmissions.

"Wow," Anta said, "you don't look like you're suffering much."

"Hi babe," Shift said. "Yeah, this hotel is awesome, at least on the inside. The grounds outside, like the rest of the city and almost everything south of central Mexico, has been retaken by the jungle. But this room is posh, for sure. Well, for now at least, until the vines figure out how to climb twelve stories of concrete and get in through the windows."

"So, what's your plan?" John Silitzer asked.

"Well, we intend to sleep. As soon as I can get Street out of bed in the morning, we'll head over to the coordinates Mike gave us. Is there anything we should know? Any more noise coming from that location?"

"Nope," Mike said. "You still have . . . holy crap!"

The volume of noise grew exponentially after Mike's outburst. "Shift! Run!"

The screaming and noise from Sunny Slope frightened the three travelers. All three began to look around, frantically, trying to see what had scared everyone so badly.

A bright light found the men through the window. As the men turned to look at the source of the light, a red dot appeared on Shift's chest.

"Drop!" Street yelled. All three men dropped to the floor just as the window shattered and laser fire rained in on the small room. The holo erupted in sparks as a beam ripped through its base, leaving the terrified group in Sunny Slope without the ability to see or hear what was happening.

As the three men began to crawl toward the doorway leading to the inner hall of the hotel, the outside wall exploded inward, raining chunks of debris down upon them. A large piece of the wall landed on Shift's left leg, pinning him to the floor. He yelled out in pain, but the sound of his agony was barely heard over the noise created by the falling debris and the ship, or whatever it was, outside.

Jon, closest to Shift when he fell, looked backward, sensing, more than hearing Shift's cry for help. As he saw Shift, not moving and covered with debris, he reached forward, grabbed Street's ankle, and pulled. Street turned, and together, they crawled back to Shift as another round of laser fire blasted the walls and furniture in the room.

"Is anything broken?" Jon yelled into Shift's ear.

"I don't think so. Get this crap off me."

Street and Jon, impeded by the fact that they were on their knees, hefted and pulled against the rubble. The large section of wall apparently pinning Shift to the floor cracked and broke apart along the edges as the men pulled. Within seconds, the remainder of the wall had fallen apart. It was then easily removed. Underneath, however, resting on Shift's ankle, was a large iron beam that probably had, until moments earlier, supported the ceiling above them.

The dust was settling around them as the room suddenly grew dark. The light from outside had moved away from the spot once occupied by a window, and the lights in the room had been shattered. Jon looked around, frantically, for anything with which they might be able to lift the beam from Shift's leg.

"There's nothing here," he said. "We need to do this ourselves; and fast, before that thing comes back."

Street and Jon each steadied themselves against a piece of furniture or pile of debris, and began to lift the beam holding Shift in place.

"Awww, wait," Shift cried. "Hold on guys. Let me brace myself."

"You ready now, man?" Street asked.

"No, but go ahead."

Straining and heaving, Street and Jon finally lifted the beam just enough for Shift to slip out from under it. As soon as Shift pulled his leg free of the tangled mess, the others dropped the beam to the floor, a loud boom sounding throughout the room. Jon carefully surveyed the room, and looked toward the gaping hole. The ship's light was returning.

Quickly, Street and Jon each grabbed one of Shift's wrists and pulled. They dragged him out of the room, his feet rounding the corner into the hallway just as the ship outside returned to the hole where the outside wall had been moments earlier. The ship began firing into the room again, causing more sections of wall and ceiling to rain down upon the floor recently vacated by the men.

"Let me crawl guys," Shift said as he tried to turn over onto his stomach. The movement caused Street and Jon to let go of his wrists. Shift got onto his hands and knees and they all crawled. Shift moved as fast as his injured leg would allow him, which was just fast enough.

Taking a left turn in the inner hallway, the men crawled toward the staircase. Behind them, as abruptly as it had started, the noise abated, leaving the three scared men on their hands and knees at the top of the staircase.

"Is it over?" Jon asked.

"I wouldn't bet on it," Street replied.

"Ah man, I can barely feel my leg," Shift said. "I hope they've left, whoever they are." Shift rolled over and laid on his back.

"I'm going to check it out," Street said as he kicked open the door to another room on the same side of the hallway. Then he crawled inside. Sixty agonizing seconds later, he reappeared in the doorway, standing.

"Whatever was out there is gone now. I even opened the window. No noise. Saw a speck in the sky in the distance just before it disappeared. So I think we're safe."

"Unless they dropped people off outside," Jon said.

"Yeah, they coulda' done that, but that would mean they left the people here, because that ship or whatever is gone."

"Okay, so now what?" Jon asked.

"Well, we gotta get out of this hotel, before it falls to the ground. Then we need to find a place to hide," Shift replied.

"How are we going to hide," Jon asked. "There are probably cameras everywhere. Whoever that was knew exactly where we were. Not just the hotel, but the very room."

"Maybe Mike can figure out how to hide us," Street said slowly, taking a deep breath. "Maybe he can shut the cameras off or somethin'."

"That may be a tall order, but it's worth a try," Shift said. "Help me up and let's get out of here."

JULY 7, 2095, 9:25PM
RIO DE JANEIRO, BRAZIL

"Are you guys okay? What was that?" Mike asked as the three men appeared on the holo. Others talked over each other wanting to know what had happened and whether everyone was okay.

As the men surveyed the anxious faces of their friends in Idaho, it was apparent that they had not been the only ones to suffer during the attack. Suvan's face was streaked with tears. Angel's breathing was still intense and her face was pale. Anta held Yurgi tight to her chest, rocking back and forth, humming the melody to an old Egyptian tune. Some wore shocked expressions while others looked more worried and curious than afraid.

"We're okay," Jon said. "Shift's leg is hurt, but it doesn't look like anything is broken. A few scratches from being dragged out from under debris," he lied so as not to distress Anta. "A part of the ceiling fell on him. Otherwise, we're more worried than hurt."

"But what was it?" Anta asked.

"We don't know," Shift said. "It was some kind of flying machine. Whoever, or whatever it was, found us easily and tried to kill us. Then the ship flew away. Maybe they thought we were dead, but they'll know soon, if they don't already, that we're still alive."

"Shift, we looked for it on USCAN after we got disconnected," Mike said. "It wasn't there. There was nothing there."

"Well, there was definitely something there," Jon said. "Was USCAN actually operational? Maybe it wasn't working right."

"Yeah, it was up. I'll keep searching for that ship, but it seems like it just disappeared. Or maybe it had some kind of cloaking device like some of the newer military ships. And whatever means it used to find you once, it will use to find you again."

"So, what are you going to do?" John Silitzer asked the three men.

"We need some help," Shift replied. "Mike, is there any way you can shut down the cameras, USCAN, or whatever it was they might have used to find us? And, can you find us a place to hide where they won't be able to find us again?"

"Maybe," Mike replied cautiously. "Let me give it a shot. I'll need your current coordinates though."

"I can send them now," Street answered.

"No, don't; not yet" Mike said. "We're going to shut off this com. I want you guys to get out of there because the bad guys may have already picked up this signal and may be listening in. In twenty minutes, I'm going to com you again on a secure channel through Shift's MEHD, assuming communications are still up by then. Then, you can tell me where you are. In the meantime, I'm going to try a few things. Signing out."

The com ended, leaving Shift, Street and Jon in the dark. They hadn't turned on the lights in their hiding place.

"Okay guys, where to?" Street asked.

"Let's get out of here and start moving. But let's leave the Fluxor. We don't need someone reading its heat signal or tracking its movements. That would be a dead giveaway. We'll come back for it later," Shift replied.

Street opened the back door to the small café where they had been hiding. Then they crept out into the night, hoping to still be alive in twenty minutes when Mike com'd back.

25

"Adal, will you come over here for a minute and look at this?" Nic asked from a computer terminal near the rear of the bunker.

"Sure Nic, what can I help you with?"

"I need for you to lift your hands into the air and keep them above your head," Nic said as he pulled a gun from his waistband and pointed it at Adal's head.

"What is this Nic?"

"This is a precaution. I know what you have done Adal. I know we're in danger. Now, I need you to walk with me."

"I think you are mistaken, my friend," Adal Jass said calmly. "The only danger here is that we run out of air. This we all know."

"No, that is what you have told us, but it isn't the truth. Now, no more talking. Walk please."

Adal Jass turned away from Nic and walked slowly away from the computer terminal. Nic followed close enough behind to keep Adal in line, but not so close as to be surprised by any sudden moves. As the two men walked toward the center of the large bunker, several others joined Nic, following close behind. Each held a gun, but none were ready to use them. Their faces betrayed their fear.

"I see you have friends to help you with whatever it is you plan to do next," Adal said. His calm demeanor was fading as he realized Nic meant business.

"Excuse me," Nic called out as his small band of outsiders reached the center of the cavern. "I need for each of you to turn toward me slowly and raise your arms into the air. Any sudden moves and Adal will feel the repercussions personally. I know you don't want that."

"What's going on?" a man called out from behind a small group gathered in the kitchen area.

"All will be explained," Nic replied. "Please gather together and keep your arms above your heads."

Nic's followers had surrounded the others, circling the edge of the large cavern. There were only a handful of them; and Nic knew they were nervous. But the people were doing as directed.

"Everybody do as Dr. Heiberg says, please," Adal said. As the words left his mouth, his eyes found those of several of his most trusted allies. They had not planned for this, but they had discussed it as a possibility. Adal hadn't known who would figure it out, nor did he know when. But he and his advisors had realized the possibility existed.

"Dr. Hieberg?"

Nic looked around for the person who had said his name. It was a female, but she said nothing more. Nic scanned the crowd that had gathered together as ordered. "Who called my name?" he asked.

Nobody spoke. Nic turned quickly to look behind him as a gunshot rang out. A man fell to the floor just three yards behind Nic. A kitchen knife clattered on the tile just before his body crumbled to the floor.

Then chaos erupted.

JULY 7, 9:54PM
RIO DE JANEIRO, BRAZIL

"In here," Street said.

Jon and Street helped Shift limp into an abandoned grocery store a couple of blocks from the café. Of course, every building in Rio de Janeiro was abandoned.

"Help me sit down guys," Shift said. "Over there by the pharmacy."

They all moved slowly toward the pharmacy. The only light in the building came from small red illuminations in signs over the doors that read "Salida", or "Exit" in Portuguese. Near the pharmacy, Street and Jon helped Shift sit on a small wooden bench where the sick waited for their names to be called to pick up prescriptions—back before the world came crashing down.

"Now what?" Street asked.

"Now we find something to splint and bandage this leg. I need to be able to walk. And there's probably some ibuprofine behind the counter somewhere. See if you can find that too."

A few minutes later, Jon and Street arrived back at the bench where Shift was inspecting the wounds in his leg.

"I'm sure it's not broken, luckily," Shift said. "Probably just a sprain. But this gash is pretty ugly. The bleeding has already stopped. So, if I clean and bandage it right, I shouldn't even need stitches. But I'll need some antibiotics to keep the wound from becoming infected."

"I found some antibiotic wash by the bandages," Jon said, handing a small, white tube to Shift. "Will that work?"

"Might. Thanks. Maybe we should look for an injection too."

"I already did," Jon replied. "Nada."

"So, Mike was supposed to com like ten minutes ago," Street said. "Is the MEHD still on?"

"Yeah, it is . . . oh crap," Jon replied. "No service."

"Well, that explains that mystery," Shift said. "Let's keep it on and keep checking every few minutes. The com system will probably come back online eventually."

"What do we do until then?" Jon asked.

"I don't know," Shift replied. "Do either of you know anything about cameras? I mean, if we looked at one, could we tell whether it was e-casting or not?"

"I don't," Street said.

"Me neither," Jon said, "but I'll go find a camera and take a look at it."

"Don't go to the front of the store. There will be a camera there, but also big, glass doors. Look by the loading docks instead, wherever those are."

"Got it."

"Maybe I should go with him," Street said quietly as Jon walked away.

"He'll be fine, but while you're up, find me something cold to drink—non-alcoholic."

As Street's silhouette faded into the darkness, Shift began to relax. The pain meds were working and his leg felt stronger already, although he knew it was just the ibuprofine working.

Street and Jon returned a few minutes later. "I couldn't find a camera in the back," Jon said as he plopped down on the bench next to Shift. Street handed Shift a can of Pepsi.

"Well then, I guess we wait," Shift replied, looking at the can questioningly before slowly popping open the cap. It fizzed and overflowed, which surprised him. Shift held it away from him as the soda ran down the can and onto the floor. "I don't think it's smart to go to the front of the store. Mike will find us. He always comes through."

"How's that Pepsi?" Street asked as Shift lifted the can to his lips.

Seconds later, Shift replied, "Aw, gross man. It's warm."

"I thought you'd love it," Street said, smiling. "Try this instead." Street produced a bottle of water from behind his back. "Warm water isn't quite as bad."

JULY 7, 11:48PM
RIO DE JANEIRO, BRAZIL

A couple of hours had passed since the men finally decided to sit and wait for a com from Idaho. Street had spent his time eating. There was plenty of canned and bottled food left in the store. Jon and Shift played cards. Shift was just about to call Jon's bluff and up the ante to eighteen chocolate chips when he heard a quiet thumping behind him. He turned toward the sound, but the blackness behind him was nearly absolute. He couldn't see anything out of the ordinary, but the sound was definitely growing louder.

"Do you guys hear that?" Shift asked.

"Yeah, stay here," Street said quietly as he rose from the ground a few feet from the card game. "It's outside, whatever it is."

Street crept slowly toward the front of the store.

"Wait. Shhhh," Jon said, holding his finger up to his mouth. "I think it's getting quieter."

The men remained still for a few minutes until they could no longer hear the strange thumping sound. Whatever was outside was gone, at least for now.

"Well, now what?" Street asked, returning to the others.

"They must not know we're here, or they would have stopped, not gone away," Shift replied. "It's probably time to look for a camera at the front of the store," Shift said.

"We'll go look," Street replied.

"Carefully gentlemen," Shift said as they walked away toward the front entrance of the store, through which they had entered over two hours earlier.

Within moments of leaving, Shift saw the silhouettes of two forms coming back toward him in the dark.

"Back so soon?" Shift asked.

"Stay where you are," a deep, accented voice said quietly from the darkness.

Shift was considering what to do when four more shapes appeared in the darkness behind the original two. Moments later, the silhouettes became people. Street and Jon were in the lead, hands held high above their heads. Behind them, four masked people held guns trained on their backs.

"What's going on?" Shift asked.

"These wipes think they're taking us prisoner or something," Street growled.

"We *are* taking you prisoner," one of the men said. "Please empty your pockets sir and lay your weapon on the floor."

"Sir?" Shift said. "You're a rather polite abductor, aren't you?"

"Yes, I am," the man replied. "But don't take that as a sign that we are weak. These guns have seen much action, particularly over the past couple of hours. We will use them as necessary to ensure our survival."

"Understood," Shift said. "Where are we going?"

"That's our secret," said a female voice with a thick Brazilian accent, from under another mask. "But you'll be safe as long as you cooperate."

"How do we know we can trust you?" Jon asked.

"Well, so far, you are still alive," the woman replied. "But, as I said, you'll only remain that way if you cooperate. And, you will not have much choice but to cooperate." Then the woman stepped forward and, forcing each man's hands behind his back in turn, handcuffed them.

"Hey, we'll cooperate. Right Street?" Shift said, looking into the eyes of his friend.

"Yeah boss. I'll be a good boy."

"Alright then, let's go," said the first male voice.

The masked figures led Street, Shift and Jon out the front doors of the store and into a waiting hovercar. One of them helped Shift up with a grip on his arm, since Shift's splinted leg was slowing him down, while another carried the men's packs. The back interior of the hover easily held all three prisoners and three of the four masked captors, who each held his or her gun pointed at the chest of one of the prisoners.

After all were seated, the hover sped away, a quiet thumping sound coming from the engine.

"What's that noise?" Jon asked, after they had settled in for the drive.

"Ah, the thumping?" replied one man. "That is the hover's way of telling us that the air outside is still contaminated. Fancy science."

"Why don't you give us our packs and we'll show you *real* science," Street said.

"We'll give you back your packs after we find out who you are and what you're doing here. There are a lot of bad guys out there."

"Funny," Street said, "I kind of thought *you* were the bad guys."

"Oh, we're not. I assure you," the man replied. "The bad guys are much worse than us. In fact, I think you already had a run-in with them, a couple of hours ago."

"You mean, back at the hotel?" Shift asked.

"Yes, that's what I mean."

"Then I guess I'm glad *you* found us instead of the *real* bad guys," Shift said.

The group rode in silence for nearly ten minutes before another person spoke. This time, it was a new voice, from the one captor who had not yet spoken. His voice shook with nervousness.

"Are any of you sick?" the young male voice asked.

"What do you mean?" Street asked in return.

"I think he wants to know whether we have AE," Shift said, looking at Street. Then, turning back to the masked man, he said, "No. We don't have Anthrax E. We've been vaccinated."

"How? Where?" the female asked.

"I assume that means *you* haven't received the vaccination?" Jon asked in return.

"No, we have not. We didn't even know anyone was alive out here, let alone someone who had been vaccinated."

"So, those masks and suits are all that's keeping you alive?" Street asked, a sinister look crossing over his eyes.

"Street," Shift said slowly, the warning clear in his tone. "These guys may have just saved our lives. Let's give them a chance to explain."

Then, turning back to their captors, he added, "We have the vaccine with us."

"Yes, Mr. Street, you should listen to your friend," the female voice said. "I will shoot you the moment I think you are up to something, and not even your vaccine will save you from that. But we will be interested to test your so-called vaccine, when the time arrives."

Street sagged into his seat, obviously realizing that the opportunity to escape these people, if there had ever been such an opportunity, was now gone.

"So," Jon said, "are you going to tell us who you are and where we're going?"

"Yes, but not yet. Please sit quietly until we arrive at our destination."

Twelve minutes later, the hover slowed and the back windows darkened and became opaque.

"What's going on," Street asked, nervously.

"Obviously, we don't want you to see where we're going," the woman captor replied.

"Obviously," Street said.

The hover began a slow, winding, uphill drive. After another ten minutes had passed, the hover slowed even more, but continued forward. Finally, it stopped moving altogether and the windows became clear again. But, the small group still could not see anything outside.

"Where are we?" Jon asked.

"A cave," one of the men replied. "Now, please exit the hover on the right side, slowly, and stand in a line facing away from it."

The three men did as they were told. Not long after they had lined up, hands still cuffed behind their backs, dim lights flickered on. They were definitely in a cave.

26

"Sir," one man said, looking at Shift. "You will all be cleansed on the outside before you are allowed to enter our home, but I am concerned that you may still carry Anthrax E internally. Have you any information that might help me understand whether that is possible?"

"Actually, yes. We wondered the same thing a few months ago. Our doctors performed some tests. They determined that, once vaccinated, your body eventually rejects the disease, not just fights against it. We don't know how long that period of time is, but it was determined that our whole group is not only immune to Anthrax E, but we also don't carry the disease inside us anymore. It has been killed, completely."

"We will test that," the man replied, producing a small machine from a bag inside the hover. He held the machine up to Shift's arm and pressed a square screen on the side. The machine whirred quietly for several seconds, then beeped once. The man lifted the contraption and looked at the screen.

"My little friend here tells me that you are immune. It also tells me that your body is not tainted by Anthrax E. It appears you have told me the truth."

"Was that some kind of trust test?" Jon asked. "I think we're the ones who should be less trusting." Jon lifted his hand-cuffed hands up behind his back and out to the side, showing the group what he meant.

"Maybe so," the man replied. Then he began to walk away. The others fell in behind Shift, Street and Jon, and indicated that they were to follow the first man.

The captives were then led down a dimly-lit corridor and into a metallic holding cell approximately four feet wide and six feet deep. Two of their captors crowded in with them before the door shut behind them with a quiet whoosh. A series of clicks sounded from around the perimeter of the door and something connected to the walls of the cell circled around them in the dark, emitting a gassy substance that smelled faintly of vinegar. Two minutes later, the opposite side of the cell opened revealing a vast, well-lit cavern filled with electronic equipment and other furniture.

The group stepped out of the cell and moved away as the remaining two captors came in behind them. After all were inside and the small cell had closed, the captors removed their masks and their outer protective clothing and placed them on hooks and shelves near the doors.

In the interior of the cave-like bunker, three people sat on sofas in a makeshift living room near the back. They all turned to look at the group as they entered the cavern.

"Welcome back Nic," a young man called out as he stood and approached. The man was overweight, but had a pleasant face. His long, blond hair was tied back in a ponytail behind his head, with a few stray hairs poking out haphazardly.

"Thank you Frans."

"So, you got them. Now what?" Frans asked.

"Now, they're going to tell us where they came from and show us the vaccine they claim to have. But first, let us feed them. Lilly, what do we have that these men can eat?"

"I'll find something."

"Frans, have you learned anything more?" the man named Nic asked.

"Any more of what?" Jon asked.

"That's none of your concern," Nic replied, as he walked away. "At least not until we decide it *is* your concern."

The several members of the group from the cave wandered off, leaving Lilly with the captives. She was strong and attractive, her tank-top hugging her curves in all the right places. Shift watched as Jon tried, mostly in vain, to focus on Lilly's face. He laughed inwardly at Jon's immaturity as Jon's eyes kept moving lower, then suddenly darting back up. It was fortunate that Suvan was not there.

"Can we take the cuffs off yet lady?" Street asked.

"Not yet."

"Then how are we going to eat?" Jon asked, quietly.

"I will feed you," Lilly replied.

"Oh, that won't be humiliating," Jon said sarcastically, looking down at the ground.

"You don't have to eat," Lilly replied curtly.

"Just kidding, feed me," Jon said. He looked back up, but his eyes never made it to her face.

The three captives sat at a small table and were fed a simple meal of water and a meaty substance the consistency of bread. While Shift, and likely the others based upon their expressions and body language, felt a little humiliated, he was so hungry that he didn't complain.

After they had eaten, the other six members of the cave group came back and sat down at the round table. When prompted, Shift began their story. The people wanted to know everything, from the beginning. Shift told them about his and Anta's discovery of the disease, their time in the bunker outside Boston, and Dr. Shevchuk's testing and solution.

After showing them a vial of E-rase, the man named Nic took one dose over to a machine and dumped it into a small container. "That will tell us what it is," he said as he walked back to the table. "Until then, let us continue with the tale."

Shift continued with their story of outrunning and killing the Skins, their escape to the moon, and their return. He intentionally left out the location of their current residence. Finally, he said, "There isn't much more to tell you guys. We were almost killed in a hotel a few hours ago, and then you captured us."

"Now it's your turn," Street said.

"Well," Nic began, scratching at several days' worth of growth on his chin, "our story is much simpler to tell." Nic was tall and thin, with a full head of graying hair and bushy eyebrows. His chin, covered with tiny hair, jutted away from his face giving him the look of a cartoon character.

"We are high atop Corcovado Mountain, in a cave underneath the Christ the Redeemer statue. We came here to hide, near the beginning. Our government selected us and so we came. There were fifty of us in the beginning, including Adal Jass, Continental Director of South AM. He directed our work, of course, and has been the only person in communication with the outside for many, many months."

Nic's story was interrupted by a quiet beep emanating from the machine where he had placed the vaccine for testing. He stood and walked over to the small lab, returning shortly thereafter with a tablet.

"The results appear conclusive," Nic said. "A comparison with your Dr. Shevchuk's final formula indicates that what is contained in this vial is safe. That is the only evidence we can muster, along with your own apparent immunities, without taking the vaccine ourselves. The only way to really know if it works is to test it."

"So, I guess you just have to decide whether you trust us now," Shift said.

"I trust them," Lilly replied boldly.

"So do I," Frans added quickly.

The others looked from one to another, expressions bordering on indecipherable. Finally, Nic spoke again. "I think I trust them too. I'm willing to take the vaccine first. I cannot see how they could possibly be alive unless the vaccine works."

"And what motivation would we have for killing you?" Shift asked. "We didn't even know you were here until you captured us."

"That makes sense to me," another man said. "I'm in."

"Let's do this," Lilly said, rolling up her sleeve.

Nic pulled a set of keys from his pocket and removed the handcuffs from the wrists of the three men. In a matter of minutes, Shift had inoculated all seven of the strangers. Instead of the relief and satisfaction Shift expected to see as a result of the vaccination, the men and women of the cave looked apprehensive.

"Cheer up dudes," Street said, looking around. "It works. You can go outside now. You're free. You can finally live a little." Street smiled, but the people from the bunker didn't reciprocate.

"Hey, you'll see," Shift finally said, knowing that they would understand soon.

A few moments later, Nic continued, completely ignoring Street and Shift's earnest attempts to ease their concerns. "So, while the world outside our doors perished, we prayed for a miracle—for somebody to develop a cure or a vaccine. We knew the vaccine had been created, and we watched the monsters—'Skins' as you say—hunt down every other survivor we could see through USCAN. We even saw them chasing you, although we were never able to see your faces clearly, and there were women with you. Knowing your story now, it couldn't have been anyone else. We watched you fighting them and hiding from them. We believed you were our only hope at freedom. And then you were gone."

"That was probably when we went into hiding in the bunker in Cabo Rojo," Shift said. "We didn't come out for a long time."

"We thought everyone was dead," Nic continued. "That's what Director Jass told us. He told us that all communication channels went dead too, leaving us with no connection to the outside world. And that's what we believed, until recently."

"What do you mean?" Shift asked.

"Well, until a couple of weeks ago, we believed that we may be the only people in the world still alive. We had a bit of a surprise two weeks ago when we learned that Director Jass had been in contact with the outside world the whole time, and had not thought to share that information with us, but instead, actively hid it from us."

"What did you learn?" Shift asked.

"And where is everybody else?" Jon asked.

"Well," Nic replied, "it is a terrible story." Nic and Frans spent the next several minutes relaying their sad story of betrayal by Adal Jass and his followers.

"So, you didn't know any of that, about the plot or this guy Jass' part in it, until two weeks ago?" Shift asked when Nic and Frans had finished.

"No," Nic replied. "We didn't know about it. But we did believe we were in danger."

"So you took them out?" Street asked, his eyebrows lifting.

"We didn't murder them, if that is what you are asking," Dr. Frans Sillman replied. "We hoped to restrain them, but there were too many of them. Even though we had a surprise attack, it was not as easy as it should have been. Luckily, we had the weapons."

"At first, we had them surrounded," Nic continued, as the story inched closer to its crescendo. "I had Director Jass on the ropes, in my site, with my team fanning out to surround the exterior of this large room. We had all the weapons, or so we thought. We never imagined anyone else would be carrying guns in the bunker, least of all Adal Jass."

"We were afraid," Frans added. "None of us had killed anyone before. We thought it would be a simple chore to herd everyone together."

"But what did you intend to do with them after you captured them?" Jon asked.

"That is the part about which I am most embarrassed," Nic replied. "In my haste, and my anger, I had not thought that far ahead. I believed, as Frans said, that we could simply gather everyone together, put Director Jass in lockup, and that everyone else would then cooperate. But I was wrong."

"So what happened?" Jon asked.

"As Adal and I inched further out into the room, Adal in front of me with my weapon aimed at his back, he began to get restless. I could see his head turn slightly here and there as though he were looking for an escape or rescue. I watched the room carefully."

"We all did," Frans interrupted.

"Yes, we were watching, looking for danger. I called out to those in the room who were moving closer together as we surrounded them. I asked them to raise their hands. I threatened Jass then, and most everyone complied, moving into a tight bunch in the center of the room.

"But shortly thereafter, someone called my name, taking my focus away from my prisoner. Then a shot rang out. I turned behind me to see a man, Henry, fall to the floor just behind me. A knife fell from his hand—a knife surely meant for me. But Lilly had saved me. Unfortunately, the confusion of the moment was all that was needed to break our coalition.

"Within seconds, or less, screams erupted. While the majority of our prisoners pushed even closer together in the center of the room, others began running for the sides and ducking behind furniture. Two men even fled through the front door. Grunting and yelling echoed throughout the cavern, intermingled with the occasional roar of a gun.

"I ducked for cover too, leaving Director Jass standing in the middle of the room. I watched him, with all of the commotion going on around us, standing there as calm as a summer day. He pulled a small ray gun from his pocket and began firing, slowly, in all directions. He was not aiming for anyone in particular, nor was he purposefully avoiding anyone either. Because his people were grouped together in the center of the room, when he turned that direction, he mowed them down. Arms, legs and heads severed from bodies, blood rushing from the wounds, coating the floor dark red. Bodies collapsed on top of others and shook and twitched as life faded. It was an awful sight—one which I do not believe I will ever forget."

Nic and his friends all looked down or away from one another, some shaking their heads side to side. Lilly's body shivered and Nic wiped a tear from his eye. Shift, Jon and Street sat silently, watching, giving the people the time they needed.

"Most of my people," Nic continued moments later, waving his hand around the room to those among us, "were hidden by that time. We had placed ourselves strategically around the room in those first few minutes, with shelter to hide behind in case it was needed. Although we didn't believe anyone would shoot back at us, we weren't certain. So we hid from Director's Jass' blasts.

"His own people, however, did not. Even many of those that had fled the center cluster fell to the powerful ray as it swept the room. I watched several of them die. It was as if they believed he would protect them. They were his allies after all. But Jass didn't seem to care. And he remained calm the whole time."

"It was like he had gone mad," Lilly said quietly. "I watched his face from my vantage point. He was smiling. He wasn't even looking at his targets. He was just shooting. Anyone in the path of the silent rays fell to the floor, dead."

"That's crazy!" Shift said. "Why would he kill his own people?"

"Because he was crazy," Nic replied. "I believe he had actually gone mad. Perhaps the stress of the situation broke him. We will never know. But in any event, he continued to shoot for several more seconds until his body had fully turned away from me. At that moment, I leapt forward, out from behind a desk, and tackled Adal to the ground.

"He grunted as his body smashed into a chair. I landed on top of him and hit him in the face with the butt of my gun. His smile disappeared, replaced by terrifying, angry eyes. I froze, my hand pulled halfway back, ready for another strike. When I saw his eyes, I stopped. I don't know why. It is not my proudest moment.

"Adal pushed me off of him, stood and pointed his ray gun at me. I trembled, knowing that my life was at an end, but hoping that my friends would survive. I didn't know how they were faring, but I had not seen any of them go down, and that gave me comfort. If they could survive, then it would have been worth it."

Frans reached over and patted Nic on the shoulder, then took over the narrative. "Nic is humble as he tells the story. Without him, I do not believe we would be alive now. What may have felt like mere moments to Nic, as he lay on the ground at Director Jass' feet, was, in reality, nearly twenty seconds. Director Jass stood there, poised as if to shoot, while the rest of us fought with the few remaining members of our former team. We struggled in hand-to-hand combat for some time before Lilly was able to reach Jass."

Lilly lowered her head as Frans continued. "Lilly shot two people as she ran toward the Director. Then, just as Director Jass looked as though he may actually pull the trigger, ending the life of our good friend, Lilly tackled him." Frans chuckled as he continued, "Her tackle was even better than Nic's."

"She saved my life," Nic said. "Lilly struggled with Jass on the ground. His ray gun went off several more times during the melee. Two or three others were shot by the random blasts. Nobody can survive a shot from a ray gun you know—not even if it is to the hand or foot. Its ray soaks into your skin on contact, and spreads throughout the nervous system, killing within seconds, or a minute at most.

"Eventually, as I tried to maneuver in to help, without getting shot, Lilly was able to free her gun and shoot Director Jass in the chest. He looked up at her, sitting on top of him, and his smile returned. His final words were 'that was a good shot'. Then his eyes closed and he stopped breathing."

"The rest of us came out of hiding as the echo from Lilly's gun faded," Frans added. "Many people were still moving, but they stopped one by one as the rays destroyed their bodies. It was a miracle that any of us lived. Every person, besides us, was slaughtered; those on our side and Jass' side—most of them killed by the very man they had supported."

"And only you seven lived?" Jon asked.

"That is probably true now," Nic said. "As for the two people from Jass' group that fled through the main doors, I am certain they will be dead within the week. They had no protection from Anthrax E. Everyone else perished in the fight or shortly thereafter. But only four of us here survived the battle. The other three were out on a provisions run when it all happened."

"And I assume you trust those three?" Shift asked, more than stated, as he looked around the group trying to see which of them Nic was referring to.

"Yes, we do," Frans replied. "Thankfully, all three were on our list. None of them had been selected by Jass to be here in the first place. Jass also selected the teams to go out scavenging. Looking through the records during our investigation into who we could trust, it became clear that he selected those who were not members of his select group to perform the dangerous scavenging missions. We were more expendable, I guess."

"So, what you see here now are all people who mean you no harm," Nic said, finally lifting the corners of his mouth into a tight-lipped smile.

"That's good to know," Shift said. "I'm so sorry for your losses. What a terrible tragedy."

"But how did Jass know we were coming?" Jon asked a few seconds later.

"I assume his contact in the United States told him about you," Nic replied. "The contact said people with a vaccine were on their way here, to Rio."

"United States? Does that mean ... ?" Jon began, but ended suddenly, with a lump in his throat.

"I think it does Jon," Shift replied. "A traitor."

"But who?" Jon asked.

"Everybody in our group has been with us from the beginning except you, Jon," Street said, his tone wholly void of accusation.

"And Marcus and Lin," Jon added hastily, unnecessarily defending against the implication.

"Don't worry Jon, we know it isn't you," Shift said, looking Jon in the eyes. Then he smiled. "You're too cute and innocent. Besides, if it was you, the message to Jass would have said '*we're* on our way', not '*people with a vaccine* are on their way'. Plus, you were only fourteen years old when all of this began. Seems unlikely you were in cahoots with such bad men." Shift smiled again and patted Jon on the back.

"Then it must be Marcus or Lin," Street growled. "And I trusted that man . . ."

"We don't know it's them," Shift replied. "We'll have Mike and John look into it."

"And what if they are traitors?" Jon asked. "What can we do?"

"I'm the mayor," Shift replied. "I'll have them arrested and we'll get to the bottom of it. If Marcus is behind this, I don't believe he's strong-willed enough to keep the secrets inside. I don't know about Lin."

"I'll beat it out of him if I have to," Street added.

"I don't mean to interrupt," Nic said, "but what are we going to do about the people who tried to kill you yesterday? That's our immediate concern."

"Well, who are they?" Street asked. "And why'd they want to kill us?"

"We don't know who they are," Nic replied. "We had hoped you could tell us that."

"How would we know?" Street asked. "We got into town yesterday and they tried to take us out."

"Well then, I don't think there is much to talk about," Nic said. "We've never seen them until today."

"Until we find some answers, we should probably stay hidden, here, in your cave," Shift said. "The weapons the bad guys had were more than we can deal with."

"Agreed," Nic said.

27

John Silitzer was at the Town Hall in the small town of Marsing, just a fifteen-minute walk from his home. The building served as both the government building and meeting hall for the group. He picked up the phone and dialed the number for Marcus' home.

The old phone rang twice before Marcus picked up.

"Hello?"

"Marcus, this is John. Can you come over to Town Hall please?"

John and Marcus were on either end of an old-fashioned telephone line that Mike had rigged up. The phone lines now connected each of the homes and other buildings utilized by the group. The lines allowed the group to make local calls to each other in town using old handsets the size of small bricks, many of which were tethered to the walls by spiral cords. Until Mike could figure out how to get reliable coms with the outside, this old-fashioned system would suffice.

"Sure, I was just sitting down to eat a bit of beef and potatoes. Spent the morning out gathering up the cows. They bust out of the fence again last night. Can it wait?"

"Sorry to hear about the cows, Marcus; but this can't wait," John replied.

"Okay, I'll be right over. Is everything okay?"

"Yep. Just fine. But we need to go over some things."

Fifteen minutes later, when Marcus pushed open the solid, wooden, double doors of Town Hall, he was greeted by John, Mike, Jonas and Hasani.

"What's going on guys?" Marcus asked, stretching out his arm to shake hands with John. When John didn't take the proffered hand, Marcus narrowed his eyelids.

"Come have a seat," Hasani said, reaching out his hand and placing it on Marcus' shoulder.

Mike and Jonas moved behind Marcus, cutting off any possible retreat from the direction in which he had come.

Hasani led Marcus over to a chair in the center of the room. Then the four men sat on chairs encircling Marcus. Hasani, sitting behind Marcus, pulled an old-western style revolver from his waistband and pointed it at Marcus' back. Nobody else could see it, but the other men knew it was there. It was part of the plan.

"Guys, you're scaring me a bit," Marcus said.

"Do you have some reason to be afraid?" John asked.

"I don't think so, but *you* must think I've done something."

"We have some questions Marcus," John said. "After you've answered them, we will all know whether you, or any of us, should be worried."

"What are you talking about?" Marcus stammered, sweat beginning to form on his balding forehead.

"People living in Brazil," John replied.

"I don't know about any people in Brazil except Shift, Jon and Street. Same as you."

"May I see your watch?" John asked quietly.

"Why?"

"Why not?"

"It's mine, that's why," Marcus replied.

"I think you better let him see it," Jonas said.

Before anyone could say another word, Marcus leapt to his feet and spun toward the front door. Hasani stood at the same time. Marcus stopped abruptly when he felt the hard metal of a gun barrel against his chest.

"You should probably sit back down," Hasani said evenly.

"Are you going to shoot me Hasani?" Marcus asked, gaining an eerie confidence.

"I have no plan to shoot you Marcus, but I know my way around a gun, and will not hesitate to do what is necessary."

Without warning, Marcus swept his right hand upward, striking the gun and sending it flying through the air. At the same time, Marcus drove his knee up into Hasani's groin. Hasani fell hard; and Marcus ran.

Just as Marcus reached the front door, a quiet click sounded from behind. He paused momentarily before reaching toward the door handle.

"I *will* shoot you," Mike said, his voice wavering.

Without turning around, Marcus replied, "No you won't, Mike."

Marcus squeezed the door handle, pulled open the door and crossed the threshold into the bright sunshine. Then he fell. All three other men looked at Mike as the smoke cleared from the end of the revolver. There were tears already forming in Mike's eyes.

"I didn't mean to . . ." Mike stammered. "I didn't mean to, honest."

Mike slumped to the floor. Hasani, still in pain, crawled over to him and put a hand on his arm. Jonas and John walked over to Marcus.

"He's alive, Mike," John said. "No worries. But we may need to get you some target practice."

"Be nice, John," Jonas said. "Mike, you barely grazed his thigh. I'd call that a great shot."

JULY 9, 2095, LATER
HOLO CONFERENCE

"He confessed," John said through the Holo. Luckily, satellite communications were operational at the moment. "He was the contact."

"I knew it," Street said from Rio de Janeiro.

"What do we do with him now?" Jonas asked.

"I don't know," Shift replied. "But since his contact here is dead, I don't know who else he can communicate with."

"Don't forget the guys who tried to kill us though," Jon said.

"Oh, I haven't forgotten about them. But nobody knows where, or who they are. We haven't seen them again. And since it appears that they received their instructions from Jass, who's dead, they may not be able, or willing, to seek us out."

"So what do you propose, Mayor?" Hasani asked.

"Well, I guess we need to give him a trial or something, right?"

"Probably should," John replied. "But that's your job Shift, since we don't have a judge."

"Okay," Shift said, "then I guess he needs to be locked up until we get back. Can you do that?"

"No problem," John replied. "Don't think of it again. We'll take care of him until you get back."

"And when will that be?" Jonas asked.

"We'll leave here soon. The others are coming with us. But we're going to do a little digging around here before we leave. These guys want to be sure they leave nothing for the bad guys, if they ever show up again. Where's Anta, by the way?"

"She was coming over, probably just got tied up with Yurgi. We'll tell her 'hello' for you."

"And I'll give her a nice, long hug for you too," John said, smiling.

"I bet you will," Shift replied. "But be ready for the sucker punch afterward."

"Yeah, I guess that could be dangerous," John replied, laughing.

"Keep us posted Shift; and be careful," Hasani said.

JULY 10, 2095
CORCOVADO MOUNTAIN, RIO DE JANEIRO, BRAZIL

"They're out there, flying toward the city right now," Nic said as Frans and Shift jogged over to the computer bay.

Nic and some of the others had been watching the monitors closely. Late the previous night a sound was picked up by one of the sensors the Brazilians had placed in the city a couple of years earlier. For the past few hours, they had taken turns watching a dozen monitors that were fed constant real-time images by the cameras hooked up to the sensors. Because Mike had been unable to see the ship through USCAN on the day of the attack, they were relying on these older cameras.

Throughout the night, the cameras showed very little. The city was too dark. After the sun rose, three hours earlier, the only sign of life was the birds. But now, the dark shape of a flying machine could be seen in the distance, apparently flying over the Atlantic Ocean toward Corcovado and the city. The USCAN system couldn't see it, as expected, but the older cameras showed it clearly.

"It looks like USCAN is still having trouble picking up this ship, like Mike said earlier," Shift said.

"Yes," Nic replied. "It likely has a cloaking device. Our country's military was implementing such devices on newer ships just before Anthrax E arrived. It is likely other countries were doing the same. USCAN cannot see it, but our digital cameras can."

"That's stale!" Jon said.

"Stale?" Nic asked. "Like old bread?"

"Nah. Stale, like totally awesome."

"I see."

"Okay, thank you for that wonderful lesson in pop culture," Shift said, chuckling.

"How fast is it flying?"

"Not very fast actually," Nic replied. "Its movements are more like a helicopter than a plane."

As the remainder of the small group in the cave hurried over to the monitors, the ship, or whatever it was, continued to grow in size as it approached the cameras on the southern edge of the city. The group watched in silence as the machine reduced its altitude. It then turned northwest, and continued to move directly toward Corcovado.

"Do you think they know what we've done—I mean, what happened to Director Jass?" Frans asked, nervously.

"I'm sure they do," Nic replied. "They may not know that their leader is dead, but they must know something happened. He hasn't contacted them in two and a half days. And they probably knew that you guys had a vaccine."

"Yeah, I imagine they're pretty confused as to why they haven't been given the word that it's safe to come on over for an inoculation and ice cream," Shift said.

The ship continued to move toward the mountain. Nic remotely positioned the angle of the closest camera, which was set up outside the cave under the statue of Christ, to view the ship. Through that camera, they could clearly see the ship, but none of them had seen such a machine. Its metallic gray exterior glistened with moisture, either from the sea or from the humidity in the air.

"It's headed straight for us," Street said quietly.

"No, I don't think so," Nic said. "It looks like it is headed straight for the camera, but the camera is set up a couple hundred meters from the cave, to the north."

"Then do they know where the camera is?" Jon asked.

"I guess we'll see," Nic replied.

Within moments, the ship changed direction and began moving to the north, away from Corcovado and toward the city center.

"I guess that answers the question," Street said. "They went right on by."

"But, if they had been receiving orders from Jass before he died, they know where the cave is, right?" Jon asked.

"Yes, that is likely," Nic replied. "They may have been doing a simple fly-by to see if anything was visible on the outside to give them an idea of what was going on inside."

"So what do we do now?" Frans asked. "They seem to be searching for something, but what?"

"We'll keep an eye on the ship," Nic replied. "If it returns to the place from which it came, during daylight hours, we may get a better understanding of what we're up against."

"I need to try to talk to Marcus—see what he knows," Shift said.

As Shift walked away from the group, the ship was picked up by another camera to the north. The group continued to watch its progress for a while longer. Soon, most of them walked away to pursue other activities.

JULY 10, LATER
CORCOVADO MOUNTAIN, RIO DE JANEIRO, BRAZIL

Shift and Street sat in a small lounge area along the western-most wall of the bunker. Adjacent to the stone wall was a large set of antique wooden bookshelves, full of books. Some of them were clearly very old, with cracked bindings and yellowed pages hanging loosely from string running down the center of the spines. Others were more modern, but well read. Two books—The Hunger Games and Circle of Reign—sat on a small table next to the chair in which Shift was sitting, placed there by someone else. Shift had thumbed through both when he first sat down, but had noticed another book on the shelf, which he was now holding.

"What are you reading?" Street asked, looking up from a game he was playing on a small tablet.

"I don't know," Shift replied. "The cover and binding are faded and the first few pages are missing."

"Who wrote it?'

"Hard to tell; but it looks like some guy named Daniel Wilde. Never heard of him."

"Me neither. Must not be too famous," Street said.

"Probably not, but the book is so worn out that it caught my attention. There was a book mark on this page with an interesting quote highlighted." Shift opened the book back up to where his finger was holding his place. "The author quotes an anonymous writer. Listen to this:

'Along the road of life, the uncontrollable shifting and twisting sands threaten to alter man's course; but he who fights to control his own destiny while on that course may be satisfied,

at the end, with the knowledge that he finished his battle. The man that will not endure, but instead bows to the crushing weight of his trials, will forever be scarred with the knowledge that his life was controlled and taken by the sands of time. The Killing Sands always shape the destiny of man; but he who stays the course, who survives and endures his trials, may look forward to a better world.'

"What's that mean?" Street asked, his face thoughtful as he pondered the words.

"I don't know. It kind of sounds prophetic though, doesn't it? I mean, here we are, probably several decades after this book was written, and only two and half years after a plague completely altered the destiny of mankind. We couldn't control the fate of the world. Nobody could. We couldn't control it—but we fought Anthrax E and the Skins. We finished those battles. We survived. Now, even though the destiny of the whole world has been altered or changed, by something we couldn't control, our fight to live has ensured the survival of the human race. We have a new world in front of us, and I think we have a duty to ensure its survival. That's what we're trying to do, isn't it?"

"I guess the killing sands didn't get all of us, did they?" Street asked quietly.

"No, they didn't."

"Hey guys," Jon called out from across the large room, "its Sunny Slope on the computer!"

Street and Shift stood up. Shift placed the book mark back in the weathered book and set the book down. Then he followed Street over to the small group that was gathering around a computer. Shift pulled out a chair and sat. He tapped the screen to accept the message.

"We're here. This is John," Shift read from the touchscreen.

"Hey everybody," Shift typed. They were using a rudimentary computer-based texting system to communicate. It would be laborious and slow, but other communications were down presently. "Did Marcus tell you anything about that ship?"

"Yes, he did," John said. "Anta coerced him into spilling the beans."

"Is Anta there? Thanks Babe."

"Yes, she's here, and she says, 'you're welcome, you sexy thing.'"

"Yeah, I'm sure. So, what did Marcus say?"

"Hi Shift, this is Anta. Marcus is pretty weak. He couldn't resist my charm. It took about eight seconds before he started talking. All I had to do was show him a little skin."

"WHAT???" Shift typed into the keyboard.

"I'm just kidding babe. All I had to do was ask. I don't think he wants to get into more trouble than he's already in. Here's what he knows: The only ship he is aware of is one that was operated by a pilot that had been in contact with the Rio group. He doesn't think this pilot had ever actually been to the Rio bunker, but he probably knew where it was. He believes the man operated the ship himself, but at the direction of Jass. And here's the kicker. The man's name: Thomas Franconi."

"Are you kidding me? You mean Latisha Bodily's boyfriend from Connecticut? Is this a joke?" Shift typed.

"No, it's not," Anta replied. "Marcus says he doesn't know Franconi very well. They've only talked a couple of times, and never met in person. But he believes Franconi was a friend of Latisha Bodily. And Marcus wouldn't shut up once he started talking. He confirmed our theory as to Latisha's role in releasing AE in the bunker years ago."

"So is this Franconi guy alone up in that ship?" Shift asked.

"Marcus says Franconi is alone, and has been for at least a year. He says Franconi wanted to join the group at the Rio bunker, but Jass wouldn't let him. Jass thought it would look too fishy to have a stranger show up after it was believed the whole world was dead. Jass knew that if Franconi showed up in his ship, they wouldn't be able to hide the fact that they knew each other and that Jass was communicating with the outside world. Jass thought that would be dangerous. So, as far as Marcus knows, Franconi has just been flying around, recharging as necessary, wherever he is, and checking in with Jass as the need arises. He's been waiting, like the others down there in Rio, for the vaccine to arrive. Then, Franconi believed he would be allowed to join the group in that bunker."

"Did Marcus say anything about Franconi's attempt to kill us back at the hotel a few days ago?"

"Yes. Marcus swears he didn't know anything about that until a couple seconds before it happened. We checked the watch Marcus had been using to communicate with Jass. There was a message from Jass fourteen seconds before we saw the ship on the holo try to kill you. Marcus says he hadn't even seen it at that point because he was with all of us trying to speak with you. So, at least Marcus wasn't part of that plan, I think."

"That's good. Maybe Marcus is a good guy after all," Shift typed into the touchscreen keyboard.

"I don't know about that, but he didn't know that attack was coming," Anta typed in reply.

"So, what are we supposed to do about Franconi?" Shift asked.

"Marcus thinks he isn't a threat, especially now that his mentor and leader, Jass, is out of the picture."

"Well, we can't really rely on that speculation, especially from Marcus, can we?"

"No, I think not," Anta replied.

"Maybe we just wait and see what comes of him. Maybe we just let him go his way. Actually, Street just said we should shoot him down."

"Street might be right. We may feel sick about it afterward, but I don't know whether we can trust him to leave us alone. We saw what his ship can do. He tried to kill you guys, completely unprovoked."

"Why don't all of you discuss it, and we will too," Shift replied. "Let's talk again as soon as we can get the MEHDs or a holo working. I love you Anta!"

"I love you too!"

"John says he loves you too Shift!" Anta typed, adding a smiley emoticon.

28

"Hey, it's so good to actually *see* all of you again!" Shift said through the holo. Communications had come back online only moments earlier, and the two groups had all gathered around holos, on each end of the line, to see each other. The group in Idaho was anxious to see the faces of those who would be their new neighbors. The group in Rio was equally restless.

After introductions were made, John said, "So, Shift, guess what Marcus has been up to?"

"Do I want to know?"

"Yes, you do."

"Then spill it."

"We gave him a computer earlier today. He's spent the last few hours trying to contact Thomas Franconi."

"Why?" Shift asked.

"Well, after we disconnected the chat a couple of days ago, we met and discussed what to do with Franconi. Steve and Marilyn brought up an interesting thought. Apparently, they've had a few conversations lately on the subject."

"And what subject is that?" Shift asked, smiling at Steve and Marilyn who were sitting next to each other on the other end of the holo, holding hands.

"I'll let Steve explain," John replied.

"Shift, this may come as a surprise to you," Steve began, "but I actually have more time on my hands than I know what to do with. The pigs and chickens at my place practically take care of themselves, unlike yours. So I have a lot of time to think."

"I don't believe that for a second," Shift said, smiling. "I've been to your farm. Those pigs are nothing but trouble. But I know you've got a good head on your shoulders. So what have you and Marilyn come up with?"

"Well, we've talked, many times over the past year and a half, about how there was something strange in the way AE returned to Earth from the moon. We all know that someone onboard Gortari II must have been contaminated. Then, when the ship was shot down, AE spread throughout Central AM on the winds of the hurricane that Marcus and his crew dispersed. But what we wrestled with was, whose bright idea was it to allow, or direct, Marcus and his team to disperse the hurricane at nearly the same time as Gortari II was scheduled to travel through the region? People must have known the ship was coming and would pass through the dispersing hurricane.

"I've done some research and the hurricane wasn't that large. And its direction of travel didn't pose much of a threat to the region. Yet, the potential for disaster if the detonation inside the hurricane occurred too close in time to the passing of Gortari II was huge. So why was that hurricane dispersed at all? If it hadn't been, then when the Cubans shot down the ship, AE may have been locally isolated, and possibly containable."

Shift opened his mouth to speak, but Steve cut him off.

"I know what you're thinking, Shift. Would we have been able to contain AE in any event? The answer, as I see it, is probably not, unless foam was dispensed like they did over El-Alamein. But it still begs the question, why risk it? Why risk dispersion of the hurricane when it could destroy the ship and kill the people on board, whether AE was present or not?"

"Interesting question," Shift said. "Do you have the answer?"

"Marilyn thought we should talk to Marcus about it, since he is the one responsible for the dispersal of the hurricane. He had a few things to say about it."

"I'm sure he did," Street growled from the background.

"So," John said, taking over for Steve, "taking Marilyn's advice, Mike and I spent a bit of time with Marcus, and he did have some thoughts about the timing issue. Interestingly, what none of us knew, until now, is that our little friend Marcus was the Director of North AM for a short while—just a couple months—until he got sacked for not doing what Secretary General Davis wanted him to do."

"Wow, that's quite amazing," Shift said. "I never would have guessed that."

"Me either. But as a result, in those days, he received his official orders in regard to the handling of storms from the Meteorological arm of the IWO. Marcus said that, on January 27, 2093, the day of the ship's destruction, he expressed his concern over the timing of the WDD detonation with his contact at the IWO. And here's the interesting part: Marcus didn't know the name of his contact. He only knew that the contact was in *Rio de Janeiro*."

Several people on both ends of the holo immediately began talking and mumbling. The commotion grew until nobody was even listening to the others anymore. Finally, Steve and John were able to get those in Idaho under control. The people in Rio, however, were getting angrier by the second. Shouts of "Jass", and "that murderer" and other similar exclamations, in English, Portuguese and German, were coming through the holo clearly.

"Shift, listen," John said loudly. "There's more."

At those words, the noise in the cave in Rio began to fade. But the anger was on the surface. The faces of the ten people in the cave, particularly those of the seven people who had lived and worked with Director Jass, revealed expressions of extreme, even violent anger. They needed to hear more, but were finding it difficult to control their fury.

"You guys under control over there?" John asked, smiling.

A few moments later, Shift replied, "Yes, go on John."

"Okay, so, in those days, Marcus didn't know who his contact was. He later learned that is was Jass, as y'all figured out on your own a few seconds ago. But Jass never explained anything. Immediately after Gortari II was shot down, Marcus asked his contact, Jass, what had happened, and Jass said it was an accident. Jass said nothing more. And, by the way, we have confirmed that timetable through the data logs on Marcus' watch."

"In other words," Mike interjected, "we believe Marcus is at least somewhat blameless in all of this. He was certainly part of the group that Jass commanded, or controlled or whatever, but he appears to have been a pawn. I really don't think he had any bad intentions. He was doing his job at the start. And then, as time went on, according to Marcus, he believed he was helping Jass and the survivors in Brazil by feeding them information about us and the vaccine."

"Then why did he keep it all a secret?" Jon Porter asked. "If he knew there were survivors in addition to us, why didn't he tell us?"

"That's the sticky part," John replied. "While Marcus was a pawn, he also continued to follow orders, even when he should have known better. As Anta said a couple of days ago, Marcus is weak. It seems he was not able to break ties with Jass, even when he became our friend. Jass still controlled him. For that, Marcus needs to be punished. But I firmly believe, as Mike does, that he intended no harm to come to us. Remember, he didn't have prior knowledge about the destruction of Gortari II *or* the attack on you guys a few days ago."

"Okay," Shift said. "You've convinced me that he isn't a real bad guy. But I'm still pretty pissed off. Is there more to the story? Why did you give Marcus a computer?"

"Yes, there's more," John replied. "Marcus told us what he knew about Gortari II, and it seems to confirm Steve and Marilyn's theory that the destruction of the ship was not just an accident. And we now know that Jass had made the decision to have the storm dispersed at that time, despite knowing the risks. What we didn't know, was whether Cuba's decision to shoot down the ship, at that precise moment, was also orchestrated."

"I'm sure it was," Street mumbled.

"You're right, Street," John said. "It was. But Marcus says he didn't know anything about that, either at the time it happened, or later. That's why we gave Marcus a computer. Mike, Lin and Marcus have just spent several hours on the net, looking for anything that would give them any idea about whether Cuba had a purposeful role in the release of AE—whether it was just an accident, as Jass had told Marcus, or whether Jass had something to do with it. Several hours after they began, Mike came across a hidden folder located on the servers of your cave down there in Rio."

"*Our* servers?" Frans asked, clearly confused. "I've had access to those servers the whole time, and I've never come across a hidden folder."

"Neither have I," Nic added. "But I guess that's what 'hidden' means."

"No, you wouldn't have seen it," Mike said. "It was well-hidden. I've hacked into a lot of servers over the years, but this one was tough. It had all of the standard IWO locks, plus many more that I'd never run across. We knew we were on to something the minute I got through the IWO lock and was faced with a *personal* passcode."

"Adal lied about that too, I guess," Nic said. "We all believed he was computer illiterate."

"So did you get in?" Shift asked.

"Yeah, we got in," Mike replied, smiling. "It's one of my greatest accomplishments."

"Sheesh Mike," John said. "You're so boastful, you arrogant son of a . . ." Mike and John both laughed, along with several others in Idaho. "Why don't you just tell them what you learned instead of gloating?"

"Fine. Anyway," Mike continued, "we got in. And the stuff in there is quite revealing."

"And revolting," Anta added from the background.

Several people nodded in agreement.

"The first thing we wanted to know was how Cuba was involved in Jass' plan to take over the world, if at all. And at least one person in Cuba *was* involved. We don't have any names, and the person is probably dead now, but someone in Cuba was in contact with Jass in the hours leading up to Gortari II's destruction. We found several communications between Jass and Cuba's Department of Defense. And, IWO logs show that Jass was instrumental in convincing the IWO to let Mexico return from the moon. Then, once it was confirmed that the Mexicans were coming home, Jass and his contact in Cuba orchestrated the launching of the missile to coincide with the dispersion of the hurricane."

"But there's something missing there," Shift said. "Did Jass know AE was on Gortari II? If so, that's pretty reckless considering there was no vaccine yet."

"But there's a deeper question," Anta began thoughtfully. "Why would Jass pressure the IWO to let Mexico come home, and then help Cuba shoot down the ship? That doesn't make sense."

"Keen observations; and I'll address each of them," Mike replied. "It doesn't appear that Jass knew AE was on the ship. With the files in front of us, and Marcus by my side, we were able to discern a few more things. Have any of you ever heard the name Alan Stein?"

Jonas and Hasani looked at each other. A moment later, Anta noticed them. "What do you two know?" she asked.

Jonas gave Hasani a slight nod.

"Yeah, we know Alan," Hasani said. "He was on the moon with us. Well, not *with us* exactly. We told you guys about him. He's the guy who fixed the communication problem we were having on the moon. We'd lost contact with Earth and the other shells. He fixed that problem. But before we could get to him, he was sucked out into space when the German Shell burst open."

"I remember the story, but not the name," Anta said.

"Well, that's him. How many 'Alan Stein's' could have been on the moon at that time?" Jonas asked.

"Well, in any event," Mike continued, "Stein was stationed in the Mexican shell and was scheduled to come back to Earth on the next ship. But then all ships were grounded and Stein was stuck on the moon with everyone else. What he did after that, I don't know, but it appears he also had contact with Rio in the days leading up to the destruction of Gortari II."

"What kind of contact?" Shift asked.

"Well, the hidden logs on the server there in Rio identify several coms between lines registered to Stein and Jass. In those communications, Stein and Jass discuss, in rather nasty terms, a potential takeover of the IWO."

Mike paused to let that sink in. Rather than the uproar he expected, most people sat silently, pondering, and waiting for the next piece of information. After everything they'd learned over the past few days, nobody seemed surprised that Jass was attempting a takeover.

When nobody spoke for several seconds, Mike continued. "So, one series of communications is interesting. Stein threatened Jass that he would reveal Jass' secrets, whatever those were. The threat appeared to be based on a dispute over the roles they would each play in the forthcoming—if Jass got his way—newly-formed IWO. And the last communication between the two was only a couple hours before Gortari II left for Earth. In it, Jass told Stein that he would regret his threat and would not live long enough to assume any role in the new government."

"So, Stein's life was threatened by Jass," Hasani said. "That must be what Stein was talking about when he told us his people abandoned him. Remember him saying that, Jonas?"

"Yeah," Jonas replied. "Let me piece this together. Stein was in the German shell when he contacted us, not the Mexican shell. That means that he never planned to leave the moon on Gortari II. Mike, did you check the IIA servers to see when Stein logged out of the Mexican shell and entered the German shell? Remember, there was a system-wide shut-down of the tubes at the time."

"Yes, I checked. Stein didn't leave the Mexican colony until after Gortari II had already left for Earth. It was many days later actually. And that makes sense, right? You guys had travel restrictions up there, as you said. But those restrictions weren't just rules; they were actual electronic blockages that shut down the tubes, right? Stein couldn't have gone anywhere until he figured out a way to get through those restrictions."

"He was a computer guy," Jonas said. "He called himself a hacker."

"So he must have figured out a way to bypass the travel restrictions after everyone else, as far as he knew, had left the moon," Hasani added. "That's how he got from the Mexican shell to the German shell where he was finally able to restore communications on the moon, just before we heard him."

"But if he left the Mexican shell, he would have been contaminated, right?" Anta asked. "Why would he do that?"

"Well, if he was as smart as your older brother—me, that is—he would have had a suit and oxygen tanks," Hasani replied, smiling. "But I'm sure the reason he went to the German shell was because the German shell had the master communications equipment. Isn't that right Jonas?"

Jonas nodded.

"So," Hasani continued, "Stein needed to get over there to get coms operating again, which he did. Then he got a hold of us."

"Maybe he didn't want to live," Jonas added. "When he left the Mexican shell, he thought he was alone. When Hasani and I went to get him from the German shell, it had bust open. We never figured out how that happened. Maybe he was trying to kill himself. But I guess it doesn't really matter now, does it?"

"But why didn't he go home on the Mexican ship with the others?" Jon Porter asked. "If he thought he would be left all alone on the moon, why would he stay?"

"The answer is possibly very simple," Mike replied. "His life had been threatened. He had been in contact with Jass and helped orchestrate the IWO's authority for the Mexicans to return to Earth. If Stein knew Jass like *we* are beginning to know Jass, he probably worried that he would be assassinated once he returned. If Stein was truly concerned for his life, he may have thought it better to just stay on the moon, even though he would be alone until his last days."

"So," Shift began, "if I'm getting all of this, you guys are saying that Jass and Stein wanted to take over the world. But they got in a fight and Jass said he would kill Stein. So Stein stayed on the moon, only to die, or kill himself later anyway. But on Earth, Jass assumed Stein would want to come home, to help him rule the Earth, so he orchestrated both the return and the shooting down of Gortari II by the Cubans to eliminate Stein. But why would Jass do it that way? Why didn't he just wait to have Stein land on Earth and then have him killed? That would have been simpler and plenty easy given Jass' apparent connections; and, it wouldn't have killed the thousands of people on the ship."

"I wondered the same thing, and that's where Marcus comes back in," John replied. "While Mike was piecing this story together, Marcus was attempting to contact Franconi. They finally spoke a few hours ago. I was in the room with them, listening, but Franconi didn't know I was there. Franconi thought they were speaking as cohorts in a plan gone wrong. Franconi said he had been trying to get a hold of Jass and asked Marcus if he had heard anything. To his credit, Marcus played dumb and they came to the mutual conclusion that Jass was either dead, somehow, or had abandoned them. Franconi said he had been searching for signs of life from his ship over the past few days."

"We can confirm that," Nic said.

"So, Marcus suggested that he and Franconi may be all that's left of the group. Franconi knew that Marcus was with us in Idaho, but didn't know that we had caught him. So, the two of them hatched a plan to meet in Mexico City in seven days, and discussed specific coordinates. Marcus told Franconi that he thought we were on to him, and he had to leave Idaho. It was Marcus who suggested seven days. He explained to me afterward that he thought it would take less than seven days for you guys down there to get to Mexico City for an ambush."

"So is Marcus really helping us out now?" Shift asked. "I mean, is he still playing us, or is this real?"

"I think he understands the precarious situation he's in," John replied. "Either he's with us or against us. If he's against us, his only ally is Franconi. Everyone else is dead. So, even if he still is an enemy, in any way, I think he really is trying to help us now. It's in his interest to cooperate with us, and he seems to do whatever is in his own best interest, right?"

"Okay, so we don't really trust his motives, but we trust his attempt to help," Shift said. "Go on."

"So, after Marcus and Franconi finalized their plans to rendezvous, Marcus asked him a lot of questions about Jass' plan, saying he had been left in the dark about much of it since he was stuck in a cabin in Alaska. Marcus did a great job playing the fool, or maybe he really is a fool. I don't know which.

"Franconi said that Jass had, through some stroke of genius or luck, come in contact with some woman in Germany. That woman had found photographs of ancient Nazi documents, digitally preserved on an old computer in the basement of a library in East Berlin. Those photographs were sent to Jass at some point in mid-2092, before AE was released from the cave in Egypt. Mike found the photographs on the hidden Rio servers. The documents pictured in the photos contain the elements and methods—basically, the recipe—for creating a vaccine against AE. And the formula is *nearly* identical to the one Yurgi finally created."

"You're kidding, right?" Street asked, loud enough to be heard over the commotion caused by John's revelation.

"No, I'm not Street," John replied a few moments later, after everyone had settled down a bit. "But remember, the documents just contained the formulas. And they weren't quite the same as Yurgi's, so we don't even know whether a vaccine based upon those formulas would have worked. We couldn't see any indication that a vaccine was ever created until Yurgi did it back in Boston."

"Actually, this makes some sense," Nic said. "We had created what we believed would be a vaccine early on, maybe March of 2093, based upon research that Jass' second-in-command was spearheading. We believed we were very close, but we could not finalize it. That attempted vaccine was probably based on the formula Jass procured from Germany."

"Interesting," John replied.

"So, tell me if I've got this right," Shift said. "The Nazis had a vaccine, or at least believed they had a way to create a vaccine, at the time that poor guy Anta and I found in the cave died, way back in the 1940's. They believed they could wipe out their enemies with little loss of life in their own ranks, if everything worked correctly, because they had a vaccine. I'm sure any actual vaccine was lost when the regime fell. But the formula, or something close to it, lived on in written documents. Then, the man in the cave died from AE.

"AE wasn't released to the world until 150 years later; but before AE ever left the cave, Jass had procured what he believed to be the formula to create a vaccine to Anthrax E. Why? Why did he need it, or seek it out before anyone ever knew the disease would be released to the world? I'm so confused."

"Me too," Anta said, a look of thoughtful concentration on her face.

Most of the people on both sides of the holo sat quietly, likely pondering what this all meant.

Finally, John spoke again. "Ladies and gentlemen, Franconi said something else, which may give us the answer to Shift's questions. He said that Jass had traveled to El-Alamein several times during the three or four years prior to December 2092. He also had extensive contact with one of the Bedouin tribes in the Qattara Depression a few weeks before AE got out. Franconi said Jass was searching for something, but he didn't know what. But Jass finally found what he was looking for in January 2093. Franconi didn't know much else, except that Jass' contact in the Qattara Depression was angry over the loss of the lives of two of his tribesmen, who looked like they had been, quote, 'eaten alive in the desert.'"

"This can't be," Shift said quietly.

"Shift," Anta said, "Jass must have known AE was out there in the desert. He had people searching for the vial. Those two dead men, the men from Riyad Shafik's photographs, were looking for the vial."

"And they found it," Shift added quietly.

"And Jass knew all along what it was that he was searching for," Anta said. "He planned to use it to destroy human kind. He already had the vaccine, or at least he believed he had the method for creating it."

"And he assembled a hand-picked team in Rio to create it," Nic said, interrupting. "But we weren't able to. The formula we tried first wasn't quite right, and now we know why; and by the time your Dr. Shevchuk created the actual vaccine, we couldn't leave the bunker to procure one of the elements we needed without significant risk of infection ourselves. That's why he had Marcus and Latisha keeping tabs on you, and why he tried to have Franconi kill you when you arrived. He only wanted the vaccine, not witnesses to his madness."

"And," John added, "to answer Shift's question moments ago: Jass didn't care about the lives of the people on Gortari II. They were expendable. It was more important that Stein die, and if it was done this way, there would be less people to implicate him in a potential assassination later, because there wouldn't be an assassination. The whole world would blame the Cubans."

"So the story comes full circle, finally," Marilyn said, after a few moments of near-complete silence on both sides of the holo.

"What's amazing is that Adal Jass had nothing to do with the re-surfacing of AE in the desert," Shift said. "The wind storms opened that cave. Jass never would have found it without the random storms. But because the storms occurred, AE probably would have escaped without Jass' involvement, at some point, either by curious people finding and entering the caves, like we did, or by the wind. And blasting Gortari II from the sky didn't cause the resulting loss of life here either. The disease was on its way back to Earth anyway. But perhaps the destruction of the ship, during the dispersion of the hurricane sped up the process."

"I guess the only thing we can really blame on Jass, apart from his evil mind, was his help in facilitating Gortari II's return to Earth," Jonas said. "If the ship had never left the moon, AE would never have returned to Earth. But then Hasani and I would be sitting up there, with Tom and Misty and Jerad, alone and scared that we would always be alone. I guess it's pretty selfish of me to think this way, but I'm glad I'm here, not there."

"That's not selfish Jonas," Shift said, looking his friend in the eyes through the holo. "We're all glad you're here. You saved lives up there. And you had nothing to do with the evil that Jass and the Nazis unleashed on the Earth and the moon. The five of you saved our lives too. Tom and Misty and Jerad, they're heroes, just like you and Hasani."

Many people nodded their heads in agreement. Several people patted Jonas and Hasani on the backs. Neirioui slipped her hand into Hasani's and laid her head on his shoulder. Anta gave Hasani a hug as tears fell from her eyes.

As the group began to fully realize the impact that they each had on the others' lives, and the reality of the storm that had befallen them, many wept openly. The details and accounts they had just heard gave some measure of closure to a terrible chapter in the human story.

Finally, Shift lifted his head and said, "Ladies and gentlemen, some of us have a date to keep with Mr. Franconi. We need to go. We'll keep in touch. We need to leave tomorrow morning to make it in time. I love you all and I'm proud to be among you. God bless."

As others said their goodbyes, Shift walked away from the holo, laid on his bed, and wept. He finally knew, after two and a half long years, what had happened to his world. And why.

29

"Good afternoon Mr. Franconi," IWO Secretary General Antonio Davis said, the venom carefully hidden beneath his cool exterior. "I didn't think we'd hear from you again after you abandoned us." SEC-GEN Davis couldn't believe his luck. While he hated even the idea of speaking with Franconi again, without him, they could not have reestablished a link with the outside world early that morning. They had been alone in Antarctica, at Victory Base, for over two years; and the Cuban, Miguel González, had made much of it unbearable.

Earlier that morning, out of the blue, a line started beeping in the ops center. Thomas Franconi, from his ship, had established a link with Victory Base. SEC-GEN Davis' clerk, Bria Newton, had arranged for a conference to occur later that afternoon.

"Thank you for answering my com, Mr. SEC-GEN," Thomas Franconi replied as small beads of sweat began to form on his brow.

"I guess I should thank *you* for reestablishing contact with us this morning, but that is hard for me to do under the circumstances."

"Sir, I'm so sorry. I made a mistake. Director Jass led me to believe that you had bad plans for me. He told me that you were going to use me and my services, and then kill me. I believed him. I was wrong. He fooled me. He fooled all of us. And now I think he's dead."

"No, Franconi," SEC-GEN Davis replied thoughtfully, "he only fooled *you*. It appears you followed him to his death—if he *is* dead—

and now you have nothing to show for your betrayal. Now, you crawl back here to plead for mercy?"

"Please Antonio, have mercy," Franconi said, the desperation clear in his voice.

In the background, Miguel González growled, "Put the call through the speaker, Davis. Now."

Before speaking again, the SEC-GEN pressed a button on the console in front of him, relaying the call from Franconi throughout the ops center. Prior to the com, Miguel and the SEC-GEN had discussed what needed to be said.

"Franconi, you have lost the right to address me by my first name," the SEC-GEN said, "but I believe I may show you mercy . . . if you will help me."

"I'll do anything you ask Mr. SEC-GEN. Name it."

"I want you to land your ship and help us off this frozen rock."

"Sir, I don't think that's a good idea. Jass had me kill the only people who might have been able to save us, four days ago. They had a vaccine. And now they're dead. And the rest of their group is going to know it was me. They won't likely be in the mood to help me, or any of us now."

"Why would you do that?" The fear in the SEC-GEN's voice was palpable. But a moment later, he continued, calmly, "Wait, you said 'the rest of their group'. Who else is out there? And do they still have a vaccine?"

"There is a group of survivors, sir. They are in Idaho, in the United States. I have a contact there who says they still have the vaccine. Its former North AM Director Marcus Dorian. But he has fallen out with them as well and plans to meet me in Mexico City in two days. He didn't seem to believe that the rest of his group would want to help us."

"Dorian?" the SEC-GEN asked. "You sure that's who you spoke with? I was sure that guy was dead. He abandoned his post a couple years ago. He couldn't do the job and took off."

"Yes sir, it was Dorian. Jass was directing *his* work too."

"Franconi," a new voice said, "My name is Miguel González. I am here with the SEC-GEN. We need your help. You will come here and pick us up. We will worry about everything else."

"Mr. SEC-GEN, who was that?" Thomas asked.

"He is a . . . friend," SEC-GEN Davis replied. "And he is right. Come here now. We will prepare for your landing. Wait for coordinates to be sent to you from my staff."

"I can do that," Franconi replied. "But I'm scheduled to meet with Dorian. What should I do about him?"

"You shouldn't meet Mr. Dorian."

"Why?"

"You said Dorian is no longer with the group in Idaho. If that is true, then they don't trust Dorian any more. We can't team up with someone who will guarantee our failure. Our only hope is to convince the folks in Idaho to help us. Dorian cannot help us there. Do you have coordinates for their location in Idaho?"

"No. But I can trace Dorian's call and get them easy enough. I'll have those before I get to Antarctica."

"Excellent. We will see you soon."

JULY 14, 2095, LATER—HOLO CONFERENCE

"I can't live with the guilt Dorian," Thomas Franconi said, lowering his eyes.

"What do you mean?" Marcus Dorian asked. Behind him, out of range of the holo screen, Dr. Jonas Sampson listened intently. All coms between Marcus and Franconi were monitored now that the group living in Sunny Slope, Idaho knew that Marcus was traitorous. Now, however, Marcus appeared to want to make things right. He had arranged for his friends in Rio—Shift, Street, Jon, and their new friends from the Rio bunker—to meet Franconi in two days. Those men would apprehend, or if necessary, take more drastic measures to put an end to Thomas Franconi's madness.

"I mean, it's only you and me now. That's not good enough. I can't live in a world with no friends, knowing what I've done. I'll probably see you in hell."

"Wait, don't ..." Marcus cut his next sentence short as they watched Franconi lift a gun to his own head. Then the screen he and Jonas were watching wobbled, tilted, and went black.

"Did he just kill himself?" Marcus asked, turning to face Jonas.

"That's what it looked like," Jonas replied, a bit stunned by the events.

"What do we do now?" Marcus asked.

"We call off the dogs. I guess they don't need to meet Franconi anymore."

JULY 14, 2095, LATER—HOLO CONFERENCE

"You guys don't need to meet Franconi anymore," Anta said. "He's dead."

"What do you mean?" Shift asked. "What happened?"

"He contacted Marcus a few minutes ago, by holo. Franconi said he couldn't live in a world with no friends, knowing what he had been involved in. Before Marcus could ask Franconi what he was going to do, Franconi put a gun to his head. Then the ship began to shake. Then the holo went black. Marcus and Jonas believe Franconi killed himself and crashed his ship."

"Wow. I don't know what else to say."

"How about you say when you'll be home so I can stop worrying about you?"

"Anta, I'm so sorry I've been gone this long. We'll be home soon. One of the women here, Lilly, is a pilot. She's finally found an old airplane. We were going to Mexico City, but now we'll just come home. We'll be in Sunny Slope before you know it."

30

Sena and Dilan Tabak huddled in the corner of the large bay as the wide metal doors opened at the rear of the A-400. Thomas had told the girls that people were going to join them, but didn't give them any details. He only told them that they should stay hidden.

Moments later, six figures in some kind of biohazard suits cautiously walked in. The one in back carried a gun, and his eyes twitched as he quickly surveyed the scene. Sena could see their mouths moving, as though they were talking, but she couldn't hear anything that was being said.

Soon, a short woman walked forward to the front of the cargo bay and stepped into the small, circular cylinder separating the front and the rear of the ship. As she stepped in, the doors through which she had walked closed behind her. The tube circled rapidly around her several times. Then the opposite side of the cylinder opened and she walked out, the tube closing again behind her.

Through the glass wall, which had separated Sena and Dilan from Thomas Franconi for nearly two years, the sisters watched as the petite woman removed her suit and dropped it into a chute on the left side wall, where it vanished from sight. Then she stepped to the side and waited as the process was repeated five more times.

After the last of the newcomers had removed their suits, and the tube shut for the final time, Dilan and Sena stepped out from their hiding place and approached the glass wall. Thomas Franconi had not told the others about the girls. But Sena knew that both they and the newcomers were safe from each other. None of these new people had been vaccinated. They wouldn't come back into the rear of the ship with the girls until they had received an injection, if they ever did.

When the people on the other side of the glass noticed the girls, there was confusion. Thomas had not turned on the intercom system, so Sena and Dilan couldn't hear what the others were saying. But their pointing and animated gesticulations told Sena that the newcomers were both afraid and angry.

Sena and Dilan watched as Thomas appeared on the other side of the glass. He spoke, and the group all turned as one back toward the girls. Sena involuntarily stepped backward from the menacing glares. Moments later, the glares turned to stares and the faces finally relaxed. Then, they all turned and walked away toward the front of the ship, leaving Sena and Dilan alone again.

"I was worried about that," Thomas said through the intercom. He had come back to the glass wall after nearly half an hour. "I didn't tell them you were here for your own safety. They had to come through the cargo bay toward me, and I didn't really trust them. I still don't."

"What are they doing now?" Sena asked quietly.

"They are familiarizing themselves with the ship up here. We plan to leave soon. We're going to Idaho, as we discussed before. Hopefully, we'll be able to meet a small group of survivors that have a vaccine. I think it's the people you told me about—the ones who you spoke to before I picked you up."

"That man, Shift, was very nice," Dilan said. "If it's the same people, I'm sure they'll be happy to see us."

"I hope so. We will be taking off in a little while." Thomas Franconi had not told the girls everything. They knew about his firing of the ship's lasers twelve days earlier. Thomas had passed it off as a test run. He told them he fired at a building to see how powerful the laser was and how much protection it could provide, in case he ever had to use it. He had not told the girls about the people inside. Now, he let them have hope that they would be able to land and stay on solid ground for good. Thomas knew, however, that the people in Idaho were unlikely to give them a warm welcome. The girls would find out soon enough.

An hour later, the girls felt the ship start to vibrate and heard the familiar, quiet hum of the engines as the A-400 lifted off the ground. They were on their way. It wouldn't be long.

JULY 15, 2095
RIO DE JANEIRO, BRAZIL

"Is everything ready?" Shift asked. Lilly, sitting next to him in the cockpit of the small airplane, turned her head to look at Shift.

"Yes. Ten seconds to lift off. Will you tell everyone back there to make sure they're strapped in?"

Shift sat forward, then turned his head back over his shoulder so he could see the eight other people in the rear of the plane. "Buckle up everyone. We're out of here in a few seconds."

Lilly pushed the throttle forward. The plane was old, and still ran on fuel, but she had figured out how to refuel and pilot the craft. As she moved the plane out onto the runway at the Carlos Jobim International Airport, past large ships and smaller jets that had been sitting idle for more than two years, a tear formed in the corner of her eye. Shift watched her wipe it away with the back of her hand before pushing the throttle all the way forward. He knew what she felt. He'd had those same feelings when he, Anta, Angel and Street had left the Boston bunker. He felt it again when they left the bunker in Cabo Rojo and when they returned from the moon. A home was a comfort that he had taken for granted before the madness of AE tore everything apart. But people were resilient. Lilly would be okay.

The airport sat on the western edge of a small island in Guanabara Bay. While the exterior of the buildings on the grounds appeared well-preserved, the tarmac at the large airport was rutted and cracked. Roots from Guapeba trees and other plants had spread across and under the tarmac in several places, causing upheavals in the once-flat airstrip. Prior to their flight, the small group had walked the runway and cleared the plants and roots that crossed the path their plane would take, but it was still precarious. They had marveled at the damage which had occurred in just two and a half years of disuse.

The small plane lurched once, twice, and then began a swift acceleration. It bumped over cracks and gouges in the concrete runway, but finally left the ground. Shift exhaled, releasing the breath which he had involuntarily been holding.

"Whoa," Shift groaned from the co-pilot seat as the plane began a steep ascent from the hot tarmac. He wasn't serving any function sitting in front with Lilly, but the plane only held ten people, including a pilot and co-pilot. He had eagerly volunteered to sit up front with Lilly, just to have a better view. Now, as the ground began to drop away, his stomach tightened and he had to close his eyes. He had never flown in a plane this small.

"I'm going to keep it low so I can follow landmarks," Lilly said. "Probably only 400 or 500 meters off the ground. I don't know any other way to get us to Idaho."

"That's fine with me," Shift replied, holding his stomach.

Several minutes later, Shift's stomach settled down and he pulled out his MEHD. "Any of you guys care if I play some tunes?" He looked around behind him at the shaking heads, then pressed the screen a few times to load a playlist. Remotely connecting his MEHD to the flight deck of the small plane, he selected a song, turned it up loud, and waited for a reaction.

The music started slowly and quietly at first, then began a slow crescendo. When the words started, Shift looked around at this friends. It was unlikely any of them had ever heard this song. When the chorus started, Shift belted out along with the music, pumping his head up and down in rhythm. The others stared at him at first, as though he were a foreign being, but slowly joined him as the melody caught hold.

"Dude, what is that?' Jon called out, bobbing his head up and down in time with the fast beat.

"It's called 'Sing' from a band named 'My Chemical Romance,'" Shift replied.

"Sing about everyone you left behind. I love it!" Jon said loudly.

"Yeah! Seems appropriate, doesn't it? Right now, we're singing for the world man. We're singing for all of those who we left behind and all those who died. We owe it to all of them to sing!"

"Great song!" Jon said. "How old is it?"

"It's ancient," Shift said. "Eighty-five years old probably."

"Ahhh, same age as you," Street bellowed to be heard over the noise.

"Just about," Shift replied, laughing.

Less than two minutes later, as the song began to wind down, Street yelled up from the back. "Do you guys hear that noise? Is that the plane?"

Shift turned the music off as people strained to hear what Street had heard. Lilly checked her gauges. Based upon her reaction, or lack thereof, Shift assumed that everything looked fine there. Several people looked out the windows. The sound seemed to be coming from outside the plane. The cheerful emotion they'd each felt as they sang along to Shift's music began to fade, replaced by concern.

"Oh crap," Jon said moments later. "Is that Franconi's ship?"

"Whoa!" Nic called out, looking in the direction Jon was pointing. "He's headed straight for us."

"Evasive maneuvers Lilly," Shift said. "If that's even possible in this thing."

"I'll try to . . ."

Lilly's words were cut off as a loud, violent explosion rocked the left rear of the plane. The plane dropped instantly, nose down, toward the ground. It began to spin as the left wing separated from the main body of the ship.

"Hold on to something!" Lilly yelled as she attempted to level out before impact with the ground.

Within moments, the ship crashed through the dense upper canopy of the Tinguá Biological Reserve north of Rio de Janeiro. As it broke through sinewy vines stretching between Murumuru palms and other large trees, pieces of the plane severed off, leaving a trail of debris 350 meters into the undergrowth. Fire engulfed the rear of the small plane as it finally came to rest in a small clearing.

A loud explosion brought Shift to consciousness. He had no idea how long they'd been on the ground, but he could hear fire crackling nearby and smoke filled the cabin. Lilly sat next to him, still buckled into the pilot seat. A thick branch had smashed through the front window and impaled her chest. Blood pooled on her lap and ran down her legs and onto the floor of the plane. She wasn't breathing.

Then the pain began—a pain so intense it threatened to immobilize Shift. But from somewhere deep inside, a voice told him he had to move. He reached down to his left leg, which had been crushed days earlier in the hotel the first time Franconi shot at them. He could feel the bone in his calf pressing against his skin, but it hadn't pierced through.

He had to get out of the plane.

Behind Shift, in the cabin, someone was groaning, but he couldn't tell who. He didn't recognize the voice and he couldn't see anyone through the blinding smoke. His eyes stung as he tried to see the condition of the cabin behind him.

"We need to get out of here," Shift croaked, the smoke burning his lungs. He hoped his voice was loud enough for everyone behind him to hear. But nobody responded.

Shift released his seat harness and tried the door. It opened. He leaned out and fell to the ground. It was soft and spongy, layered with fallen leaves, moss and probably thousands of bugs. His leg was definitely broken, but he was alive. He needed to help the others, but he could barely move. He crawled back toward the rear door, searing pain shooting through his leg and into his hip, as it dragged behind him. He reached the back door and attempted to stand. He couldn't reach the handle from the ground, so he pushed against the underside of the plane and slowly moved his good leg under him. Just as he reached for the door, it opened. Nic appeared, standing upright.

"Are you okay?" Shift asked.

"Yes, I'm fine, but others back here are not. Help me get them out, quickly."

"I'll try," Shift replied. "But my leg is broken. I can't walk." A gut-wrenching cough erupted from his mouth as his smoke-filled lungs tried desperately to keep him alive. He dropped to the ground as his body convulsed in a smoke-induced spasm.

"I'm here," Street said, carefully stepping to the ground holding Jon in his arms. He laid Jon on the ground a few meters away and then climbed back into the cabin.

Within minutes, Street and Nic had removed everyone from the rear cabin. Through the smoke that billowed from the cabin, Shift thought he could see some of them moving. Only Lilly remained in the plane, still strapped into the front seat.

"She's dead," Shift said, as Street moved toward the front of the plane.

"I'm still getting her out."

"Okay." Shift tried to stand to help, but his leg wouldn't support his weight and he lowered himself back to the ground.

As Street moved around the front of the plane, a deafening, concussive blast threw him from his feet. Shrapnel shot through the air alongside Street's body, suddenly limp as a rag doll. Fire surged in great torrents from the front of the plane as Street was propelled into a nearby tree. He fell to the ground in a heap, fifteen meters from the plane.

Shift and Nic both tried to move toward Street—Shift on his hands and knees—but the flames now separating Street from the others hindered their progress. Shift fell to his face in pain. The leg was only part of the problem now. His skin felt like it was on fire, pierced by dozens of metal shards shot from the plane in the explosion. His friends were spread all around him on the ground, bleeding, moaning, coughing. *How many are alive?* He wondered. Some stirred, others did not.

"We're in trouble," Nic said quietly, crawling over to Shift. "You need to warn your people."

Nic helped Shift sit up. He pulled his MEHD out of his pocket. It still worked, and communications were up. He pressed an image of Anta on the front screen. As it dialed, his head began to swim. He wasn't going to make it. He didn't feel like he was dying, but he couldn't breathe.

"Hi Shift!" Anta said. "Where are you?"

"Anta, listen. Franconi isn't dead. He's . . . coming . . . hide."

Shift fell back to the ground, his forehead impacting the soft leaves of the dense jungle floor.

31

"Shift!" Anta screamed into the MEHD. "SHIFT!"

"What's going on?" John asked, his nerves causing his voice to crack as he ran to Anta from across the room.

"That was Shift," Anta began, her voice lowering to only a whisper as she tried to stifle her emotions. "Something must have happened. He sounded hurt. I think they're in trouble."

John and Anta were at the City Offices in Marsing, going through some information they had downloaded from the internet many months earlier. The electric delivery system from the hydroelectric dam upstream on the Snake River was acting up and the power had been going in and out at some of the homes where lines from the wind turbines had not yet been connected.

Mike, Hasani, Jonas and Lin Zheng had spent the last few hours at the dam, trying to figure out what was wrong.

John and Anta had returned to Marsing to see if they could find any information to help. They had arrived at the City Offices only moments before Shift's call.

"What did he say Anta?" John asked. He pulled Anta into a hug and wrapped his arms around her tightly.

"He said Franconi is still alive and that he's coming. He said to hide."

"What?"

"Hide."

"Why would we need to ... oh crap. Anta, Franconi's coming after us, isn't he?"

"I think we're in trouble John. What should we do?"

"I don't know, but let's start by getting everyone back from the dam."

John placed a call to Jonas and explained the situation while Anta summoned everyone else. Thirty-five minutes later, fourteen members of the group had gathered in the City Offices. Marcus Dorian was also in the building, but in a separate room under lock and key. Most didn't know why they were there. After John and Anta had finished speaking, the room was silent. The silence stretched on for minutes.

"Are they okay?" Suvan asked, very quietly.

"I don't know," Anta answered. "Something bad happened, and it has to do with Thomas Franconi. But I don't know how bad it is."

"Okay people, it's time to move," Hasani said. He had been holding his three-month-old daughter, Sami, but handed the young girl over to his wife Neirioui before walking forward and standing next to Anta and John. "We need a plan. If we can lure Franconi into a hand-to-hand fight—get him out of his ship—then we can't lose. He's alone in that thing, right?"

"That's what he told Marcus," John replied.

"Then let's set the trap. We'll be ready for him when he comes."

JULY 15, 2095
IN THE AIR OVER BRAZIL

"Antonio, we didn't need to do that." Thomas Franconi was nearly in tears as he watched the small plane crash into the trees north of Rio.

"We didn't have a choice Thomas," SEC-GEN Antonio Davis replied. "You know that was Jass. Who else could it have been? If Jass beat us to Idaho, there's no way they would ever let us land peacefully. We had no other choice. Plus, he abandoned you, remember? He left you out in the world to die. Don't forget that."

"But what if it wasn't Jass? Dorian thought Jass was already dead."

"It was him!" the SEC-GEN replied. "You said it yourself—Jass controlled Dorian. Dorian would do whatever Jass wanted him to do, even lie to you."

"Stop squabbling over such a simple matter," Miguel said from behind the SEC-GEN. "With this Jass out of the way, we have a better chance of securing the vaccine and getting me home to Cuba."

Thomas sat in his chair at the helm of the beautiful ship that had been his home for over two years. A tear formed in his eye and he wiped it away before it dropped down his cheek. He had not been this man before. He had wanted to reform the government peacefully through ConControl, starting in Connecticut, with Latisha Bodily's help. But things had not turned out as he had planned. Even a few days earlier, when Jass had ordered him to shoot at the people in the hotel in Rio, he had protested. But Jass had convinced him they were a threat to the Rio bunker and had to be eliminated. Now, this latest shooting, even though Miguel González had actually pulled the trigger, left Thomas feeling like only a shell of who he had been.

During his stay with the small tribe in New Zealand, he had actually been happy—until they all died from Anthrax E. After he rescued Dilan and Sena from the monsters, he felt his happiness return. Now, two years later, he was involuntarily part of another murder. There were so few people left alive on Earth. Who knew how many had gone down with that old plane? They didn't actually know who was onboard, but Thomas felt that Jass was not.

It would only be a few hours until they reached Idaho, a place he had learned from tracing Dorian's com was called Marsing, Idaho. Everyone on board, except Dilan and Sena, knew the reception was likely to be unpleasant. And Thomas was worried that he would be the sacrificial lamb when they arrived. Miguel was in charge, despite what the SEC-GEN said. And with a man like that in charge, who had no misgivings when it came to killing, things could not turn out well in Idaho.

32

The A-400 approached Marsing from the south. Thomas was flying low and slow. Nobody wanted to surprise the group on the ground, even though they knew the sound of a flying machine of any kind would still be a surprise.

As they passed by the large city of Boise, Bria Newton, SEC-GEN Davis' clerk, looked down at the city. "It's beautiful down there, isn't it? Not like the jungle-covered cities in South AM."

"It *is* beautiful," the SEC-GEN replied. He reached over and held Bria's hand. Then, giving it a squeeze, added, "I need to get up front now. None of us know what to expect, and we need to be prepared."

SEC-GEN Davis left Bria in the lounge area of the ship and arrived on the bridge to find Miguel and Thomas arguing about the approach into Marsing.

"Gentlemen," Davis said, "This can't be that difficult. Miguel, how many times have you flown an airship?"

"Never."

"Then why don't we let Thomas figure this one out. We all know who's in charge here, but *he's* still our pilot. He will get us down safely."

Miguel looked at Davis, then back to Thomas. Miguel hadn't let both of them out of his sight once since they left Victory Base. They had been free to leave his presence one at a time, but never together.

Miguel must have known that the other two couldn't be hatching a plot under his nose. "Fine," Miguel finally said through clenched teeth.

"So, what's the plan after we land?" Thomas asked.

"It is simple," Miguel growled. "You will go out and tell them we are here for the vaccine. If they do not give it to you, I will come out and force it."

"You think it will be that simple?" Davis asked. "What if they're armed?"

"Why would they be?" Miguel asked. "Did one of you tell them we were coming?"

"Not me," Thomas replied quickly.

"No Miguel," Davis said. "But would you be sitting around unarmed in this world? You haven't set aside your gun in two years, even though you knew we were no threat to you. Why would you expect anyone else to act differently?"

"The difference is that they have been living here peacefully for all this time. They have no reason to suspect us."

"Uh . . . remember that I shot their friends down in that hotel in Rio?" Thomas reminded them both. "They must know their friends are dead. I don't think they will believe that their lives are perfectly safe. They will suspect. When they hear my ship, they will be afraid. If they have guns, they will be armed."

"Thomas makes sense," Davis said. "I suspect they will be armed."

"Then Thomas, I suggest you start practicing your most pitiful, sorrowful face. Because you are going out there to get the vaccine."

The A-400's onboard computer announced their arrival in the airspace over Sunny Slope and Marsing. Thomas had programmed it to land on the long, straight highway west of Marsing. His traced call from Dorian had been from a large building in Marsing. So that was where they would start.

Every adult but Neirioui was in Marsing. Neirioui had stayed at her home across the Snake River in Sunny Slope with the three children and Suvan. Even though some feared this could be a bloodbath, which could leave three young children without family, they needed superior numbers. They didn't know who else might be on board with Franconi.

"There it is," Anta said. "Can you hear it?"

"I hear it," John replied. "Radio to the others to watch. We need to know where they're landing."

Anta sent a com to the four other groups situated in various buildings throughout Marsing, reminding them to watch the sky from their hidden vantage points. Each group reported that they were ready—at least as ready as they could be for a ship that could blow apart buildings. They were armed, but their armaments would only work if hand-to-hand combat ensued.

Soon, the noise from the approaching ship was loud enough that everyone in Marsing could have heard it. Moments later, it appeared, flying low over the small town. It was headed west, but circled around and came back, landing softly on Highway 55 leading into Marsing from the west. After landing, it rolled several hundred meters, finally stopping just 80 or 90 meters from the building where Angel and Mike were hiding.

"He's very close to us," Angel com'd to the others. "We have him in our sights. If that door opens, he will be in our crosshairs."

"Good," John replied. "Remember, we think he's alone, but there could be others with him. Watch carefully."

"We've got him too," Jonas added. "I suggest John and Anta move up from the middle, but leave Steve and Marilyn on the east side of town. If anyone else is with Franconi, we need that end of town covered."

"Agreed," John replied. "Steve and Marilyn. Keep eyes on that end. Even if you hear shooting, stay there. We don't want anyone sneaking up on us through some kind of diversion. Hasani, stay where you are too. Your middle ground should allow you to move either direction if necessary, but wait for a signal from me or Steve before you move.

"Roger," Hasani replied.

John and Anta moved forward from their location near the middle of town. Three or four minutes later, they arrived on the other side of the street from where Angel and Mike were planted. The door to the silver ship had not yet opened.

"You think he's got some kind of infrared or heat detector on that thing?" Lin asked Jonas, who was stooping three feet to her right, peering out a window.

"If so, we're in trouble," Jonas replied.

Moments later, the large hatch on the back of the ship began to open.

"He's coming out the back," Angel said. "We've still got eyes. John, Anta, watch that side in case he goes around your way. We'll lose him very quickly if he goes right instead of left."

"Roger," Anta replied.

Nothing happened for three minutes. Then, two young, thin girls stepped out of the shadow of the hatch and moved to the left.

"That's not Franconi," Mike said. "It's two young girls."

"Keep your eyes on them," John replied. "We're moving toward the back of the ship. The girls are a diversion. I want to get around the back and see if we can see inside."

John and Anta crept out the back door of the building in which they had hidden, and moved quietly behind two more buildings until they reached the last structure on their side of the street. From their position, they could see partially into what appeared to be a cargo hold at the back of the ship. The girls were still standing there, holding hands, and clearly nervous.

Jonas and Lin also moved forward. They positioned themselves behind a small convenience store to the right of the ship, near the front, close to the location recently vacated by John and Anta.

"We've got your spot covered John," Jonas com'd. "Do whatever you need to do."

"Roger," Anta replied. She moved in a crouched position to the other side of John to get a better angle, but stopped suddenly and dropped to the ground when a voice boomed out through the still air.

"Hello, my name is Thomas Franconi. I am here to receive a vaccination from you. I need nothing more. My young friends, who you see outside my ship, will acquire it for me. We will need two dozen vials. Please proceed with haste. Otherwise, I will move to Plan B."

Thomas spoke the words as though he had rehearsed them. In reality, he had been handed a script by Miguel. Miguel had said that it would be Thomas going out first, and he had been frightened but ready. Although only Sena and Dilan had been vaccinated, Miguel was apparently confident enough in his 'negotiating' skills, that he didn't fear Anthrax E. Either that, or he was truly insane.

Just after landing, Miguel changed his mind. He would send Sena and Dilan. Miguel explained that Thomas was much more likely to cooperate if the girls were in harm's way. He had been right. Thomas read the words exactly as they had been written.

"What do you make of it?" John asked through the coms. "Anyone?"

"If those two girls were on the ship with Franconi, it seems possible there are others too," Jonas replied.

"We can't go out there," Lin added. "If this is a trap, we can't fall for it. Plus, he's not going to hurt those girls. Look how young they are."

"You may be right about that," Anta replied. "But remember that he shot at Street, Shift and Jon in Rio. Then he did something else to them while they flew back here. He may not be as nice as you think."

"I'm sorry Anta," Lin replied. "I forgot about that. You're right. We can't trust him."

"Who's got that megaphone?" John asked.

"We've got it," Angel replied. "You want one of us to say something?"

"Yes Angel, I want *you* to say something. Why don't you call out and ask the girls to walk away from the back of the ship toward their left, toward you. Let's see if they move away from the hatch—away from whatever guns might be pointed in their direction."

"Roger," Angel replied. But before she could speak, the voice of Thomas Franconi filled the air again. This time, it was hard to miss the sound of fear in his voice.

"My friends, please cooperate with me. Please send someone out with a case of vaccines. Then we will leave."

"A *case* of vaccines?" John repeated through the coms.

"Hurry," Franconi said. This time, the fear was palpable. Something was wrong.

The group all watched the back of the ship. Four seconds later, a shot rang out and one of the girls dropped to the ground. The other screamed, letting go of her partner's hand; but she stood frozen in place.

"They're hostages," John hissed into the com. "I'm going in."

John stood and moved toward the front of the building. Anta grabbed him by his shirt as he passed by, but her fingers slipped as John turned. As he cleared the front edge of the building, he yelled, "Run."

The other girl, who was now stooping over her fallen sister, looked up at the sound and moved away from the downed girl.

"Run," John called out again as he neared the rear of the ship. The girl continued to move away from him, but was not running. Her head swung left and right as she looked from the ship, to the man running at her.

Moments before John would have reached the girl lying on the ground, gunfire broke out from the ship and bullets scattered all across the ground in front of him. He came to an abrupt stop, turned toward the side of the ship and ran in that direction. The gunfire stopped as John cleared the open hatch.

A second voice called out from the ship. "That was not very smart amigo. It was a simple request. Now, you have killed a poor, innocent girl. There will be others if I do not see a vaccine in ten seconds."

Miguel knew he had their attention, but time was not on his side. They had now all been exposed to the contaminated air outside the ship, and the clock was ticking. He needed to return to his family. It had been too long. They may already be dead, but he needed to know.

Shooting Dilan was just the beginning. Miguel shoved Thomas Franconi out the hatch and then grabbed Bria, pulling her close. Thomas landed on his face on the hard pavement. Blood immediately began to pool around his head. He didn't get up. Miguel shivered only slightly before regaining his composure. He had become numb to the violence and death, and didn't really care anymore.

Inside, Miguel turned back toward the interior of the ship, holding Bria around the throat in front of him. SEC-GEN Davis and the other three men on the ship all stopped moving. As Miguel had surmised, the others would likely revolt. Now, with Bria as a shield, separating him from the men, he would remain in control of the situation.

"Let her go," SEC-GEN Davis said, his voice strong.

"Why would I do that?" Miguel replied. "Right now, she is the only thing keeping me safe from the likes of you."

"Just let her go," another man standing to Miguel's right side said. "We'll all go with her. Then you can get your vaccination and leave on the ship."

"That sounds like a wonderful plan, but I don't think it will work."

"Why?" the man asked. "We'll go quietly. I swear." There were tears in his eyes as he finished speaking.

"How about you stop your groveling and be a man?" Miguel said. "You disgust me." Miguel lifted his gun and fired, intentionally missing. But the bullet ricocheted off the floor near the man and pierced his leg. He fell. The other three men paused only momentarily, then rushed forward. Miguel's gun went off again, hitting Bria in the back as the men collided with Miguel near the rear hatch. Bria fell to the floor, writhing in anguish.

SEC-GEN Davis and the two other men rolled toward the open hatch as Davis tried to pry the gun from Miguel's hands. The gun went off again, the bullet hitting the tarmac only inches from Sena's feet. She screamed again.

During the struggle, Davis looked up to see Bria's neck constrict before sending vomit and blood spewing from her mouth. Then she stopped moving as her last breath hitched in her throat.

Davis moaned and renewed his attack on the man responsible for the death of his lover. More shots were fired as the melee continued inside the ship.

"They're fighting," John com'd. "Now's our chance. Let's go."

Anta rushed out toward John on the right side of the ship. Angel and Mike rushed from the left. More shots rang out inside the hull of the ship and more screams of agony, both male and female, accosted the ears of the would-be rescuers. Jonas and Lin moved forward cautiously from the right front corner, separating so that one went down each side. They kept their guns trained on the doors to the ship on each side. There was no movement in any of the windows up front.

John approached the corner near the hatch carefully, crouched down, and peeked his head around the edge. On the other side of the ship, Mike did the same.

Another round fired from inside, sending a bullet into the street near Mike's side. Mike and John both backed up instinctively.

Anta approached John, stopped, and listened. "They're fighting inside," She said through the coms. Then, to John, "We need to get in there."

"How?" John asked.

A thud sounded from inside the ship as if something large and heavy had been thrown against the wall right next to John and Anta. Then there was silence.

John and Mike both peeked around the edge of the hatch again. Another report rang out and Mike dropped to the ground. John looked over at him. Mike hadn't made a sound. There was a small hole in the middle of his forehead. It hadn't even started bleeding yet. Then another woman screamed. It was Angel.

"No!" John yelled into the coms. Then he rushed into the back of the ship, his own firearm in front of him at chest level, hoping to catch whoever was firing off guard. He immediately ran into a man and together, they crashed to the floor. John's gun was knocked from his hand and slid across the floor of the ship, coming to a stop next to the wall on the opposite side. John turned and dove for it, sliding across the floor, now coated with blood. His left hand grasped the weapon just as a heavy weight slammed into his back. He felt a cracking sensation and let go of the gun. The other man reached over John and picked up the gun. He stood, facing John and pointed a gun at John's head. Hearing a quiet click, John rolled over and froze. He hadn't thought it would end this way.

Blood was running from the man's mouth and his clothes were torn. He was missing a shoe. But whatever he looked like, he had the upper hand. John knew he was going to die. He stared at the man as the man's trigger finger slowly pulled inward.

John closed his eyes. The roar of a gunshot echoed through the ship. John didn't feel any pain. Then he heard the sound of rushing footsteps and a familiar voice.

"John, John, open your eyes."

Anta.

John slowly opened his eyes. They were filled with tears.

33

The quiet words of the song faded out as the group finished a tribute to the unknown dead from the ship. They hadn't wanted to bury the people so quickly, but they had other concerns to deal with. Shift, Street and Jon were somewhere in the Brazilian jungle.

After Anta shot Miguel, two survivors on the ship appeared from dark corners. Everyone else on the ship had died in the melee, including the Secretary General of the International World Order. Thomas Franconi also lay dead in the street. The young girl, Dilan, had been shot and was confirmed dead. But her sister Sena had survived.

One by one, the dead were carried from the ship to the side of the road and placed in a row. The three survivors from the ship, a woman named Tal, a man named Nenka, and the young girl, Sena, grieved for their lost friends. Nenka and Tal had been given injections, almost immediately, to ward off AE. Then, less than two hours after the battle ended, Nenka passed away as well, having suffered the loss of too much blood from a bullet shot to his leg before he could be tended to. Now, all eight bodies had been laid to rest. Only Mike's cold body remained. The Sunny Slope survivors hoped to find Shift, Street and Jon, and let them say "goodbye" before burying their friend.

Having concluded the short funeral, John, Jonas and Marilyn were preparing to leave in search of the others. Steve didn't want

Marilyn to go, but she was the only one with medical training. If their friends were hurt, she needed to be there. Anta was desperate to find her husband, but John convinced her that Shift would want her to stay and take care of Yurgi.

Tal had told the story of the airplane they shot down over Brazil. It had been a mistake. The SEC-GEN had thought Director Adal Jass was on board. Of course, Tal made sure the group knew that she and Sena had nothing to do with it. They claimed to be hostages to Miguel as well. And the small group in Sunny Slope believed them. Wherever their friends were in Brazil, they would be found, and Marilyn would heal them, if possible. They would take Tal and Sena with them. Sena had not ever actually flown the A-400, but she claimed to know how. Thomas had told her it would pilot itself with the right control settings. And Sena had memorized them.

They would leave as soon as possible.

The small group moved away toward the gate of the Marsing Cemetery. As the group left, Hasani moved into position to begin shoveling dirt onto the second casket. He had volunteered. He wept as he sent shovel after shovel full of dirt into the ground. He didn't even know these people, but they had been alive only hours earlier. Now, the world had lost more of the very few people who had survived AE and the Skins.

Two meters away, Sena knelt down and threw a handful of dirt onto the pile of freshly moved dirt that covered her little sister's body. She sobbed and fell to the ground, grasping at the dirt and pulling it away. Hasani walked over to her and knelt down next to her. He placed his hand on her back and began to sing. The lullaby he had learned as a child was in Egyptian, but it didn't matter. Sena's crying quieted and she leaned into the man she barely knew. He pulled her close as he continued his song.

Moments later, Neirioui and Suvan approached and knelt down too. They understood her grief—everyone did. The four of them knelt next to Dilan's final resting place for several minutes until Hasani's singing died out. He lifted Sena's head and smiled at her. No words were spoken. Then Sena leaned in and hugged Hasani. As they embraced, Sena reached out and grabbed Neirioui's hand and pulled her close too. She felt a warmth from these people that she hadn't felt in a long time.

After the funeral, Tal had helped John and Marilyn load gear into the A-400. She had explained that she was a nurse in a former life, but had very little actual training or experience. In Antarctica, there were few injuries or illnesses needing her attention, and she had been there for years. Nevertheless, she told the group that she wanted to help. She and Marilyn determined which gear and equipment needed to go, in order to be prepared for any kind of catastrophe, and they loaded the ship.

Now, they were flying south over the jungle north of Rio de Janeiro, Brazil, and closing in fast on the location where Tal and Sena believed the airplane had crashed. John hoped it would be as easy as seeing smoke rising from the jungle. The plane had been shot down less than 36 hours earlier. But as much as they hoped for smoke to guide them, they also feared what smoke would mean—fire, or worse.

"There!" Jonas called out. "Smoke, right there." He pointed down and to the right of the A-400. Everyone moved to that side of the ship to look. Jonas was correct.

The smoke was thin and wispy. If they hadn't been paying close attention, they would have flown right by it.

Sena moved to the control panel and input instructions to slow and descend. As they approached the smoke trail, gently lifting from the jungle, the destruction of the forest became more obvious. Dozens of trees were crushed and broken. The undergrowth was ripped apart for several hundred meters leading directly to the location from which the smoke slowly drifted. Trees were charred and parts of the plane littered the ground. But there was no fire. Then they saw the wreckage. Marilyn gasped and placed a hand over her chest. Jonas reached toward her and pulled her close. "We don't need our doctor to pass out and become incapacitated too," he said.

"Land the ship about 100 meters from the wreckage," John instructed. "We don't want a secondary explosion to knock us out too."

Sena did as she was asked. As soon as the ship touched ground, she shut it off, releasing the internal locks. John opened the right side door and jumped out. Tal followed.

"I'm okay," Marilyn said. "Let's go." She pushed away from Jonas and the two of them followed the others out the door. Together, they approached the mangled wreck that had recently carried their friends.

"Be careful," Jonas said. "Just because we don't see fire, doesn't mean there isn't danger. The plane could cause us problems if anything electrical is still functional in there."

It took more than five minutes to reach the ship, their progress hindered by the debris and broken tree limbs in their path. As they finally closed the last few meters, the sound of quiet moaning reached John's ears from the right. In a small clearing, no more than twenty or twenty-five meters from the plane, a man coughed and then vomited. His clothes and hair were scorched. From the back, John couldn't tell who he was.

As they approached the man, he quickly turned. His face registered surprise that surely equaled that on the faces of the five rescuers.

The group slowed as the man's features became clearer. His face and head were completely free of hair. Marilyn breathed the word "Skin" before recognition hit. The man wasn't a Skin. It was Jon.

Jon Porter fell to the ground, long sobs suddenly breaking the silence of the jungle. Jonas and Marilyn rushed to him and knelt down. As John rushed up behind them, he looked around. Scattered around the clearing were the broken and charred bodies of five other people. He peered at the remains of people who had obviously died very recently, looking for faces he recognized. It was clear that the people lying on the ground were from the Rio bunker. John recognized some of the faces, but only from the short visits with the bunker a few days earlier.

"Jon," Marilyn began quietly, "where are the others?"

Jon raised his head and looked at Marilyn, then over at John. The vacant look in Jon's eyes was frightening. But he slowly raised a finger and pointed. They all followed his gaze. Near the front of the ship, three people sat or crouched on the ground, hunched over, seemingly looking at something near their feet.

"Why didn't they hear us?" John asked. Then, looking at Jon Porter, he asked, "Jon, can you hear me?" Jon's eyes closed slowly, then opened. He pointed at his left ear with his left hand and shook his head. Then he spoke, his voice choking as he pressed air from his lungs, "The explosion. I can't hear very well." Then Jon coughed again, the spasms rocking his body.

"The explosion must have been so loud. They can't hear," Tal said. John had come to the same conclusion.

"Let's get over there," Jonas said, "but be slow about it. They may be armed and we don't want to surprise them. They'll recognize us, surely, but a surprised injured human can do crazy things."

"Tal, stay here with Jon please. See how you can help him." Jonas said. Tal sat down next to Jon and held out her hand to shake his. Jon slowly lifted his hand and took hers. A moment later, Tal opened a small medical kit and began rummaging around inside, as the others moved toward the nose of the plane.

As the group approached those gathered in the trees just a short distance from the nose of the plane, it became apparent that there were three men or women sitting—it was hard to tell given the burnt and shredded clothing—and one person on the ground behind them. Likely sensing their approach, one man turned and looked at the approaching group. The corners of his mouth turned upward as he stood.

"Dr. Nic Heiberg, it's good to see you," John said, reaching out to shake the man's hand.

"It's good to see you too," Nic said loudly. "I'm sorry, but I'm not hearing too well." Then he tapped the other two on the shoulders. Each of them turned to look. One man, who some of them recognized as Frans from the Rio bunker, stood. The other man was nearly unrecognizable. His clothing had been shredded and blood coated much of his body. His hair, like Jon's, had been burned from his head. But then he smiled.

"John, it feels like forever since we last saw each other."

"Shift!" John and Jonas both cried out at the same time. Then they dropped to their knees and embraced Shift.

"Owww. Dudes."

"Sorry Shift," Jonas said.

"Shift probably can't hear you," Nic said. He and Jon were very close to the plane when it blew. But I think they are both regaining a bit. I think they'll be alright."

Suddenly, Marilyn gasped again. The others moved to see what she was looking at. It was Street, his body lying on the ground behind Shift and Frans. He looked worse than Shift and he wasn't moving. Street's right arm was bent at an odd angle, the shoulder drooping away from his body. Blood coated his chest and face, and an obvious gash stretched across his forehead. The bleeding had stopped, but Street's skin was pale and cold.

"Don't worry everybody. Street will be fine too. He's lost a lot of blood, and he's unconscious, but his vitals are stable as far as I can tell." John found Nic's confidence comforting.

"Nic, what kind of doctor are you?" Jonas asked.

"The right kind," Nic replied, smiling.

Marilyn pushed past the others and bent over Street. She pulled some digital equipment from the bag she had carried from the ship and began checking Street's vitals. Moments later, she announced, "I think Nic is right. Street should be fine. The scanner doesn't pick up any internal bleeding, his pulse and breathing are fairly normal, and it appears the only broken bones are his collarbone and shoulder."

"That man is a rock star," John replied. "This is the guy that a Skin couldn't even take down."

The others laughed, but not for long.

"I better check out Jon and Shift too," Marilyn said. "Nic and Frans, I'll get to you next."

"Thank you . . ."

"Marilyn." She finished Frans' statement for him.

Hours later, Nic, John, Jonas, Tal and Marilyn had finally loaded everyone into the back of the A-400. Jonas had radioed back to Sunny Slope with the news and they all eagerly anticipated the reunion. Jon, Shift, Street and Frans were all loaded onto beds in the cabin area of the ship. Marilyn had determined that Frans had fractured several of his ribs in the crash. Nic, surprisingly, was uninjured apart from scrapes and burns.

Jon would be okay, once his hair and hearing returned. Marilyn couldn't see any major burns that she wasn't able to treat topically. Shift had broken several bones in his leg, but Marilyn had set the fractures and molded a cast around the sensitive areas. She was confident that he would heal and that his hearing would also return, at least most of the way.

Street was in stable condition, and Marilyn, like Nic, believed he would recover. The gash in his forehead gave Marilyn concern, but the effects of the head injury might not be known for weeks or months.

The bodies of the five members of the Rio team that had not survived the crash were carefully strapped down in the hanger.

"I'm sorry about your friends," Marilyn said as she placed a white, linen sheet over the last of the bodies.

"Don't be sorry," Nic said. "We'll miss our colleagues; but a few days ago, we feared that every one of us might die during the battle we waged inside the Rio bunker."

"That's when you wrestled for control against Adal Jass and his team?"

Nic nodded. "We'll mourn, but we finally have hope for a better life."

The flight back to Sunny Slope was long. Jonas instructed Sena to take it slow. Even though the ship was comfortable, changes in air pressure still moved the ship. Marilyn had asked that the journey be made as comfortable as possible for the injured in the back.

"Tal," John began, his curiosity finally finding a time to express itself, "that guy Miguel, why did he take all of you hostage?"

"He said he wanted a ride back to Cuba, with vaccinations for his whole family."

"We would have given that to him."

"I know. But nobody knew that until now. None of us knew who you people were. And Miguel had already been burned by Director Jass and the SEC-GEN, or so he said. He didn't trust anyone."

"I guess that makes sense," John said. "Where was his family? He couldn't have really believed they were alive."

"Oh, he believed it. He said they were in a bunker, with thousands of people, and that they were all alive."

"Did he say anything else about the bunker?"

"Not much. He said it was a government bunker in Havana."

"A government bunker huh?" John thought for a moment, then said, "Excuse me." He stood and walked toward the sleeping quarters where Shift was strapped down.

"Shift, can you hear me?" John asked, peeking his head into the room.

Shift's eyes opened and he turned his head toward the door. "Yes John. How can I help you?" Shift smiled wide, but his smile quickly turned into a frown. "Ouch, that hurt my face."

John laughed. "Still the same Shift I see; always worried about what you look like. That's good. And I'm glad you can hear again. Although I'll have to be quieter now when I make fun of how you look. I don't think Anta will even love you anymore. You don't have any hair you know?"

Shift laughed aloud, but cut that short too. "Owwww. My face. Dude, be nice to me."

"I'll try. Okay, maybe you can help me out. Remember back in Cabo Rojo, when we were contacting all of the bunkers around the world, trying to find survivors?"

"Yeah."

"Didn't you talk to someone in Cuba, in a government bunker of some kind?"

"Yeah."

"What happened to them?"

"He was the last person alive. I think they were in Havana. They had starved to death, he said. 3,000 people or something like that."

"Oh. Bummer."

"Why do you ask?" Shift asked.

"We started to tell you about the fight we had in Marsing, just before we came to get you. Well, that guy, Miguel, who had taken everyone hostage; he said he had family alive in some government bunker in Havana. Could that be the same bunker you spoke with?"

"It was the only bunker of any kind known to the guy I spoke to. What was his name? Colonel Fonseca, I think. Yeah, Fonseca. 3,000 people in there had lived for about six months or so. Then the food spoiled and the water ran out. They thought they could make it for a couple years in there, but they didn't. Fonseca said the bunker wasn't designed to hold that many people."

"And there are no other government bunkers in Cuba?" John asked.

"Fonseca said he didn't know of any others—government or private. Remember, we were trying to contact everyone we could find, to see if we could get them to the Cabo Rojo bunker. We heard about the bunker in Cuba from someone else. And Colonel Fonseca said they were the only one in Cuba that he knew of. So, yeah, it was probably the only government bunker in Cuba."

"Then I guess there's no reason to stop over there on our way home?"

"I'd rather not. I have no desire to see 3,000 more corpses. We've seen enough. But maybe we can try to contact the bunker again when we get back, just in case."

"Good plan boss." John softly rubbed Shift's bald head and walked away.

34

We arrived home to a warm welcome this morning; but the celebration was short-lived as we gathered together for another funeral. This time, we buried a great man—one who aided our survival as much as anyone else had.

Mike Petrovsky, the computer geek whose skills and talent helped us watch and prepare for the world as we left the Boston bunker so long ago, will be sorely missed. His death, like that of so many before him, reminds me of our frailties. I'm told he died trying to save others—people he didn't even know. He wasn't the first, and he won't be the last; but his heroism and the wonderful, kind man that he was, will not be forgotten.

I watched from a padded chair as my friends lowered Mike's casket into the ground. I couldn't breathe as tears streamed down my cheeks and a lump formed in my throat. I couldn't speak, and thankfully, nobody expected me to. The grief threatened to overwhelm me; but I took some comfort knowing that others shared my sorrow.

The others from Brazil, people most of us barely knew, had been buried minutes earlier. But we all shared the pain. The human race had taken another hit.

After the funeral, some members of the group helped Nic, Frans, and Tal settle down in the small hotel in Marsing, just across the river from most of our farms. Hasani and Neirioui asked Sena to stay with them. Their stay in the hotel will be temporary—just as long as it takes to find permanent homes nearby. I look forward to getting to know Sena and Tal, and hope they will be able to contribute to this new society we're trying to build.

Marcus will learn his fate in a few days, once I've healed a bit; but his help has caused me to lean toward some measure of leniency. Besides, we need him as much as he needs us—the human race needs him.

On our trip home from Rio, lying in bed for several hours, and missing my hair a great deal, I thought a lot about our experiences, starting from the day I met Anta in January, 2093—such a short time ago—back when the world was relatively peaceful for the first time in its history. Little did either of us know how our lives would turn out.

Now, as I prepare for sleep, my thoughts have turned to the future. We seem to be safe now. There may be others alive in the world, and we have a place for them here, if they'll come; but only if they'll obey the rules we've laid out.

I can't help but feel like the few of us remaining on this Earth have a deep responsibility to it. We're possibly all that's left of the human race. The killing sands have twisted and shaped the Earth and the destiny of mankind upon it. But we made it. We're alive. We will survive; and we can thrive, if we're careful.

It seems as though the page has turned. This chapter of our lives has come to an end. I lie in my bed next to Anta, with Yurgi sleeping soundly in the next room. I'm watching Anta's quiet slumber, her chest rising and falling with each peaceful breath. Man, I love her. It's impossible for me to describe. I'll do anything to protect her—and Yurgi. Nothing has changed. Nearly everything I've done for the past two and half years has been for her and my friends.

We've been given a second chance. I hope that we'll be thankful for the opportunity ahead of us and use this Earth and its resources wisely. But most importantly, I hope that we will love each other as we look forward to building a new world.

AUTHOR'S NOTE

Thank you for reading the Killing Sands series! It has been an amazing experience creating the lives and stories of the people about whom you've just read, and I hope you enjoyed reading the story as much as I enjoyed writing it.

As with so many products for sale today, much of what drives future sales are positive reviews from people like you. If you have a couple of minutes, I would appreciate your honest feedback through a product review on Amazon. It's easy: just login to Amazon.com and click on the "Orders" tab. Then, find my book and click on the button that says "Write a Product Review".

If you didn't purchase the books through Amazon, but would still like to leave a review, search for the name of the book(s) on Amazon's website. Click on the book's title then scroll down to the Customer Reviews section. Click on "Write a Customer Review". You can leave a separate review for each of the three books in the series.

Thanks again!

I didn't decide to write this story until just before I published *Tomorrow We Rise*. The story didn't feel complete. In the first two books, I left little pieces of the story unanswered. I debated about whether to let my readers imagine what happened with those little side stories, or whether I should tell my readers what I thought happened.

I knew some astute people would wonder what happened to those teenage girls in Russia, or what it was like when the people fleeing Argentina got caught by the Skins near the Panama Canal, or whether

Anthrax E was purposefully released from the killing sands of the Sahara Desert.

So, after much internal deliberation, I decided to answer those questions rather than leave yawl hanging. I'm pretty considerate that way.

Like the books before it, *Now We Survive* certainly isn't the final chapter in mankind's struggle for survival, but it's almost certainly the final chapter in this little book series.

As with my first two books, I received tremendous, valuable help and constructive criticism from several people while writing Now We Survive, including Steve Wilde, Susan Niedert, Brian Dickinson and Chris Palmer.

As always, my wife (Chandi) and kids (Sage, Roston, Aspen, Rader and Loch) were patient with me as I spent late nights writing this book. They even let me take another trip back to the Coral Pink Sand Dunes in southern Utah, the site of the picture for the cover of *Today We Die*, where I took the photograph for the cover of *Now We Survive*.

ABOUT ME

I grew up in Taylorsville, a suburb of Salt Lake City, Utah. My teenage years were spent skiing, golfing, mountain biking, hiking, camping and dating. After high school, I spent two years in Scotland on a religious service mission. During college, I met and married Chandi, and we started a family.

I graduated from the University of Utah with a bachelor's degree in mass communications in 2003—Go Utes! Since my only job prospects with a degree in mass communications included writing obituaries and teaching mass communications to others, I went to law school in San Diego, California. Boogie boarding became my favorite pastime. I graduated from law school in 2007 and was offered a very nice job at a small firm in St. George, Utah, in the southwest corner of the state. I practice law in both California and Utah.

My family and I have lived in St. George for eleven years now. It's hot, but incredibly scenic here and my life couldn't be better. I'm a husband and a father of six (one deceased). My wife and kids are amazing and keep me busy and young-ish. My wife is still as beautiful as she was the day I met her—more than nineteen years ago. I'm a father, husband, lawyer, pianist, percussionist, Sunday School teacher, soccer dad, armchair quarterback, outdoor enthusiast, and "author". In the very little free time I have, I camp (in a trailer, not a tent), cliff-jump, kayak, golf, do yardwork, and hike with my family. On the rare occasion I have free time after all of that, I write.

Keep up with me at *www.danielpwilde.com*,
www.facebook.com/danielpwildeTKS, or
e-mail me at *danielpwilde@gmail.com*.

www.ingramcontent.com/pod-product-compliance
Lightning Source LLC
Chambersburg PA
CBHW031952120726
47898CB00002BA/360